Sports Car Menopause

Sports Car Menopause

a novel by
PAGE STEGNER

AN ATLANTIC MONTHLY PRESS BOOK
LITTLE, BROWN AND COMPANY
BOSTON · TORONTO

FIRST EDITION

T09 77

LIBRARY OF CONGRESS CATALOGING IN PUBLICATION DATA

Stegner, Page.
    Sports car menopause.

    "An Atlantic Monthly Press book."
    I. Title.
PZ4.S8164Sp [PS3569.T3394]   813'.5'4   77-5505
ISBN 0-316-81224-2

ATLANTIC-LITTLE, BROWN BOOKS
ARE PUBLISHED BY
LITTLE, BROWN AND COMPANY
IN ASSOCIATION WITH
THE ATLANTIC MONTHLY PRESS

Designed by Susan Windheim

*Published simultaneously in Canada
by Little, Brown & Company (Canada) Limited*

PRINTED IN THE UNITED STATES OF AMERICA

To My Father:
for his wisdom, counsel, and faith.

Part
One

One

I AM A GRUMPY RISER. MANY OF US ARE, OF COURSE, BUT irritability in the morning hours has had a more wide-ranging effect on the people around me than I should ever have allowed.

The problem, put simply, is that I am not really in control until I have been up and moving for at least three hours, and there's nothing much I can do about all this because I refuse to have commerce with the surly son-of-a-bitch I wake-up with every day until he can at least be civil. A lady whose work I admire once started a story with the lines "Jesse awakes startled," and I remember the lines because they are the way my story always starts, every morning when dawn begins to leak into the eastern end of the room, every beginning of every day when I awake, startled, and then mad, because it is five-thirty not seven-thirty and I have two hours to kill before I can permit myself to get up and three more before I begin to

I

function. Before I was married I blamed my father for my internal alarm. After I was married I blamed Erica. And did my utmost, I confess, to see that she shared my suffering.

The routine usually went like this. Surprise myself in the act of waking, lie a moment growing irritated, throw off the covers, swing out of bed with a thump, go in the bathroom to pee and leave the door open. Bang the lid. Flush. Land back in bed as if it is a trampoline on which I'm reaching for a back one-and-a-half with a double twist. If she sleeps through the first act, she is awake for the second. Well, why not? How many times, after all, did I tell her to get some backing for the bloody curtains? How many times did I explain, patiently, with medical footnotes, with annotated bibliography, that some people, unlike herself, wake up at the crack of dawn if the room isn't absolutely dark. Some people have a hair-trigger retina. Some people are affected by the slightest alteration in light. It did me no good. I complained, but the same old hopsacking hung over the windows, and the dawn spilled in as if through a sieve. By the close of my fifteenth year of marriage to Erica I was becoming increasingly tyrannical, on the one hand, and on the other more withdrawn and reclusive than ever. When I was playing the tyrant, she quite appropriately responded with cold hostility. When I was playing the troglodyte, she would pester me continually, just to see if she could get a rise out of me, and in the end our respective "give and take" resulted in an explosion — not a very dramatic display of mega-tonnage, more like the muffled thump of a cherry bomb in a toilet bowl, but nevertheless sufficient to blow things apart. I can remember very well the morning when I woke up, as usual, at five-thirty, looked at Erica sleeping next to me, and decided for the hundred and fiftieth time in a month of weeks that I had had it. Perhaps my decision wasn't consciously articulated, but her mouth was open and whistling away, there were creases in her neck and at the corners of her mouth, and I thought, Jesus! Middle age. I lay there wondering what had ever happened to the girl with the tight, clear skin, darkening under a day's sun and glowing beneath the light film of its natural oil; the trim figure with no softness around the belly or accumulation of flesh between the thighs or veins beginning to show at the back of the legs, no stretch marks, wrinkles, open pores. What ever happened to lovemaking in the afternoon, midnight caresses, hard-ons at dawn? Why joke? What's funny about going to pot? At forty I wasn't exactly peaches and cream myself. Also, it should be said, I was having a hell of a time with the narrative voice in my latest novel, and when things are not going well with our fictions, our facts tend to sour.

The bedroom doorknob at which I was starting began to turn, clockwise first, then counterclockwise, neither direction relevant since the internal mechanism was lacking its latch. The door slowly opened. An inch. Two inches. Then wide enough to admit the body of our four-year-old son, who entered the room with his thumb in his mouth. It discouraged me. I watched him hesitate at the foot of the bed, unsure which lump in the tangle of sheets he wanted, then pad around until he was peering into my face.

"Get your *thumb* out of your mouth," I growled. "Don't you ever learn?"

Erica suddenly stirred beside me, turned, and half sat up. I knew perfectly well she hadn't been asleep for at least fifteen minutes. "Leave him alone," she said. "You're the one who never learns anything. Come here, Pickle, get in by mommy."

Christ, I thought. Here we go again.

3

The trouble began the night before when I was trying to get some thinking done before dinner. I had been working day and night for almost a month trying to get my book going again after an enforced layoff, but I had gotten myself into a serious bind by locating my point of view with an omniscient narrator. From that stance I could only *comment* on my protagonist, I couldn't permit him the liberty of *self*-irony — with the result that he kept turning into an unrelieved peckerhead whom I knew nobody in the world was going to stand still for. I had a contract; I'd spent a considerable advance during the past year; I was getting really worried that there wasn't a book there after all. I rewrote the first hundred pages in the first person, and simply wound up creating not a fictional persona but myself, at my very worst. A month of hard work and I was back to Go. And I had just filed all that agony in the wastebasket, and was making notes for the opening of a new chapter when Erica burst into my study (an agreed upon sanctuary) full of chatter about some vacation idea she had just learned — from Iris Gorton, wife of a linguistics professor on loan from the University of London. It seemed you could rent these little motor launches that would sleep six or eight, and you could tour all through England on canals, stopping in quaint little villages with two-hundred-year-old pubs, ruddy auld sods walking the cobblestones, drink Watney's Stingo and eat fried parsnips and pork. I heard *from the Thames . . . Iris says . . . in July and August because . . .* and my name.

"What?"

"You haven't listened to anything I've said, have you?"

"Everything."

"What was I talking about then?"

"Punting on the Thames. Come on, Erica, you might have noticed when you intruded here that I'm trying to

4

work. We're not taking any boat trips with Tulips Gorton and her sniffy old man . . . I can assure you of that. So kindly spare yourself the heartburn of preseason planning and me the headache of listening to it."

"*Iris* Gorton. I wasn't suggesting we go anywhere with them, I was talking about us, alone, *sans enfant*. I was daydreaming a romance. I was drumming up conversation." She came over and stood by my shoulder. "You know it wouldn't kill you to practice spoken English for fifteen minutes a day. I realize I'm pretty boring company, but I try now and then to pretend that I live here, that I'm your roommate at least and that we've been introduced socially, you know? Here's this guy, I say, and here's me. That's two of us. With two people you have enough for a conversation, a dialogue, an exchange of words and ideas. Only you're a mannequin, and it's not a dialogue, it's a monologue."

I offered a sinister smile. "A dramatic monologue," I said; "my last duchess."

"You are a teacher, aren't you?" she said. "You do talk up there in front of a class?"

"You are a housewife, aren't you?" I asked. "You do cook? Why don't you just get the beans on the table and let me worry about the life of the mind." I waited for her to slug me, but she turned and left the room. I could hear her mood by the way she not quite slammed the dishes down on the dining room table, but for some irritable reason I compounded my felony by bringing my notes to supper. Where I read them to myself.

Silence. We eat, more or less, in silence. In silence, more or less, we eat. What it comes to is that we weren't speaking to one another. A typical evening at home. Erica devoted her attention to the baby, feeding him, though he was perfectly capable of feeding himself, talking gibberish at him, and then sweeping the plates off and bringing me a half grapefruit before I'd finished the main course. I ignored her. I continued to revise my notes and took my coffee into the living room. Ten minutes later she appeared in the doorway with Lenny in tow. "Would you read to him before he goes to bed? I want to finish the dishes."

I suppressed an impulse to point out again that I was busy, that I had a book to get out that I had already spent the money for. I nodded. "Sure. Okay," I said.

"Go see Daddy, Pickle," Erica said. "Daddy's going to read you a story."

Pickle, alias Leonard Savage, after his maternal grandfather, trailed in with his thumb in his mouth and a tattered copy of *Fox in Socks* under his arm. I had read it to him so many times that the print was worn on the page. Jesus! Groan! The interruptions, the intrusions! Is there no peace? I don't mind reading to the little mutt, I thought, but the same book every night? He's as bored with it as I am. I think his mother produces it just to persecute me for my addiction to solitude and the pleasure of being alone in my study.

"Get your thumb out of your mouth," I said. "You're going to push your front teeth straight through your upper lip if you don't stop." Erica refused to see it as a real problem. There are orthodontists, she liked to say. Yes mam, at six hundred a throw. You'll make him a neurotic, she liked to say. It's him or me.

On page three of *Fox in Socks* I noticed that the old thumb was back in its peg and that Lenny was rhythmically bouncing his feet on the arm rest of the sofa, paying little attention to the story. Naturally. He knew it by heart. "Hey listen," I said. "Do you want me to read, or what?"

He nodded.

"Then sit up and pay attention." The feet stopped and

the eyes turned toward the book. They seemed vacant, dulled by the bedtime ritual that had become only a ritual. If we could try on something new, maybe we could engender a spark of interest. But I had tried that before. And engendered only tears. Complaints.

I began to read once again. Before I had finished the page, the feet were back in action and all attention had reverted to the thumb. I decided that I had really, finally, irrevocably had it. Calmly, in the softest of voices, I said, "You wait here just a minute, Pickle, and Daddy will be right back. I have a little surprise." In the kitchen I rummaged through the spice cabinet until I found what I was looking for, went back into the living room, and sitting down beside him I said, "Gimme your thumb a minute, honey. I've got something for you."

He took his thumb from between his teeth and looked dubiously at me. His scowl indicated no particular distrust: it was simply his everyday expression. "Whazzit?" he said.

"Something you'll like. It's sort of candy, as a matter of fact. Let me have your hand, Pickle."

Pickle innocently presented his palm, fingers spread, and I carefully applied a poultice of cayenne pepper to the damp, pink thumb. "Now pop that in your kiss," I muttered, and after a tentative inspection of his appendage, he did just that very thing.

For a few moments nothing happened. Then, as I was sneaking a look at the label on the can to see if I had somehow made a mistake, my little gherkin began to make terrible flatulent noises with his lips, like a horse trotting up hill. Lava began to course down his cheeks. He wiped at them, beginning to whimper, the whimper turning to a howl, to a shriek as he foolishly smeared pepper in his eyes. The results were far more spectacular than I had anticipated. Pickle turned into a smoldering volcano.

BBLLAAAARGG, he said. He reminded me of a crawdad trying to scramble its way out of a pot of boiling water. I expected at any moment a terrific explosion. The poor kid's head would launch into orbit like a champagne cork, through the lath and plaster and redwood shakes, straight up into the night sky like a flaming gobbet of jellied napalm. Good Christ, what have I done?

Somewhere in the midst of all this, Pickle was rescued by his hysterical mother, who hauled him off to the bathroom and half drowned him in a tub of water, yelling abusive epithets all the while at the monster in the living room. The monster, to tell the truth, began looking for a place to hide.

When one's contrition is great, when one knows that one has invented poorly, what one emphatically does not need is an *explication de texte* to point out the limitations of one's creative gift. It is not helpful to have some authoritarian critic standing around saying, "Shame on you, you creep, look what you did in your hat." My problem with Erica, at least in part, was precisely that kind of carping. She was not stupid, or unaware of my various moods. She knew when I was sorry for something that I had done, yet she could not resist rubbing the dog's nose in his mess. The dog's defense, quite naturally, was to flee the scene, and that's what I did after I set fire to Lenny. I drove up the coast and looked at the moonlight in the surf.

When I came back she was in bed. I prayed, without much hope, that she was asleep, but she was not, and after I had undressed, climbed between the sheets and waited through ten minutes of penitential silence, we began another routine. "Why did you do that?" she said.

What was maddening about the question (a typical Erica question) was the assumption that no matter how much time had passed since the crime, no matter what else might have transpired in the history of the world, she and I and *it* were still unresolved, she and I had but one point of departure, and I, of course, was as eager to unburden my guilt as she was to hear my confession. If I ran off and stared at the ocean for fifty years, I thought, I would come back and Erica would give me ten minutes of cold shoulder and ask "Why did you do that?"

"I did it to encourage him to stop sucking his thumb," I said.

Another pause. "Don't you think it was just a little bit cruel?"

I recognized the opening. It was Erica's *I have been injured* gambit, justified under the circumstances, and even tolerable if it did not lead inevitably into her *now we are going to have a meaningful little talk;* her *I will ask probing questions, and you will struggle with answers, and come, in the process, to know yourself better.* I suppose some people enjoy that kind of entrail inspection. I suppose it's popular in this day of sensitivity exercise to break down communication barriers, tear down the defenses, but I was never able to play that game with anyone, and Erica knew it. If I thought I had been cruel, it was my business to do something about it, not hers.

"I bet he keeps his thumb out of his mouth," I said.

"Maybe he will, I don't know. But don't you think maybe that even if you won a battle you lost the war?"

"What is that supposed to mean?" I asked her.

"Maybe he won't suck his thumb anymore, but it'll be a cold day in hell before he trusts you again. He's been burned in more ways than one. I wish you could have seen him when he finally stopped crying and went in to bed. 'Daddy hurt' he kept saying. 'Daddy hurt.'"

"Oh come on, Erica." I rolled over and presented her with my back, but she had gotten the knife in. Daddy did hurt, which she might have found out had she not been so busy playing prosecuting attorney.

"Well, it *could*," she insisted. "I don't see why you find the idea so absurd."

"Because it is," I said. "And anyway, if it keeps him from making a shelf out of his front teeth, then it's well worth it. I'm tired. Good night."

We both lay there rigid, each knowing the other was shamming sleep. I tried deep breathing in an attempt to fool someone . . . myself maybe . . . and the electric clock made a humming noise every time the second hand swept past the six. I began to count.

Erica's voice came to me unattached out of the darkness, floating, oddly pitched. "Is it me? Is it something I do to you?"

"No."

"It must be. It must be something I do to make you behave this way. You never used to be this way . . . impatient, distant all the time. You act as if you just want to get away from all of us, and go live by yourself."

I refused to be drawn.

"Won't you even talk to me?"

"I'd prefer not to."

She was quiet for a minute. Then she said, "Well, maybe you ought to go see someone."

"See whom?"

"I don't know. A psychiatrist maybe. Somebody who could help. That seems to be what you need."

"All I need," I said, "is to go to sleep."

Things were no better in the morning. By the dawn's early light it was obvious that I had not only lost the war, I had lost the battle as well. My Waterloo was snugged in there in the protecting hollow of his mother's flank, his head under the covers. The day began to leak in through the curtains. I lay with my sullen thoughts and waited for the hour to arrive when I could get up and escape to the office, cursing Erica because she was cursing me, cursing because I was cursing. Psychiatrist, my ass, I thought, what I need is to get out from under. My life has become suffocating and boring.

If I had gone to a shrink what would I have told him? That I had been a breech birth and had ruined my mother for further childbearing? That I would not breast feed? That once when I was being ridden on the back of a bicycle to nursery school I stuck my foot in the spokes because I was mad at somebody, and broke my leg so badly in the ensuing fall that I was in a cast and brace for over a year? That I was a difficult child and an impossible adolescent? That I had been rejected in the seventh grade by a raven-haired beauty who had looked blankly at the Saint Christopher medal I dangled over her shoulder in social studies class and laughed out loud when I asked her to go steady? In high school I had my revenge (her moustache developed nicely; her breasts not at all). None of these scattered memories suggests abnormal warping.

My loneliness.

Should I tell him that I was quite nearsighted by the time I was thirteen, but that I told anybody who wanted to know that I was farsighted? Or that I wished to be a hundred-and-ninety-pound meathead, but was, in fact, a hundred-and-forty-seven pound lamb chop. I was not good at sports, but I lived a fantasy life of athletic prowess. I *was* good at school work, but I despised it, and eventually managed to achieve fairly reprehensible marks. Perhaps I should tell him that at the time Portnoy was sneaking off to molest himself in the can, I was sneaking off to lather up. No peach fuzz grew on my sallow cheeks, but I changed my blade every third day. On the basis of these marginalia he could deduce that whatever I am, I wish I was not; whatever I am not, I wish I was.

Only that is not my problem anymore. I weigh a hundred and ninety pounds, have found sports that I am quite good at, shave twice a day (if I have to go out at night), and for some reason my eyesight has returned to normal. Analysis will have to go deeper into the murky depth where behavior can be defined and catalogued, but not easily explained.

Why, for instance, have I always been fascinated by caves? Freudians know, but I do not find their moist smiles reassuring. When I was six I built canopies over my bed and rearranged the furniture so that I had to crawl through a maze of dresser drawers, toy boxes, book cases, and chairs to reach the snug security of my nest. When I was ten my parents moved into a new house, and I was assigned a room with a large, double-doored closet. I managed to get my bed, my desk, and all my valuable possessions (carved kukri knife, empty cigar boxes, sacks of steelies and aggies, comic books) into that hole in the wall. At college I was an avid rock climber, but I preferred spelunking to ascending mountains. Blame it on Tom and Becky and Injun Joe. That's where I first heard about caves.

I will tell him instead that I am an only child. That will explain it all. We all know the trials and tribulations of the only child. To people who asked what it was like, my standard response was that it provided the undivided attention of one's parents, three hundred sixty-five days a year. No move went unnoticed. The lingering breath of a cigarette in the downstairs bathroom could not be blamed on a sibling. The four ounces of whiskey missing from the sideboard decanter was easily traceable. At the dinner table there was no one else to tell what he had "learned in school today."

And by the time I was fourteen or fifteen I wasn't learning anything. I was too busy trying to be a big shot, "one of the boys," as the phrase went, and academic achievement was decidedly not the measure of success in my school. It was considered suspicious. A kid who was a "brain" was also queer. Everybody knew that. The highest compliment I could imagine was to be known as "the guy who could do it if he wanted," but whose indifference was so supreme that he was, on the contrary, the champion fuck-up of his class. The above phrase (the one in q otes) is how I was remembered in the yearbook, Class of '55.

But there is a brighter side. By the time I was a junior in high school I had learned that "the loneliness of the only child" could be used very effectively on certain women; that the more lost, isolated, and generally twisted around you appeared to be, the more mysterious and attractive you became. You didn't have to be a great athlete, as long as you didn't fall down when you walked; you didn't have to be terribly handsome, as long as your acne wasn't terminal. You could score rather well with "the girls," who hung around with and dated only "the boys," if you were sullen, mildly cynical, and gave the impression that you marched (out of vast and wearying experience) to the beat of a different drummer.

I wasn't an athlete, but I was rather good looking in a sulky sort of way, and I had an attractive, sexy smile. It was generally known. People noticed it, I imagine, because it appeared so infrequently, like an eclipse. What was not so generally known was that I practiced it in front of a mirror until I had it down. It began with a slight lifting of the upper lip on the left side, developed slowly into what the observer feared was going to be just another sneer, then broke finally into a lopsided grin. The difficulty was in keeping the right side of your mouth immobile. The charm of the whole thing was in its surprise. Whew. He isn't going to be a shitmist after all. How nice.

Of course, to make the whole thing work you had to be a study in brown most of the time. Otherwise nobody would be pleased when you were not. It was a role that gave me trouble for a while, because it wasn't all that much fun to play, but it got easier. By the time I met Erica it was so easy I felt as if I'd been acting in the same stage production for fifty years. So I terminated the gig and got married.

But maybe psychiatrists aren't interested in all that regressive personal history stuff anymore. I don't suppose they even use a couch. Methodology, like the times, has probably changed. If I had a psychiatrist I probably wouldn't tell him anything at all, just clam up and let him beat his brains out trying to pry me out of my hole and engage in a bit of normal conversation. Style counts for a whole lot. You shouldn't be too quick to alter it. What I need, Sir, is more freedom. What I am suffering from, quite obviously, is a bad case of sports car menopause. Figure that out. It took me long enough.

Two

BY EIGHT-FIFTEEN I WAS STANDING ALONE IN THE FACULTY lounge at my college (the university being comprised of ten such units — a mini Oxford), staring out into the fog and stirring a cup of day-old coffee. I had just read the agenda for an afternoon faculty meeting, and I was wondering idly whose idea it had been to divide a university into colleges in the first place, thereby doubling everybody's administrative load, when I happened to see two naked girls appear out of the early morning mist and walk jauntily across the courtyard toward the Provost's office on the other side. The taller of the two, the one with stupendous breasts and long, brown hair, paused a moment before the door, and then entered. The other seated herself on a low concrete wall and awaited, I assumed, an interview on her own. She was close enough that I could see the muscles of her buttocks tensing against the cold, damp surface.

I stood there sipping my coffee in a rather pensive manner, and I remember thinking that what was interesting about this whole scene was that in a sense it *wasn't* interesting. Two nubile sweethearts walking around without a stitch right outside my window, and I didn't even find it surprising. In 1965 my eyeballs would have been soldered to the glass. In 1975 I suppressed a yawn. In the aftermath of recent administrative measures to discourage open cohabitation in sexually segregated dorms a series of "nude-ins" had broken out at the university and my college perhaps because it was the center of a cluster of six, had become the hub of exhibition and demonstration. The Provost still fought it, still declared himself for decency. He had finally given up sending his secretary out to issue dress-code proclamations and pleas (unheeded) for moral re-evaluation, and had himself accosted a half dozen sun lovers on the lawn in front of the library, telling them they could either get dressed or resign from the campus. When he returned thirty minutes later, only four had departed. The two who remained, their backsides an alarming though appropriately protestant red, were not only adamant in their refusal to cooperate, but rather abusive as well, and the old boy had no choice. On this cold and foggy morning, two days later, the girls were obviously appearing before him for disciplinary debate, and had chosen, with somewhat opaque logic, to reinforce their position by doing so in the buff.

I could imagine the chaos that was taking place in Dixon's office. "Miss Allencraig, get your twat off my couch." Hardly. Poor old Dixon would be running his fingers through his silver hair, wondering how in God's name a long and distinguished career had come to this, wondering what had ever happened to the demure student who pursued his or her prospective profession with mature dedication and a love of learning, wondering what was the infernal obsession with asserting the right to make an ass of yourself? His essential decency and his complete confusion would render him helpless. Miss Allencraig had his ticket and she was going to punch it.

Harry Weisberg, ex-psychiatrist turned professor of psychology, came in while I was observing this whole scene, and I thought to myself, well, this ought to be good, the campus mammaephile and world's most unsuccessful cocksman is about to realize his wettest dream — a dolly without her duds. "Good morning," I said. "A bit damp with this fog, what?"

"It'll burn off. It burns off by ten-thirty or eleven up here."

"I know that, Harry, I work here too, remember? What I was doing was making small talk, right? Chitchat, by way of acknowledging your presence, to let you know I care." Actually, I always liked Weisberg. He was a bright, perpetually horny intellectual from New York whose only affectations were sartorial. That month he was doing Woody Guthrie with pukka shells.

"I see we're in our Tuesday mood," he said, fishing administrative circulars out of his mailbox and throwing them away without reading them. "That stuff drinkable?"

"If you like sewage."

"Yuk," he said, peering into the urn. "Yesterday's instant. Suppose it's better than nothing."

"Not really."

Harry depressed the handle and then came over by me at the window, perched himself on the edge of the secretary's desk and began blowing gratuitously into his lukewarm cup. Immediately he launched into a blast at the California legislature for cutting capital improvement funds to the university system, and I started to wonder how long it would take him to notice the girl out in the courtyard. Not long, as a matter of fact. In the middle of his seventh subordinate clause he stopped dead and glared out into the fog. I looked at him expectantly. "Yes? You were saying about the council of higher education . . . ?"

He was actually a little bugeyed. He compressed his lips (at least he didn't lick them), stared, and finally turned on me with a foxy squint. "So how long have you known she was there, smartass?"

"Who?"

"Don't 'who' me, kiddo. That little honey-pot out there in front of the Provost's office."

"Honey-pot?" I said. I offered full concentration to the area at which his index finger was pecking; then gave him a puzzled shrug. "Are you okay?"

Harry glanced at me wildly. "What do you mean am I okay? Right there on the wall, turkey, that girl right there. Jesus Christ!" He slopped coffee on the pant leg of his Can't Bust'ems.

"Oh, you mean *her*." I said. "Sure. What about it?"

He was hardly listening. "She naked," he croaked. "She fantastic. She beautiful. Oh, fuck me, I'm in love."

I shook my head sadly. "Harold, she's wearing a three piece tweed suit and a hat, and you're in big trouble, pal. I told you about smoking doobies on the way to work. It rots the brain. It's a problem we literary people see quite a lot of. Illusion becomes reality, life imitates art . . ."

"Cut that shit out, will you," Harry said. "Appreciate, putz, that broad is beyond belief."

"That's what I'm trying to tell you, Hal."

"Will you look at those cannons. My *God*, I'd give my retirement benefits to swive her little squash."

"I like the other two better," I said.

I had him there. He did a classic double take and nearly slid off his perch. "Where? What other two?"

"You don't see them do you," I said, regarding him again with sad dismay. "Poor Harry."

"You ass," he said, punching me in the arm. "Don't you have to go teach or something? Aren't the bootless and unhorsed lined up waiting for you outside your office? Jesus, I don't know what they pay you a salary for, Warren,"

"For what they pay me," I told him, "they're getting overtime."

I watched for a few more minutes to see if anything exciting would happen, like an explosion, or the arrival of the National Guard, or Dixon running out and committing hara-kiri in the library fountain, but nothing did so I left. The faculty office building was a short walk from the lounge, and it was one for which I had a considerable fondness. A path led through a stand of second growth redwoods, along a hill crowned with poison oak, and then down into a ravine where classrooms, labs, and offices had been hidden to protect the natural beauty of the landscape. From the lower parts of the campus one could hardly tell that there were any structures on it at all, and while I knew that growth and more indifferent administration than the present would eventually foul it up, it was this atmosphere that had attracted me to the school in the first place. It was more like working in a national park than a university.

I paused for a moment as I came out of the trees, and looked out over sloping fields to the bay several miles to the south. The fog had already burned off, and the deep blue of the water with white caps forming out beyond the point made me wish I had a boat and the freedom of dark swells and the wind. A good tide was running. I could see six- and seven-foot waves breaking in Steamer Lane, rolling in for a quarter mile before they dissolved harmlessly on the littered beach by the boardwalk. I should have been a marine biologist. Or a surf bum.

Two students approaching along the path reminded me that office hours were waiting — which meant Michael Arington and his short story — and that I was dawdling because I didn't much want to confront what was inevitably (from that particular moron) an argument in the defense of illiteracy. Consoling myself with the idea that it was better sooner than later, I hurried down the last hundred yards and entered the building. Arington was propped in the corner outside my office reading an abused copy of *The Thief's Journal.* I muttered an apology for being late, to which Arington gave no acknowledgment other than to close his book, follow me through the door, and lean himself in the same corner inside the office. It was one of Arington's peculiarities to avoid, if at all possible, sitting down. He would stand in class unless forced by threat of eviction to take a chair. Wiesberg opined he had hemorrhoids. Others thought him merely eccentric. I thought he did it out of some notion that it gave him psychological advantage over those he addressed.

"I got my story back with your comments," Arington said, getting right to the point, "and, like, I would like to rap with you about it because you didn't pick up on it at all, man, for accuracy. Like, you get zero, you know? Zero. What I wish to impart here is that you didn't *read* it right, you didn't understand it, your comments are not relevant." He stopped abruptly and cocked a furtive glance at the ceiling, pursing his lips all the while as if he were about to kiss something.

"Let me see it," I said. "Why don't you sit down." I waved a hand at the chair. Arington took a soiled manuscript out of his duffle coat pocket, unfolded it, laid it on the corner of the desk, and said he'd just as soon stand. I shrugged and flipped to the end where I always put my general remarks. I couldn't for the life of me remember having read it at all, but there in my familiar half print, half script was a page of reactions beginning with *I haven't the vaguest idea what you're trying to do here* . . .

"Like I'm not pissed you didn't dig it," Arington said, "only just a little saddened, you know? Disappointed that you missed the point. I mean I don't get uptight about it if people don't dig my stuff, just as long as they see what I'm doing, because I've been writing for a long time, man, and I mean like I know I can write without people all the time having to tell me my stuff's the greatest, but the thing here is you didn't *read* it right. So obviously it's gonna sound like shit."

I began turning pages in a half-hearted attempt to remind myself of their content, saw only sentence fragments, typos, the stained imprint of a coffee cup, the alliterative gibberish of what I have come to call student submission #1, *The Roadmap of My Mind.* I contemplated contesting Arington's claim that he was a writer by reminding him of Malcolm Cowley's remark that a writer was somebody with readers, but I knew that would lead to student defense #3, *I don't write for readers, man, I write for myself.* So after what I guessed was an acceptable pause for reinvestigation, I handed the manuscript back. "I don't read you at all," I said. "I look at nine-and-a-half pages of unpunctuated, uncapitalized, misspelled nonsense that is devoid of plot, ideas, characters, setting, focus, reference, form, content, you name it. There is nothing here but words. Words I can read in a dictionary. What do you want me to say about it?"

"Oh man," Arington groaned, "not words, man, word *patterns.* The warp and woof of word texture."

I looked at him blankly, keeping my expression pleasant while trying not to appear encouraging.

"I mean of course there's no plot or characters. That's old-time shit, man, really it is. Henry James. Whereas this stuff here is, like you say, words, just a head talking beautiful words, making images, man, spinning a tapestry out of threads of words. You're not *supposed* to understand it, like with your mind or anything, you're supposed to groove on it. Like it's a different form of communication, right? It's nonlinear. You gut-respond in an organic kind of way, right? With your balls, man, not your head. It's definitely a different trip."

"My mind is not located in my balls," I intoned, still smiling.

"I can dig it," Arington said. "Listen, I read this piece to the dude I live with . . . a prose-poem is what it is . . . and it blew him away."

The time was at hand. Terminate this interview, I knew, or I would get involved in a defense of my critical abilities against Arington's speed-freak roommate, a dropout poet named Kirschner, panhandler, author of a free verse epic entitled *Spare Change,* and a builder of collapsible geodesic domes. It had happened before. "Look, Arington," I said. "We're not really getting anywhere with this. My opinion is my opinion and you can take it or leave it. For all I care you can write any damn way that amuses you, but if you're going to hand in this kind of thing . . . this journal of your latest high . . . then you have to be prepared for people telling you they don't understand it, don't respond to it, don't *dig* it, because the only person in the world who is interested in your head trips is *you.* I don't want to be a drag, but I'll tell you another reason why I can't get too excited, and that's because I've read it before, man, a hundred and eighty times in the last six years, and my reaction on the hundred and eighty-first is a carbon copy of my reaction on the first. It stinks. If you want to jerk off with a typewriter don't wave your soiled drawers in public!"

Arington's face registered something between amazement and irritation. Noting this, I began to back off a little. I was not given to angry outbursts, even to students I disliked, and I was just a little ashamed of myself. I had written some pretty self-indulgent prose in my life, and if someone had tromped on it, I had had at least the satisfaction of its having been in print. "Look," I said, repenting. "I'll tell you what we're going to do. Maybe I'm wrong. Maybe I just need *my* head opened. You read it tonight in class and we'll see what kind of response it gets from guys who are closer to it in spirit than I am. I mean, my ear is subjective and conditioned like everybody else's, and I could be way off pitch. You read it, and then we'll kick it around."

Arington merely shrugged. Christ, I thought, maybe I've really wounded him. He comes for advice and he gets abuse. But he's not after advice, he's after confirmation. Still, maybe he deserves better than an irate put-down by some guy who has had a bad morning with his wife. "The piece is not all that bad," I said, and immediately wished I hadn't. "Let's see how the others react to it."

Another shrug. Arington picked his manuscript off the table and left. I sat behind my desk with my chin in my hand, unable to decide whether I was more angry with myself for having lost my poise or for having capitulated on a judgment that I knew to be correct. Why couldn't I tell him his stuff wasn't worth a tinker's damn and leave it at that? Why did I have to reverse my field and score for the other team? What was I trying to do, win a popularity contest? Here lies Eliot Warren, loved but unrespected.

What you've got to do, I told myself, is make up your mind about who you are and what this office you hold is all about. Thank you! I've been considering that issue for some time. On the one hand, as the resident writer on campus, a position I consider slightly blemished by the fact that I also have a degree in literature, I sincerely feel my allegiance ought to be with resistance, rebellion, and death, and not with the "establishment." I have, in my own special ways, been running from, rejecting, or ignoring institutional involvement all my life (until recently), and for most of the same reasons that the current crop of students are now taking *their* stand. Who ever liked to answer for his actions, to be judged and held accountable by someone other than himself? Like all members of the species, I profoundly believed, through my teens and early twenties, in spite of evidence to the contrary, that I was a definitely superior creature and above the critical prying of others. In the rare instance when I have been forced to accept the fact that my judge is morally, intellectually, and experientially twice the number I am, my reaction has generally been outright rebellion. To hell with it. Who needs it? In my students I think I see something of the same impulse for negative self-preservation.

On the other hand, I find myself increasingly irritated by youth cults, subcultures, whatever the popular phrase is — irritated more by its inability to articulate any idea more complex than simple want than by its postures and poses. I am generally weary of the suffering adolescent with pebbled chin and frazzled hair and a hand-me-down conviction that every institution from the American family to the U.S. Government is conspiring with single-minded devotion to co-opt him into society, divest him of his marvelous, albeit fragile, individuality, corrupt his artistic soul, and utterly destroy his humanity. I am profoundly bored by the unshakable belief, expressed in halting non-sequiturs by one quivering sensitivity after another, that the boughs of all evil emanate alternately from the mega-corporation, the military-industrial complex, holders of private property, or a materialistic set of two-in-the-garage, split-level, suburban Los Angeles parents. End of speech.

They have passed through my office for ten years. They seek me out because they hear on the grapevine that I am not like most professors, that in spite of my credentials I am not really an academic at all, but an art*eest* of some sort, and therefore in possession of vibrations that approximate their own. They hear that I am indifferent to, if not downright disrespectful of, institutional practices and protocol, that I avoid departmental meetings and college social functions, and they assume on the basis of this evidence that I am someone who can be reached, someone who will respond in kind to their Snyderian utterances and lend substance to their search for new forms of non-verbal communication. Nuts. My real problem, as I see it, is that I encourage these seekers through equivocation. I am such a series of contradictions myself that it is easier to agree with whatever muddled argument confronts me than to take a contrary stand.

At that moment my debate with myself was interrupted by a knocking at the gate and I barked something in the vicinity of "come in." Willy Ward, an on-again, off-again graduate student whose association with me went back to his undergraduate days, walked in with a big grin and a howdy-do, look-at-me, I'm-home-from-the-wars handshake, and plunked his six and a half feet of carrot topped angles and dangles into the chair by my desk.

"I'll be damned," I said. "I thought you were supposed to be drudging in the British Museum. You wear London out already?"

"I think it wore me out," he said. "All that crummy weather and poorly heated flats and prices you wouldn't believe."

I could see he wasn't kidding. He had always been a

wiry string bean with a high-domed forehead and receding hairline — a kind of composite basketball player, Irish priest, Yogi, but now he looked thinner and more ascetic than ever. His hair was cropped close, his face drawn, and his nose, hatchet thin in the best of times, honed to razor sharpness. "To tell the truth you don't look so hot," I said. "In fact you look worse than when you came back from Vietnam with dysentery and a drug habit. What were you living on? Potatoes and water?"

"Fish and grease. And love. Actually it wasn't all that bad. We had pretty decent digs above an antique store right on Kings Road in Chelsea, but then Frankie had a miscarriage and I got hit on my bicycle and broke my collarbone, and we finally decided to pack it in. I wasn't doing pididdle on the thesis anyway. I wrote three hundred pages of a novel instead."

"Hang on here," I said. "What's this love business? Who's this Frankie? What miscarriage? "

He looked sheepish. "Guess I wasn't a great correspondent, huh."

"You never are. The year you spent in that Tibetan ashram, or whatever it was, I think I got one card."

"Yeah. Well . . ." he uncoiled himself from the chair and fished in his back pocket for his billfold. From one of the plastic inserts he took a picture and handed it to me. "That is Frankie," he said, collapsing again in a pile of bones. "It's funny. I hold you indirectly responsible, so I guess I sort of assumed you knew. I guess I should have written."

"Telepathy has always been my short suit."

"Back when I was just a hungry undergraduate scrounging meals off my favorite guru I used to look at your tranquil domestic scene and say to myself, 'boy, if I ever find a good woman like Eliot Warren's got, I'm gonna marry her and settle down to slippers and pipe.' So when

26

I found her, working for a collection agency I had a little altercation with, I whisked her off to England and made her mine. How *is* Mrs. Warren . . . Erica?" He blushed, caught in the middle. No longer a boy, not yet an equal.

"She's okay," I said. "She'll be delighted to see you." To change the subject I told him I was sorry to hear about a miscarriage. Tough break. Erica had been through one herself.

"Oh, I don't know," he said. "To be strictly honest about it I don't know if we wanted to celebrate or go into mourning. The idea of a baby was a disaster at first, what with no money, no prospects, and my book hardly begun . . . wait till you read it. It's GREAT . . . but anyway, we retooled to meet the future and got our faces all fixed, and then when she lost it we felt sort of cheated. I did, anyway."

"So you grew a mustache to hide your doleful puss," I said.

He looked puzzled, then blushed. "I got tired of everyone telling me I looked like a Hari Krishna. But listen, I didn't come by to talk about my troubles. I just wanted to say hello and . . . well, actually there are a couple things I wanted to ask you."

" Fire away."

"Only if I don't get a cup of coffee I'm going to croak. You mind if I run over to the cafeteria and bring one back? "

I did not mind. Besides, his absence gave me a chance to fill in the record and reflect on the minor changes in Willy's appearance that might or might not be important. That mustache there, I told myself, is a metaphor for change, significant because it is *not* accompanied by any of the other trappings and paraphernalia of the post-modern world — no long hair, no leathers, no hiking

27

boots, no costume jewelry, no patches on his pants. It shows us that Willy is capable of concession to his fundamentalist upbringing, but just barely. And not much. He always was, and still is, the straightest young man I have ever met. Obviously gets his ears lowered once a month. Buys his moccasins from L. L. Bean. Stern, intense, serious. His wire frame glasses are not a sartorial gesture. He wears them because the army issued him two pairs, and he is, among other things, frugal. He is also a compulsive worker, and very bright.

Willy, I remembered as I sat there waiting for him to return, began his career as student at just about the same time I began teaching in New England. I had two sections of "bonehead" English in those days, and one of a survey course that led the yawning scholar from Grendel's lair to Gray's churchyard in twelve easy lessons, one lesson a week. Eight centuries in thirty-six hours. A kind of whistle-stop tour through the *Norton Anthology of English Literature, Volume 1,* with a layover in Crabbe's "Village" because the chairman of the department (a scribbler of notes and queries to the PMLA) thought Crabbe one of the great neglected realists of the early nineteenth century. The only thing that saved me from weekly self-mutilation as I plowed dismally through "Twickenham Garden" and "A Voyage to the Country of the Houyhnhnms" was Willy Ward.

"The plot of Congreve's *The Way of the World,*" I would announce, having never read Congreve, and having lifted my question from some guide to Restoration comedy, "is deliberately complex. The author deals out his secrets so gradually that they assume an intricacy far beyond the actual situation in the play. Now why do you think, you there with your hydrocephalic head on your desk, that he does this? What does he gain by exploiting the schism between appearance and fact?"

Twelve yahoos regard me dully. Schism? The radiator hisses and clanks and somewhere in Passaic, New Jersey, two Youth-for-Christers set fire to a muttering drunk. Outside a light rain is falling, and if the sky doesn't clear tonight the drainfield for the septic tank will overflow. "I think," Willy Ward says, after an appropriate pause, waiting to see if anyone wants a shot at it, "that Congreve is testing the differences between emotional and dynastic reality. The play criticizes appearances which are not the natural outgrowth of an internalized, that is to say, emotional, reality." Ah! Is he dealing in the same brand of horseshit I traffic? Dynastic reality? Is he trying to beat the master at his own game? We continue this exchange for the remaining forty minutes while the philistines belch and sweat and doggedly eyeball the clock.

Willy came back with his coffee. We talked for a while about reverse culture-shock, soaring prices, outrageous rents, and the apparent decline of student radicalism — "a return to the fifties mentality," he called it. Like most academics, budding and otherwise, he liked to speak with authority about subjects he had never actually experienced. Then we reminisced awhile about the good old days in New Hampshire before I came to California and he eventually followed suit. Finally, he got to the real point of his visit. "I wonder if there is any way you can get me a teaching job for the spring quarter?" he said. "I'm so broke I don't know week to week where the groceries are going to come from."

I scratched my face. "I don't know," I said. "I don't really have anything to do with teaching assistantships, and I imagine you've used up your allotment anyway, no?"

"Yes, but I wasn't thinking of being a T.A. I was hoping maybe there would be some soft money around to do a course of my own. I could work up something on Hesse, or the Bible as Literature, or the role of Seventh Day

Adventism in a structuralist approach to literature; heck, I could even teach a fiction writing course, if you needed somebody."

"Did you talk to the chairman?"

"He was pretty evasive. Talked about National Defense loans and the like. But he did say if one of the colleges would come up with half the salary, the department might find the rest. I thought maybe you could pry something loose up here. I wouldn't ask, but I'm desperate, and if I take any job other than teaching I won't get the book finished."

"I can try, Willy," I said. "That's about the best I can tell you right now. It's fine with me, but I don't control the purse strings."

"I'd appreciate it," he said. "We've already rented out the garage for a student to live in, and Frankie has a line on a job, but England set us pretty far in debt even with the fellowship. So whatever you can do."

"I'll talk to the Provost this afternoon."

He gulped down the rest of his coffee and threw the paper cup in the wastebasket. "There is one more thing, since I'm begging favors. Honest, Eliot, I wouldn't have the audacity to ask this of you if you hadn't been so damn decent to me ever since I started my checkered career . . . something of a paradox, what? I inflict myself on those who are nicest to me." He held up his hand like a street beggar and crossed himself.

"Okay okay," I said. "Skip the *patrone* number."

"Yes, I know. But what's happened is I've changed my direction a bit. (Two hands this time, to ward off my groan.) I've moved into the History of Consciousness program because it allows me to stay in graduate school with what amounts to an undefined status. An actual degree no longer seems very important to me. Basically all I've ever wanted to do since I defied my mother and refused to go into the seminary is write fiction, and the His-Con people will let me work on my novel as a major part of my program."

For the second time in the space of less than an hour I was confronted by a young man whose creative aspirations exceeded his abilities. Not that Willy was in any respect like Arington. He was infinitely brighter. But I had read some samples of his fictional endeavors long before he went to England to work on this thesis, and imagination, the ability to invent, Willy surely did not have. Perhaps that was one of the reasons he went about so busily assimilating other people's lives.

"I suppose you hold me indirectly responsible for the new directions too?" I said.

"I always acknowledge my sources."

"Good boy. And you want me to read the novel."

"Yes."

"Is it any good?"

"It's great."

I hesitated, then made a stab at being candid. "Sure, I'll read it, but I really think you're making a mistake. I think you ought to stick with what you know you're good at and not gum up your career trying to play Renaissance man."

Willy looked at me shrewdly. "Well, you know one of the reasons I came out here in the first place was to learn from the pros. I notice you manage to combine the interpretive and the creative process."

I squirmed uncomfortably. I enjoy an ego massage as much as the next man, but there was something just a tad unctuous about Willy. "I don't do either very well," I said. "I'd be better off if I could put my mind and energy on one thing. And I think you would too. All you get by splitting yourself in half is ulcers and a skin rash."

"What would you get if you didn't even try?"

"Peace. Tranquillity."

"I think you'd feel that you sold out."

"Okay," I told him sternly. "Leave us not get into that can of figs. I said I'd read your book. But when you wind up on welfare don't say I didn't warn you."

He smiled. "I need a couple of weeks to polish the last section before I'll have a draft I like. Then I'll bring it to you."

"I can hardly wait, William. Every morning I'll get up wondering if the day has come."

"No, you'll like it. It's all about sin, guilt, and redemption in the sixteenth century."

It was almost noon and my stomach was roaring. I walked him out to the parking lot, promised once again to speak to the Provost about funds for a course, and headed for my own car to go home for lunch. Among other things I was hoping to make restitution with Erica. Harry Weisberg caught up with me halfway and bummed a ride down the hill. "I have some tragic news," he said. "Those two beautiful, nubile, lovely, luscious lassies? Sassy assies? Classy chassies? (For Christ's sake, Weisberg.) Well, the old man has just turned their case over to the Committee on Disciplinary Action and eat your heart out, Eliot, because I am the fucking *chairman* of that committee. And I use the adjective advisedly, pal, in the same sense as hanging-judge Roy Bean. Fucking chairman Harold Weisberg. That's me."

Three

WHEN I ARRIVED HOME THAT TUESDAY FULL OF GOOD INTEN-
tions and discovered that Erica was not there and that
there was nothing for lunch I went into a snit. There
was a time when I would not have given a damn (or would
have given a damn, but for better reasons); in fact, until
the last six months of our living together, if the thought
had ever crossed my mind that she ought to be home, I
would have rejected it out of hand as absurd and un-
desirable. Domesticity to that extent had never been a
part of our scene. In Cambridge, where we spent our
first year and a half in a small apartment off Prospect
Street, we had been completely independent of each other
at all but dinner and bedtime. Erica was dressed and gone
to work before I was civil enough to carry on a conversation, and didn't return until five-thirty or six. I left
for the university around eleven, and was almost never
back before seven. More often than not we ate out during

the week, and on weekends, except during the winter, we would cook over a hibachi on the back porch of our apartment. The porch was screened and half-covered with vines. With the front door open a breeze blew down the hall keeping it cool and rustly. My favorite recollection of that time and place is dozing in the hammock of a Sunday afternoon, Erica sprawled on the throw rug with a pillow bunched under her chest and the Sunday paper spread around her, the Boston Symphony on the radio. The phone would ring. Let it ring. Better answer it, it may be your mother. Then you answer it, she's your mother. But it's another graduate student couple engaged in the same lazy Sunday afternoon, suggesting dinner, someplace cheap. Maybe take in a flick after. And why not? It's a full life. Time for everything. The only problem is, it doesn't last.

When we left Cambridge in 1960 with the start of my thesis in one box and the start of a novel in another, there seemed no particular reason to hurry to take a job. We had lived on my fellowship and the GI Bill, and Erica's earnings had all gone into the bank. Her father offered us the use of a farmhouse he had bought for his retirement in Canaan, New Hampshire, and we took him up on it. Work on the thesis. Work on the book. Be together, all the time, for the first time.

Except that it had been me who had accepted the farm and dreamed up the togetherness. Erica liked her job in Medford, and over the year had been given an increasing amount of responsibility. She was editing films, traveling to places like Stowe and Bar Harbor and Marblehead to do promotional work because the firm had branched out into fifteen-minute tourist quickies for "sports" resorts. She didn't want to leave Boston. "Why can't we just stay here the way we are, and you work on your books, and I'll keep my job and make us gobs of money?" she asked.

"I'm sick of the city," I told her. "I want to get out in the country where I'm not interrupted all the time, and where I can go out for a little air without freezing or frying or choking on carbon monoxide."

"But think of the money, Eliot. We're saving almost four hundred a month now, and anyway I'm just really getting into this job. We could stay another year, you finish your thesis, and we'll have enough to go to Italy or Spain for a year. You can write two novels and two theses if you have nothing else to do."

I told her she was an incurable romantic and that I was temporarily sick of Cambridge right then, not in a year, and for about a month we discussed it until one day, after a session during which I hammered in a number of old bromides such as "it's a woman's place to follow her man wherever he goes," she gave in. Reluctantly, but with grace, I thought, she gave the company notice, and a month later we moved. To make the whole thing more financially acceptable, and to offer up a sacrifice of my own, I landed a teaching job at a nearby college and spent eight hours a week imparting the secrets of English composition to knotheaded prep school failures who hadn't made it into Princeton or Yale.

It has been said that there are only two things to do if you live in a small New England town — and you can't fish in the winter. In the spring of our first year of freedom, Erica found she was pregnant. This crisis was tougher to deal with. It was not a joyful discovery. "I want an abortion," she said, and burst into tears.

The time was 1961 and abortions were not legal. They could be had, but they were expensive and dangerous, and in any case I was not sufficiently modernized to take the rejection of an heir without having my feelings hurt. I didn't even want to discuss it. Erica tried reason, plea bargaining, and finally anger. "Do you want it?" she asked.

"No," I admitted, "but one pays for one's pleasures."

"Please don't give me that bullshit."

"I'm perfectly serious."

"Look, Eliot, I don't want a baby, not now and maybe not ever, if it's up to me. If you want kids, okay, but later, definitely not now. I'm twenty-six, for God's sake." She stared dismally out at the rain-soaked field below the house. The clouds were down in the treetops. "Honey, we've hardly had two years together, remember? And you in school. I want to live a little before I become some scout's mother."

"Maybe it'll be a girl," I said.

She actually began to cry. "This isn't a joking matter. You don't have any idea how I feel about it. I don't want it."

Maybe because I had twenty-five themes to read, or maybe because I had been up half the night trying to fix one of the oil furnaces, or maybe just because I was secretly a little proud of having reproduced myself, I got self-righteous and vanished into my study, banging the door. I expected a long and quite possibly bloody war, but oddly enough it was the last discussion we had on the subject. Erica, for reasons she chose not to divulge, accepted pregnancy, and went about preparing for the addition with a curious calm that I found, under the circumstances, completely disconcerting. I too, however, kept my feelings to myself.

We were spared major alteration of our life-style when Erica miscarried and we did not change our pattern. Moving to the Midwest for a two-year hitch and then to California in 1965 we did. The move from the isolation of New Hampshire back into the mainstream of urban life seemed to reactivate in Erica some of her yearning for an independent existence — or at least a degree of independence that being a housewife didn't provide. She received ample encouragement from women around her, the wives of my colleagues, most of whom were beginning to be crazed by the thought of equal rights. Then Pickle came along.

And the university, for all the talk about its elitism and distance from "real life," was as shifting and unstable an environment as one could possibly find (unlike the farm); a microcosm of human discontent where, as I saw it, envy, spite, greed, self-aggrandizement, backbiting, entrail gnawing, hairsplitting were carried on with such an intensity that they pervaded not only one's professional life, but one's private life as well. Not only did I have to suffer the accusation of the department's matrons that I was a male chauvinist (which, of course, I was — and probably still am), I was getting echoes of the same line at home. The more time Erica spent drinking coffee with other faculty wives, complaining, I imagined, about the absence of day-care centers that would free them for jobs they did not really want, nepotism rules that kept them from accompanying their husbands to the office, discriminatory practices that prevented them from becoming oil riggers and truck drivers, the more angry I became with what I saw as her abdication as a housewife. Pickle didn't change a thing.

And so it was with some irritation that day that I noticed, on entering the bedroom to hang up my jacket, that the bed was not yet made, that the ashtray on the night stand was overflowing, and the dirty laundry was tossed in a corner. "I wait for enough to make a load," was Erica's excuse. Already there was enough for a laundromat. In the kitchen the breakfast dishes sat on the sink counter, and the garbage bag was propped against the back door, as if she had started to dump it and had been interrupted Or said the hell with it, which was more likely.

I looked in the bread drawer for the foundation of a sandwich, but there was none, and I wound up making myself a salad out of some limp lettuce, tuna fish, and the remains of a bottle of Miracle Whip that had not yet completely transformed itself into penicillin. In the ice-box there were some highly suspicious bowls of leftovers, loosely topped with waxed paper and rubber bands, which I dumped into the disposal along with a half carton of bruise-colored yogurt and a solidified lump of sour cream. My mood was not enhanced by the discovery that the coffee had been boiled at least once since breakfast, but I drank it anyway. It gave me an acid stomach.

When I finished I washed the dishes and put them in the drying rack. Then I went into the bedroom and got the ashtrays, dumped them irritably in the garbage bag, and, belching fire, took it out to the service yard. The neighbor's dog had once again turned the can over, and I was trying to tip it upright, balancing on one foot while using the other to snag the handle and flip it on its bot-tom, when the sack in my hand broke and I found myself cuff deep in coffee grounds and spoiled cabbage. Enraged, I flung the soggy bag against the wall, kicked garbage all over the walk, and was on my way in to commit suicide when Erica drove up and deplaned from her hideous Citroën, dragging Lenny with one hand and a ten-pound sack of nitrogen with the other. We had a little collision in the kitchen.

"Hi," she said, handing me my son and offering a poof of imaginary exhaustion. "Thought I'd give the lemon trees a feeding." She put the nitrogen on the counter and turned to wash her hands at the sink.

"That's nice, Erica," I said, glaring at her neck. "That's very thoughtful. Only if they're on the same schedule as everybody else around here they're probably DEAD by now, and you're going to go out and put your 'spoonit' on next winter's FIREWOOD, not live, vigorous juicy TREES. Because they'll be DEAD, ERICA, LIKE EVERYTHING ELSE AROUND HERE! FROM TOO LITTLE TO EAT." Pickle sat down on the floor, and I took a deep breath. "Well, at least it's not for our consumption. Jesus, I wouldn't be surprised if Adele Davis recommends it for a healthy prostate or something."

"Wow," she said, "you're really freaked today. What's the matter with you anyway, you get fired?"

"What's the matter with me," I intoned, in the calmest voice I could conjure, "is that there is nothing to *eat* in this house, there is *never* anything to eat in this house, I am growing *cobwebs* in my ass on account of the lack of eats in this house! That's the first thing that's the matter with me. The second is that there is filth in every room because you are so goddamn lazy you won't pick up a broom and clean it. The third thing is that I have exactly one T-shirt and no shorts and no socks in my dresser drawer because you can't find time in your busy schedule of coffee clatches and harpie happenings to drop a little soap in the washing machine and turn the *dial*. There's a lot more wrong with me, but that will do for openers."

Erica shrugged. More battles that we'd been through before. "The washing machine is fucked. I told you that two weeks ago."

I stared at her, my hands on the doorjamb above my head. "It's *what?*"

"It's fucked. I told you three weeks ago to call the plumber, or whoever you call." She was rummaging in the icebox, no doubt wondering where the tuna fish had gone.

With my hands still above my head, I turned around and shuffled into the dining room. "My favorite washing machine is fucked," I informed the ceiling. Holding a make-believe telephone in my right hand, I put through a

call. "Western Appliance? Gimme the service department on the double. This is Dr. Eliot Warren, Ph.D.,
Harvard, '63, professor of the king's English. I'd appreciate it very much if you would get over here *tout de suite*
and look at my bloody washing machine. It's fucked."
I hung up and turned to peek at my wife. "Where do
you *get* that kind of talk?"

She regarded me as if I were a harmless though irritating lunatic. "What's with you, anyway? You're not
exactly Mr. Clean in the language department, not that
I've ever noticed. I don't know where I get it. Everybody
says that now when something is busted. It's current
usage, professor, though I suppose if it's not in the OED
it's inadmissible in your repertoire. And as for the rest
of that crap you just dumped on me, you can go fly it.
There's plenty to eat around here. If you want Langen-
dorf bread and chocolate milk like your mother weaned
you on you can eat out, and if you want clean shirts every
day of the week, take 'em to hell to the laundry yourself.
Try making out by yourself for a change."

"You know something, Erica," I said, "I think I might
just do that. I think I might just move myself out of this
slum. I think that might be one of the better ideas you've
had in a long time."

"I think it's pretty good myself," she snapped.

"Well, fine," I said, "fine. I'm goddamn well going to
do that."

I would like to have left on the tails of a more snappy
retort, but I couldn't think of anything And I was just
a little amazed that it was really happening. Was this
typical? Was this the collective experience, the whimper
on which the great institution comes to an end? "Fine.
Fine." Mumbling off to collect shorts and shirts and the
blue dress socks with a hole in the heel? Surely I should
have raged, torn up several acres of planet, brought down

the universe, committed murder. Anything but "fine, fine," and out into the hot afternoon sun with my brief-case full of dirty underwear to check into some miserable "Bide-a-Wee" Motel. I suppose I felt abused. The whole damn day, starting with Pickle's thumb sucking at five-thirty A.M., quiff and quim parading through the fog of my morning coffee, and Arington capping whatever seep-age of humor might have finally leaked through the fis-sures of my crusty soul, had been a conspiracy leading to the plank. Walking out on my wife (or being thrown out, depending on how you wish to view it) was a fitting con-clusion. I mean, how else would you wrap up a Tuesday?

Part Two

One

HOIST ON THE PETARD OF ERICA'S FEMINISM, OUSTED FROM
the comfortable clutter of my own house and grounds
(the terms of my self-pity then), cast into the stucco nightmare of housekeeping apartments, motel rooms, condo-
miniums-by-the-week, beach cottages — all the stains
and smells, peeling plaster and rotten plumbing of the
short-term lease, I was finally rescued by Harry Weisberg.
He lent me a room above his garage, and I spent a week
or so fixing it up and making it more or less habitable,
getting a bed from the Goodwill, a purple couch with
matching chair from the Drug Rehabilitation Center (remade junk and junkies, said Harry) and building myself
a desk out of an old door and some redwood two-by-fours
I found in the rafters of Harry's garage. In the same place
I also found a stack of girlie magazines and a dirty comic
entitled *Tits and Clits*. My Cyprian landlord must have
stuck them there and forgotten them, though a few, like

the comic and a "collector's series" paperback with a lurid cartoon of an Al Capp mountaineeress propped against a loblolly pine, fellating a banana the size of an atom bomb, were of contemporary vintage. I think the title of the collector's item was *Three's a Sandwich,* and was positively not for sale to minors — a curious restriction, since only a minor could have been entertained by its hieroglyphical prose anyway. Took it to my room and installed it in my library.

Spring quarter began, as it always did, with students trailing in to get their study cards signed, to beg for an independent study in Vonnegut, Dylan ("no, man, *Bob* Dylan, the *poet*"), Carlos Castaneda, whoever happened to be the sophomore rage at the time, or to inquire about the requirements of a particular course. ("Papers! Oh shit, I can't write papers!") Two girls outside my office thumbed through the catalog while they waited for an interview with Ted Helton, "Chairperson" of the Ecology Department. "I got it figured out for my religious studies course," one of them said. "Like I'm going to do women in the church. And like for my sociology course I'm going to do women in South America. But I can't figure out what I'm going to do for calculus."

"Really!" her companion said.

Just before noon on that first day of registration Willy Ward dropped in to see if I had plans for lunch. I didn't and we walked over to the dining common together and went through the line. I asked him how things were going. He allowed smoothly enough. The job I had engineered for him wasn't precisely what he had hoped for, lower division, and not as much money as he thought he was worth, and not offered in fulfillment of the degree requirements in literature, but it was a job. He thanked me profusely. Without it he would have been on the hook. To make him feel better I grumbled a little about the submissions I was reading from supplicants to my fiction writing workshop — "emissions" I think was the way I described them — and we got into the first phase of what was to become a patterned conversation.

"They're not any good?" he asked.

"If I ever get a story from a student that isn't about the discovery of the self, that has more than one character in it, and that goes on for more than six pages, I'll submit it for a Pulitzer."

"Didn't you ever write six pages discovering yourself?"

"Never."

"I would think that people write better when they write about something important."

"They write better when the thing that is important ceases to be themselves. How do you suppose it's possible to make Jell-O taste this way? You think they put mortar in it?"

"I'm serious. If you're eighteen years old why not do something that forces you to confront yourself in a formal way?"

I noticed that Willy had been out in the sun a good deal since his return to California, and had acquired the kind of parboiled coloring of a red haired man who doesn't tan. He wore a faded green shirt that was frayed at the cuffs and a white knit tie, and in spite of his resemblance to a seedy Christmas package, he didn't look well. I considered telling him to relax, take things a little easier, the quarter was just beginning.

"It seems to me," he went on, "that working on your own case is the logical place to start writing anyway. 'Be thyself, young man. Go forth to create the features of your face and race.' "

"With a footnote to Joyce," I observed. "But actually, why be yourself when you could be somebody interesting?"

"You don't believe that. You know perfectly well that beneath the crusty surface of every student there is enough of interest to sustain a hundred stories."

What the hell was he talking about? Beneath the crusty surface? I should pass out soap and towels with the class cards? For self-discovery, just add water?

"Don't forget, I've known you a long time, Professor. I've studied the mold. All you really lack, now and then, is a little compassion."

I looked at him in amusement. "Ah, that's it," I said. "Compassion. Well, thank God we have your vast storehouse of experience to draw on, I thought I was just bored."

"Like with Arington. You didn't treat *him* with much compassion."

Now I was truly amazed. "How do you know Arington?"

"He rents my garage."

"You're kidding."

"No. He and a guy named Kirschner have fixed it up into a pretty nice living space."

I started to laugh. The contrast between those two stoned freaks and the sober, intense Mr. Ward was too much. "At least they won't require plumbing," I said.

"They use our bathroom," he said.

"How nice for your wife."

He blushed and ducked his head. Obviously it was not so nice for his wife, but in the interests of the rent money she had given in. "What I meant about that self-discovery stuff," he said, "is that I think students are pretty complicated human beings at an especially complicated time of life. They need an outlet from their chemistry labs, their math problems, and it's better they learn about themselves in a writing class than grind away at accounting or engineering and wind up ten years later on the psychiatrist's couch trying to figure out what went wrong."

"Better for whom?"

"For them, obviously."

"But what we are concerned about here is *me*."

A tall, good-looking girl in a pair of shorts and a halter sort of top that looked, for all it covered, as if it might be the undershirt of some NFL linebacker stopped at the table where we were eating and asked if I was going to be in my office during the afternoon. I said I was. Would I have time to see her for a few minutes? *What more of her was there to see? Well . . . some . . . between thigh and navel, of course, and, well, yes, I would like to see that, though I seem to remember . . . but those shorts, then, you would perhaps remove them? Sir? By all means! My Christ, where was it, dammit, lummox, dimpled buttocks, shivering, shankers, that tush, luxuriant bush, cush, smoosh, I know your case is familiar, common to girls of your particular complexion and hair coloring. I'm worse than Weisberg. My mother was a Sicilian, Sir. Was she really now? Fascinating, absolutely . . . but your eyes, love, lovely, surely they are more Nordic? Ice-blue, pale, and your temper a bit mild. A Latin lass would break my fingers for me. Oh, but I like your fingers, Sir. Don't be smutty, precious, remember I'm twice your age. May want you for dinner tonight, to invite you for dinner, to dinner, know this little Mexican restaurant with the most exquisite* chile rellenos *north of Paso Robles, the cook a personal friend of mine, of course, knows precisely how I take the* GUACAMOLE *on my* FLAUTAS, *hot, wash with* TRES EQUIS, *cold as your eyes, dearie, I know of only one other place where* TRES EQUIS *can be obtained in the entire state of California . . .*

None of this took place. Not, anyway, in the order that

I've set it down. Willy was just becoming tiresome with his prattle about compassion and self-discovery and I did a little Ali shuffle to break away. But it did actually happen, in an altered sequence and form. I kept trying that afternoon, as I sat at my desk listening to Nina Allencraig describe a project she wanted to pursue involving Goya, Otto Rank, and Norman Thomas (I have total amnesia regarding her proposal except its stolen title, "What if Goya had a Guggenheim?") . . . I kept trying to remember where I had seen her before. Or more precisely, where I had seen that *body* before, bulging beneath my bloodstained eyeballs. Mona's Gorilla Lounge? Dona's Drink and Diddle? My nose was beginning to run.

"Have you been in a class of mine, Nina?"

"No."

"Hmmm." In the dirty books that Weisberg leaves around his office (in the hopes that some coed will catch the drift of his interests) such pulchritude is generally greeted by catchy expletives like WWHHUUNNGGG! and AARRGGHHH! I should be more demonstrative. "Hmmm."

"So, like I said, the idea that reaction generates action, or if you want to put it another way, frustration generates creativity (it does, my dear, it does), seems to me a reasonable idea, even if Otto Rank overextends it."

"You weren't in Schiller's seminar last quarter, maybe? American romantics? I lectured twice."

"And if we accept the theory that art is a creative release from our anxieties . . . maybe I should say created *as* a release *for* our anxieties . . . Mr. Eliot, are you listening?"

"Warren. Mr. Warren. Call me Eliot, though."

"Mr. Warren, are you following me?"

"Say again."

"I mean, because if you're trying to remember where

you saw me before it was out in the courtyard about ten days ago, only you probably don't recognize me with my clothes on. So if we could get back to my project . . ."

WWHHUUNNGG! and AARRRGGGHHH! "Nina, would you care to meet me at, say, seven at the Azteca? We could run through this Rank stuff once more over a bottle of *San Miguel* and a *burrito*."

"Sir? Oh, well gee . . . Mr. Eliot."

"Just call me Warren, Nina."

"Warren. I guess I could, but . . . I mean, aren't you married?"

"I'm only asking you, Nina, to share my *burrito*, not my bed."

"Well, gee. Okay, then, I guess I could. I guess that'd be swell, El." Ha ha. Nina was the only person who ever called me that. I am still out of sync.

Willy's wife, whom I still had not met by the third week of the quarter, found herself a job at the yacht harbor selling slickers and swedges and sailboats (whatever it is they sell in marine hardware stores), and Willy had access to all the various gear they rent to inland weekenders and would-be surfers from the San Joaquin Valley. He took up skin diving, and like all latecomers to the faith, became a fantatic. On a number of occasions he tried to coax me out into the bay to prowl around with him through whatever weedy murk lies below its metallic surface.

Even in summer there is nothing terribly inviting about the waters off northern California. They are not only opaque and troubled, they are cold. Willy had a long and involved argument with me in which he attempted to demonstrate an existential relationship between one's soul and the force of tides and currents and the shafts of sunlight that filter weakly through the kelp, but I told him I took my teleology above wave, preferably on a comfortable boat of not less than forty feet, preferably with a gin and tonic in my hand. The pug-uglies of the deep would have to get along without me.

More and more often my conversations with him (which usually took place in my office or at lunch) turned into dialectics. I would be drawn into making some off-the-top-of-the-head statements about teaching or students or women's rights or the price of bean sprouts, and all of a sudden I would find myself defending an ill-considered point of view that I had no commitment to or interest in, and I would more often than not wind up entangled in contradictions that were not even, it seemed, of my own making. It was bizarre. I don't know how I let myself get sucked in. It was the same kind of number I was always getting into with Erica back when we were trying to outdo each other in unpleasantness. Once, I remember, Erica was furious about the intellectual limitations of a local group called Citizens for Decency, who had launched a rock-throwing campaign at the town's only porn shop in an effort to close it down, and I was sitting in the kitchen one day, lunching on garbanzo beans and lecithin-laced orange juice, when finally her strident denunciation of a bunch of people she knew nothing about got to me. "I think the Citizens for Decency are right on, God damn it," I said. "That place is evil."

Erica, naturally enough, was surprised. "Are you kidding me?" she said. "Nobody says you have to go there if you don't dig it. Nobody forces you."

"Right," I told her. "But assume I'm as obsessed as the next guy, and I go, I've been, in fact; not to this one, but to others, they are all over the place, and they are the skuzziest dumps you ever laid eyes on, honest to God. They absolutely kill the senses, dry up the juices, deaden the appetites . . ."

"So stay out. That doesn't give you the right to start throwing rocks and depriving other people of their rights."

"That's not the point," I said. "Listen, Erica, the thing is this. When I was a kid, okay, I used to get a big bang out of underwear ads. In the Sears Roebuck catalog, for instance, I was quite literally crazed with lust by all that 'nylon tricot' or whatever it was, and I'd sneak off to the can with number 4785 in my shirt, 'Matching bra and panty set in blue, gold, white. Matching slips and garter belts.' *Garter belts.* Just *thinking* about garter belts would turn me to froth. But now . . . *now* . . . every time I turn around there's another muff staring me in the face, and I can't even get a tingle anymore. I'm saturated with skin. I'm festooned in pubic hair. I want to go back to the good old days when sex was dirty and playing with your wick was a sign of insanity and your old man gave you lectures about wind sprints around the block. When you had to be furtive just to get a peek at a girl's drawers, Erica, it was *fun.* Now it's just boring. Thanks to all this freedom."

"All of which has absolutely nothing to do with what we were talking about," Erica said. "All of which is completely beside the point about censorship and one group's right to interfere . . ."

"It has everything to do with it," I said. "When you make things too easy, too available, you diminish their ultimate value. Too much freedom dulls the appetite."

"I think you are completely full of shit. If somebody wants to dull his appetite, that's his business. You give me a headache."

"Why don't you take an aspirin?" I sneered.

"It's bad for your stomach."

I stomped into my study to spend the rest of the evening reading Emerson. There, at least, was a moralist to reckon with. Crazy. I had nothing against porn.

My standard counterattack with Willy, however, was to turn the whole debate into a joke at some point and refuse to address myself seriously to the points he would try to raise. It frustrated him (which is why I did it), and a curious kind of hostility began to surface in his voice and his gestures, a bitterness that I realize now I hardly recognized and certainly ignored. He only checked his irritation, I suppose, because I was still his teacher and mentor, and in some way he had chosen to pattern his life after the image he carried of mine. I was, also, of course, responsible for the job he held at the university.

And held very well, I should add. The students liked him. He was conscientious, thorough, had a lively classroom manner. A couple of writing students (not the easiest types to please in a class devoted to literary criticism) remarked that he was "one cool dude" at the seminar table. Asked to explain: "Well, it's like he sits there, you know, at the head of the table, no jacket, no tie, and he's picking his teeth with a toothpick and staring out the window like he's thinking about the beach or his lady or something, and right at the point where you're absolutely sure he can't have the slightest idea what's been going on for the last ten minutes, he swings around, points his toothpick at some creep who's been doing a critique and says 'Has it occurred to you, Smithers, that the reason Lawrence's mature verse seems technically original is that it has a metrical norm that is different from most English poetry?' or something like that, and everybody lays back and goes 'farout.' Smithers is wiped away, but he doesn't know it because he's got all this heavy shit to think about, stuff that's actually simple and out front, but then the whole seminar turns into an intelligent discussion instead of the same old lit crit recap number that most guys lay on you."

I mentioned this to Willy but he was not particularly

surprised nor flattered. "They're a good bunch of kids," he said. "All I do, actually, is throw out a few one-liners and they carry the ball. They're very sharp."

"One-liners, huh."

"Isn't that what you told me once. Learning to teach is learning to con people into thinking you know your stuff when in fact you haven't ever read the book?" His faint smile said that if I had told him such a thing he didn't believe me, and in any event it wasn't a con he would ever employ. For every one-liner he threw out I'm sure he prepared two or three hours.

"I had a friend in graduate school," I told him, "who did better than that. He didn't just pretend he'd read things he hadn't, he'd *invent* a book, start talking in very pompous terms about its 'machinery,' to see if he could sucker anybody into the discussion, always nailing the hapless ass who wished to please in the middle of some pomposity about the limitation of the novel in question being the author's failure to make a felt distinction between the self and the work of art, something vague enough that would apply to anything, and then he would rear back and cackle, point an accusing finger at the speaker and say "You fool, there is no such book. I made it up."

"That's pretty cruel," Willy said.

I glanced over at him. I could see that the idea really offended him, that he was actually upset. "Well it was just a game. The fraud test we called it. Lots of people failed."

"You say this man was a friend?"

"A friend, yes. An acquaintance." I studied his pinched frown. "Willy, it was a joke. The guy who invented it had it played on him often enough, you can be sure."

"Why would you be friends with someone like that?"

"For Christ's sake, don't be so sententious. I told you it was just a game, a kind of initiation rite over a pitcher of beer that we used to pull on new graduate students. We weren't interviewing them for jobs."

"Who is the fraud in that situation? The one who fails the 'test'? Or the ones who administer it?"

"I'm not going to continue this discussion, William," I said. "I'm sorry I brought it up."

He rubbed his face in his hands for a few minutes and then looked at me with bright eyes. "You're right," he said. "I'm so damn tired I'm losing my perspective. Nothing strikes me as very funny anymore."

What puzzled me about Willy as the first weeks of the term progressed was not only the increasing tension he seemed to be under, but, given the kind of success he was enjoying in the classroom, the self-doubts that began to surface at our lunchtime arguments. He acted toward me as if I held some great, dark secret down inside of me that he had to get hold of in order to adjust the direction he was taking, in order to put himself in "perspective," as he said. Because now, more than at any previous time in his life, he was questioning the limitations of a career teaching people how to be analytical about a work of literature. He had been moving in that direction ever since coming back from England, but the classroom procedure he was subjected to three days a week brought the dilemma home in very concrete ways. "How do you justify it to yourself?" he would ask. "How do you sit there dissecting some magnificent passage of poetry as if it were a frog on the laboratory table, and then go home and put on your other hat and start creating worlds out of words?"

"Is that 'you' in the generic sense?"

"No, that's you, Eliot Warren."

"I eat a lot of Tums."

Willy wanted answers, not jokes. Probe, probe, probe. He managed finally to get on my nerves because I was not prepared to give out answers. I just did what I did. Figure out your own life, I began to think, and stop borrowing mine. In fact, *why* are you borrowing mine? What is this apostolic business, anyway? Why be me when you could be somebody interesting? The more I thought about it the more peculiar it seemed, and I never really did figure it out. Actually, I suppose one of the reasons I had always rather liked Willy was that he was such a curiosity and a contradiction — a pacifist who joined the army, an ascetic who became a short-term junkie, a Catholic who practiced Buddhism — maybe it had to do with wanting to be a writer. He just went around endlessly absorbing other people's worlds.

One Saturday I was called to the phone at chez Weisberg and again invited by Willy for an afternoon of fun in the sun. Frankie's boss had invented a new kind of wet suit, he said, and I just had to come down and help him test it out. It was a hot day. The chapters I was working on were not moving. I decided to accept the offer and get it over with.

Driving down into town I could see across the bay where the mountains behind Monterey faded into whitish haze, part mist from the surf, part smoke from the Moss Landing power plant, part heat. As I neared the ocean it grew a bit cooler, but the mast pennants and wind indicators on the boats in the harbor were motionless, and the oil slick water was glassy and calm. I parked in front of the boat shop, asked for Willy, and was told he was up in the weather station on top of the building.

Once on the roof I paused to look out over the beach below, only mildly crowded for a Saturday, and devoid of the usual contingent of body surfers because the shore break was too small to attract. I could see a couple dozen boards out by the point. From a half mile away their riders looked like seals, black bodies rolling over the crest of the swells, waiting for a decent set.

Willy was sitting on an air mattress on the lee side of the weather shack, his back against the wall and his eyes closed. He held a pair of binoculars loosely in his lap. "Afternoon," he said, without moving his head or opening his eyes. "Pull up a chair and explain to me why you think Sut Lovingood is a funny man."

"Is that what you do down here?" I asked, sitting on the end of the mattress and picking up the glasses. "Read *Sut Lovingood*?" I fiddled with the focus wheel of the binoculars. "Sut is funny for the same reason it would be hysterical if you fell off this roof and cracked open your skull. Side splitting when somebody's maimed or killed. Read Bergson on humor."

He ignored my answer, if he even heard it. "Look down there toward the end of the jetty," he said, "and you'll see a young lady with no top to her suit."

I adjusted the focus once more and followed the line of rocks out toward the harbor mouth. On a boulder just above the surf line there was an older woman in a blue jumpsuit with a girl of about six wearing only a pair of shorts. She was eating a sandwich and drinking a bottle of pop. "Very funny," I said.

"I told you she was a *young* lady."

"You raised an old man's expectations."

"Glad you can still raise something."

I trained the glasses on the surfers by the point, then out to the open ocean where a few small whitecaps were beginning to peak. "Little wind coming up," I remarked.

"Generally get an offshore about this time," he replied.

We studied the horizon in silence, as if concentration might produce some dramatic alteration in the pale, almost invisible joining of sea and sky. After a few minutes Willy turned a little toward me. "I need some advice," he said.

"Troubles with the book?"

"No, not that kind of advice." He picked at the corner of his mouth with his thumbnail. "It's nothing very specific. In fact, I'm not quite sure even how to phrase the question."

"I see. You want to borrow ten bucks."

Willy didn't smile. "I mean, this is an incredibly naive question, I realize, so spare me the guffaws, but do you think it's common for two people who have been married for a while to want a sexual relationship with somebody else?"

I couldn't help it. I dropped my jaw and stared at him crosseyed.

"Wait a minute. Let me rephrase that. Do you think there's really anything there *between* them if they want that? And never mind what it says in *The Swinging Housewife* or *The Sensuous Commune*."

"I wouldn't say you were peculiar, in the sense of being an outrageous mutation, if you were tyrannized now and then by your gonads. No."

"I wasn't thinking so much of me ... of men as of women."

"I don't know. I've never been one."

"But you've known ... some."

"None who've been anxious to discuss their sexual fantasies with me."

"What would you think if they *were* anxious for that kind of a discussion?"

"I'd think they were probably laying the foundation for something. Are we talking about anything specific, or are you just normally speculative?"

"If you really loved someone more than anything in the world, how would you handle that sort of thing?"

"With an overhead smash down the line."

He made a *tch* noise with his mouth and turned back to the beach, obviously disgusted.

"Willy, I don't know!" I said defensively. "I don't know if such a thing is a problem, or why it's a problem, or whose problem it is. I'm not sure fantasies are to be dealt with as if they were realities. Your question is not only naive, it's vague as hell."

"I suppose." He leaned back against the weather shack. "Actually, what set me off is I just got a letter from my mother saying she's planning her marriage to number five. I've been trying to figure out what women are all about."

My sideways glance conveyed a degree of cynicism, but apparently it was the best evasion he could think of.

"The last time I *saw* my mother she was planning her marriage to number five, only a different number five, a dance instructor at one of those social clubs single matrons on the decline seem to find so attractive. You know, where you learn to waltz and foxtrot and relax with your pink daiquiri on the rooftop garden . . . midst potted palms and plastered companions of the same vintage and persuasion. Leon Fossum was his name."

I coughed politely into my hand.

"See, in order to get Leon my mother had to become a lifetime member in his establishment. This, then, entitled her to a complete course in the ballroom dance, the annual picnic up the Hudson River, and two free drinks at the roofgarden, and, of course, Leon . . . all for ten grand. I give her credit for being a little suspicious. Like the roofgarden seemed always under construction and couldn't be visited, the two or three other 'members' she met seemed dragged out of some Forty-second Street peekorama, the picnic on the Hudson got canceled, according to Leon because the boat sprung a leak and had to be dry-docked for repairs. But eventually her hormones got the better of her and she forked over the ten big ones, and the next time she went boogieing over to the studio for a rhumba lesson she found the place rented to a sail maker."

"Is this a typical performance for your mother?" I said. In truth I was relieved by his diversionary tack.

"More or less. I think what really tweaked her was she never learned to rhumba. Getting left in the lurch was pretty familiar."

"Your father?" I said.

"He left when I was four or five, and there were two others after him, though I don't think she actually married the last one; he wasn't around long enough. Truth of it is, she's so sententious and domineering that nobody can stand her for more than a year or two. She's like one of those arctic icebreakers, plowing through the frozen wasteland of her life, never altering her course for anything, or anybody."

I said nothing, sat looking at the bathers, black against the glaring backdrop of bright water and pale sand, not sure why Willy had manipulated the conversation to include me in the personal aspects of his past — and maybe his present as well. I had a strange feeling, though I can only identify its origin with an unsatisfactory cliché — vibrations — that it was now my turn to talk about *my* parents, *my* wife, and that through the sharing of private histories our relationship would be strengthened. I kept silent.

Willy stood up, pulled on a striped T-shirt, and said, "Come on down to the workshop. I want to show you this million dollar invention."

I followed him down the stairs to the beach and around to the side door of the building. The shop was a litter of rubber suits, tanks, boat rigging, rope, surfboards, outboard motors, and Willy picked his way through the mess to a large wooden table in the corner on which lay what appeared to be an ordinary rubber suit.

"Have a look at this," he said. "Revolutionary, what?"

I looked. "Everybody should have two," I said, "but I'm missing the point, I think. A wet suit is a wet suit is a wet suit."

"Except," Willy said, "this ain't a wet suit, it's a dry suit. No water gets inside at all. The valve on the front there you use to blow in and let out air."

"That's wonderful, Willy," I said. "A dry suit. So what?"

"Well, air is a better insulator than water, it's warmer, plus you can regulate the amount you have trapped inside, and thereby determine your buoyancy. You can blow yourself up like a condom and float around until you starve to death, if you want to. Or if you're into some diving and you want a bit of R-and-R, you don't even have to tread water. Or if you're a small-boat sailor and you dump it a mile out in the briny and can't get it up, there's no way you're going to get cold or tired and drown."

"Pearson should put that in his ad," I said. "If you can't get it up, blow it up."

"Right now he's applying for a patent on the valve, and of course the zipper is something of a hassle, to make one that won't leak, but the navy's interested, and it looks as if it's going to go. You want to try it?"

"You're really excited about this?" I said. "You really think this hunk of rubber is like the wheel and sliced bread?"

"Come on," he grinned. "Mine's in the office. Let's go out and do it."

To impress upon me the strength of heat-sealed seams, Willy took a tank of compressed air, attached the hose to the valve on his suit, and blew himself up until he looked like something you see floating down Fifth Avenue on a string during the Easter parade. He indicated that

62

I should do the same, and together we waddled out of the shop, twin fat boys out of rubber and glue, and stitched up the middle by a leak-proof Talon zipper. We rolled, whooping and hollering, into the surf, and the little girl in the topless suit came out on the end of the jetty to watch us bob in the current that surged in and out of the harbor mouth. Lazy day. I closed my eyes and let myself drift. Felt good, as if I were weightless, suspended in a vacuum. Sensational. Good for you, Willy.

Eventually we were swept in past the dredge where one of the workmen came running out on the foredeck with a boat hook held like a harpoon, yelling "thar she blows." Neville Horn, whom I had sailed with occasionally during my first years at the university, was returning his Erickson sloop to her berth, and he threw a dill pickle at us as he passed, backed his engine and depth charged us with two cans of beer. We sipped our way on down toward the yacht club, chatted for a while with the crew of a big ketch just in from San Diego, wafted over toward the fuel docks, paddled in and out of slips to talk with various harbor bums Willy somehow knew, and eventually begged a tow from the patrol boat out to open water and beyond the jetty. From there we swam back to the beach and let the waves tumble us ashore.

For the benefit of two girls and their hysterical terrier, Willy rolled himself up the sand like a huge beach ball, then opened his chest valve and suddenly deflated. The dog went out of its mind and was last seen a quarter mile down the beach, still running.

"Thanks, Sut," I said, as we hosed down our suits with fresh water and headed for the shop to change. "It would have been better if you had really self-destructed there, you know, BLAM, guts and hair and shredded rubber all over the beach, but not a bad performance all in all. I enjoyed the whole tour."

"I thought you might get a kick out of it," he said. "You looked like you needed something to get you out of your shell." He was hopping around on one foot, trying to peel off the remaining leg of the wet suit.

"Me?" I said. "The Protestant ethic has never afflicted me. I am frequently found at play."

"I was afraid I might never woo you away from that overgrown teenybopper they say you've taken up with." He was regarding me from under his eyebrows, watching for my reaction.

"*They* say? Who says?"

"She the same one who propositioned you at lunch?"

"Wait a minute, hoss," I said, "if I have taken up with anyone, which I haven't, yet, it's ... personal."

"Fooling around like that seems like a bad idea. Dangerous."

"Willy!" I cried. "It's none of your business."

"Sure," he said.

"It's nobody's business."

"Sure," he said. "Sorry."

I tried to ignore this suddenly sour turn of events, and brush the whole thing off. "Come on over to the Crow's Nest," I said, "and I'll buy you a beer."

He hesitated for a minute, and then smiled. "I'll tell you what, it's almost five and I've got to pick up my wife downtown in ten minutes. If you can wait for us, we'll meet you back here. Anyway, it's high time you met Frankie."

"Time," I said, "is what I've got in abundance. Today is my day for having time. You'll find me perched in the bar." We were over the bumps, but I noticed a tenseness back in Willy's face, as if a comfortable, relaxing day hadn't done him any good at all. The heat was back under his pressure cooker.

Two

THERE WAS TIME, EVEN TO DOWN A COUPLE OF SCOTCH
and waters, before Willy returned, and to wonder briefly
if I was being overly standoffish, too insistent in my mind,
if not in my actions, on the distinction between student
and professor (I should probably say young man and
middle-aged man — Willy was no longer my "student"
exactly, even if we both had trouble remembering that
fact), but I had had problems before with kids, different
kinds of kids than Willy, to be sure, who snuggled in too
close, and screwed up in some way, and pleaded amnesty
on the basis of friendship. One particularly painful lesson. One self-appointed disciple whom I liked pretty well
had cheated on his term paper, and when I forced myself
to confront him with those sections he had copied from
an obvious source he went down on his knees, literally,
to beg. On his *knees*, yet. "You fail me in the course
and I'll be below a C average," he cried. "I'll get sus-

pended, I'll lose my deferment, I'll wind up on a platter in Vietnam. Remember how I gave you a ride to New York over vacation? Give me a break, Sir, I can't get thrown out, I don't want to die in some foxhole, my parents will kill me . . ." On and on. I was revolted, horrified. I leaped out of my chair as if it were wired and somebody had thrown the juice. "Get up, you silly bastard," I shouted, "and don't you *ever* grovel like that again. Jesus! Act like a man, you worm, you schlock! Get off the floor or I'll kill you myself." But his tactic worked. I let him do the paper over and passed him without looking at it. I would have done anything to get him out of my hair. At the same time I vowed never again to put myself or let myself be put in a position where my professional judgment could be compromised.

Some vow. It had all the force of a New Year's resolution. Willy was into me, obviously, or I wouldn't have worried about it. And then there was Miss Allencraig. Nina yum-yum. When she sat in my office, crossing and uncrossing her long shapely legs, dangling one arm languorously over the back of my armchair as she explained Koestler on creativity, she could have been telling me she was going to set fire to my mustache for all the interest I took in professional relationships. Nina and I pretended for quite a long time that the pleasure we took in those tutorial sessions was largely intellectual, but I think that neither of us was very much fooled. She *did* have a bright, quick mind, but her physical presence was just too powerful to ignore.

I ordered another scotch, put a couple of bills on the bar, and went into the men's room. Harry Weisberg was standing at parade rest in front of the urinal and I made some unmemorable crack about how difficult it must be for him to pee standing up — which set him grumbling about drunks always accosting him in restrooms.

66

"I didn't see you come in," I said. "Since when did you start hanging out in straight bars?"

He hoisted his middle finger without turning around. "I'm here with a lady. If you feel like joining us please don't, we'd like to be alone. Unless you have any money."

"I'm meeting your friend Willy Ward and his wife," I told him. Harry and Willy had not gotten on well the few times they'd met. Harry was much too obscene to be a molder of young minds, as far as Willy was concerned, and Willy was as square as a packing box as far as Harry was concerned. "We'd love to join you."

"The invitation has been rescinded."

"His wife has a forty inch bust."

"Reinstated."

"Don't forget to zip up."

Harry's lady, to my surprise, was not the vacant, toothy type of clinger he was normally attracted to. She was probably in her late thirties, though it was only at close range that the smile creases and crow's feet around her eyes were evident — and they didn't do any serious damage. She looked more like Belvedere or Atherton or the north shore of Lake Tahoe than San Jose State, where she taught sociology, as though she spent more of her time poolside or on the links than in front of a lectern — and judging from the only finger on which she wore no ring, I guessed her to be divorced. She had nice teeth. Harry introduced us. I muttered something and shook the handful of rocks she presented me. And at that moment Willy and Frankie Ward came out onto the terrace, spotted us, and made their way through the maze of late afternoon drinkers to our table. We all ran through the "how-do's" once more, and I noticed the coolness with which Willy and Harry greeted each other. They seemed determined not to let social amenities get in the way of their mutual dislike. Fortunately Frankie sat down between them.

Now I freely admit that all women have a tendency to look alike to me — or at least within the general categories by which I define them they look alike. There is the obvious distinction between good looking and bad looking, but there are also a number of subgroups, which for catalog purposes I give labels like Freaking Fay Frightwig and Horsey Hannah and Lovely Loretta Modern (and so forth and so on), and Frankie was the quintessential Loretta Modern. Bone straight hair parted in the middle and falling in a gothic arch down either side of her face to below the line of her shoulders, no makeup, no ornaments (except two gold hoops in her ears), no bra. No obvious need of one, for that matter. (Sorry, Harry.) My initial impression, as I sat there sipping my drink and listening without comprehension to Helen McGinnis finish some story she had been telling earlier, was related only to ways in which Frankie appeared to resemble all twenty-one-year-old girls in all California costume communities from San Diego to Fort Bragg — which is to say that she did not impress me as a person so much as a visual event, and a common one at that, like a tree or a tricycle or a slab of cement. Then I noticed that she had a face with a rather pretty mouth and high, prominent cheekbones, and large, gray eyes that moved in self-conscious distraction around the patio and came to rest on mine every few moments, briefly, for a sip of nectar, before fluttering off across the clover in search of sweeter flowers. I was taken in. My ego began to puff like a blowfish. Some women let you know they are interested by staring directly into your eyes, boring in, it's me and you, kid, and electricity, but others, infinitely more mysterious and alluring to me, convey the same information by a flickering glance, repeated but never held for more than a moment. Frankie's was not an original performance, but it was good enough. I began to tingle wherever it is one tingles. The harbor was behind her, and through the scotch and fading twilight and candles floating in their little ruby pots on the tables everybody began to look a whole lot better to me than they really were — especially myself.

The McGinnis woman asked what college I taught at. She had to ask twice. I was wondering how Frankie would look if her hair were shorter and less of an accentuation to the length of her face, and maybe a touch of the pencil just to give those pale eyebrows better definition. Lips should be fuller, but just a tad, or a scosh, or a hair more than a teense. "Excuse me?"

Harry helped out by explaining in a facetious tone that courses could be given or taken by anybody at any one of the colleges, that the college as an academic unit was spurious, and that while professors were called "Fellows" of a particular unit their teaching was more or less structured through traditional departments; "unless," he added, "they are really interdisciplinary kinds of courses that departments can't offer because they don't fall strictly within the perimeters of the more conventional areas covered by said departments, which incidentally have no geographic base, and *these* kinds of courses can then be offered by the colleges upon the approval of the academic standing committee that is charged with the responsibility of preventing duplication of functions. You follow?" Ms. McGinnis put her index finger in her eye and rubbed. His tone implied exactly what he thought of the system.

I dragged myself back into the present and smiled a day-dreamer's smile at Harry, whose scowl forecast poor weather ahead. "I think what he's trying to say is that nobody has ever figured out what a college is all about, or a fellow, or for that matter, a department, which we call here 'boards of studies.' We love the British. We borrow their labels, but we don't understand their application. Mostly what we do here at old S. C. is reevaluate our position every year to figure out what we're going to do *next* year, but actually it's not that interesting a subject. Would anyone like another drink?"

"Fiat Lux," Willy said.

"Is that a drink?" Harry asked.

"It's the motto of our institution," Willy said.

"That's *Ex Lax*," Harry said.

"No," said Willy, "it's Fiat Lux."

"What is this Fiat Lux?" Harry asked. "A foreign car?"

"All right, gentlemen," I broke in, "let's not be infantile. Please don't spoil the cocktail hour, because I've had a long day."

For a while things went smoothly enough. Idle chatter. McGinnis was interested, for some reason, in the effects of a no-grade system on career planning, and it was all pretty boring and artificial, and everybody drank too much to compensate. I had about decided I didn't like Harry's friend. She was the kind, I guessed, who ten years ago was teaching courses on the population crisis, changed her act about 1968 to include the black experience (a sociological perspective), and retooled three years later for the contemporary woman (frontiers of sociology). Nothing against the subjects, understand, just suspicious of the people they attract. Causes dehumanize.

Then, somehow, Fiat Lux came around again and Harry and I got into one of our routines. "Come on, Willy," I said. "Just because the sign on the gate says that doesn't mean anything goes on inside that is either innovative, intelligent, or enlightened. The truth of it is, I think the sign should say *All hope abandon, ye who enter here*."

"I think it ought to say Fat Lox and Bagels," Harry said.

"Since the theme of the place is best described as 'know thyself,'" I explained to Ms. McGinnis, "some of us find it a little difficult to take seriously, 'academically-wise.'"

Harry poked his swizzle stick around in the ice in his glass. "Watch it, fella. You're talking about the trough I feed in. Anyway, why do you always talk shop when you're drunk? You're such a bore."

"Don't put on airs before the ladies," I said.

"I wouldn't listen to them," Willy suddenly broke in. He was addressing Helen McGinnis. "They amuse themselves by putting down any place that thinks of itself as a community and promotes itself as a community."

Harry looked at me and crossed his eyes. "To simpleminded persons like ourselves," he told Willy, "the celebration of community consciousness that goes on around here is rather limiting."

Willy didn't smile. "Consciousness celebration is what college is about."

"Only if you consider college a place where people go specifically to develop their interpersonal relationships," Harry said, laying his index finger beside his nose and turning to stare out the window at the harbor. He was either growing irritated or bored.

But Willy was like a dog with a soup bone. "You don't think a university should concern itself in that area?"

"No," Harry said. "I don't."

"Why not?"

"Well, I'll tell you . . . because a university is not an encounter group, it's an institution of learning."

"That's right. But among other things it should teach you how to live with your fellow man."

"Ha," Harry snorted. "I'm sorry. I'm not sucked in by all the horse manure spread around by the exponents of new relevance in education. We send children to pre-school to learn how to get along with one another. They get to practice the art for twelve years before they're presumed grown up and ready to fly on their own, and I don't believe any more in the university teaching Dicky how to relate to Danny than I do in its trying to teach him how to write a grammatical sentence, or add six and eight. Dicky should know these things before he goes to college. If he doesn't he has no business there."

"The thing about Harry," I spoke up, trying to interject a little humor into the proceedings, "is that he just *looks* hip."

Nobody laughed.

"You have to face facts now and then," Willy said, "and the facts are that most students don't know how to relate to their peers when they suddenly have to live with them twenty-four hours a day. They have no idea how to create themselves. They have to be taught. In just the same way, incidentally, as they have to be taught to write a grammatical sentence."

"The problems to which you refer are completely irrelevant to a university," Harry said, dismissing him.

It was the wrong move. Willy grew livid. "Oh marvelous," he said, "marvelous. The fact that Suzy doesn't know a preposition from a proposition is irrelevant, is that it? The fact that Johnny is hostile, insecure, regressive, and spends his evenings picking at his penis in his closet is irrelevant, is it? No problem, no need for solution. Mister, you've got your principles and your realities all fouled up."

I held my hand up in a peace sign, trying once again to put an end to all this before it got really ugly. If Willy's wife hadn't been there I would have told him to shut up and mind his manners, but I didn't want to embarrass her. The waitress thought I was signaling her and came over to take orders for another round, so for a moment there was a lull in the storm.

72

But Willy was seething. When the waitress left he said, "You don't take me seriously, do you, Weisberg?"

"Not particularly," Harry said. "Should I?"

"You're just like your compadre here. (Pointing at me.) You treat anyone who hasn't yet reached your exalted position like a child. You amuse yourself at their expense. Administer fraud tests."

I looked at Frankie and shrugged. "What'd I do?" I said. She sat there placidly as if she had seen this play before and didn't care about the dénouement one way or the other. She seemed, actually, to be rooting with her eyebrows for the enemy camp.

"I ceased to be amused quite some time ago," Harry said.

"You and Warren sit around playing this little game," Willy said. "A couple of good ol' boys sitting around spitting tobacco juice and bitching about the loss of standards, everything's going to hell, charlatans in the classroom like me teaching love and compassion and creative development instead of an endless stream of heartless facts. You don't approve that we mix a little humanism with our statistics."

Harry leaned back in his chair and pointed his glass at Willy. "I don't approve of you, Mr. Ward, because you and those like you are a third-rate gaggle of orgasmic healers and psychic chiropractors, and I object to your style because it appeals primarily to the genitals, and I dislike your opinions because they are constructed entirely from abstractions. You and those of your general persuasion have turned this place into one of the greatest sanitariums in the state of California. A rest home for the mind."

"I notice," Willy said acidly, "that there are still lectures, seminars, papers, exams, and several hundred courses . . ."

"Courses!" Harry scoffed. "Sure there are courses. In

I Ching, Tarot, Sufi dancing, biorhythms, dream interpretation, ESP, palmistry, Rolfing. There are seminars in spiritual ecology, healthy-happy-holy, inter-trips hibernation and biomagnetic psychles for insight and self-liberation. For students who remain compulsively ego-oriented, 'freshpersons' who still remember the A's and B's they competed for to get into the system in the first place, we offer a simplified system of rewards and punishments. Pass and No Record. How progressive. Impossible to fail. Impossible to be categorized into brighter and dumber. *But,"* (Harry raised an exclamatory finger) *"But,* if a kid remains heavily into power trips and *insists* on being competitive, his kin group leader can suggest a bit of psychic surgery to help him along the healing journey to inner peace. He can be assigned to a dormitory where the doors have been removed from the toilet stalls. . ."

Willy had scraped his chair back and was standing now, staring fixedly at Harry, his untouched drink in his hand. McGinnis had been rendered comotose by the whole event, and Frankie sat as placidly as ever, watching from behind her Gioconda smile.

". . . the underlying principle of which, philosophically speaking, is that to hide in a steel cubicle and do your business in secret is not only noncommunicative and socially regressive, it is nondimensional as well. Imagine the core experience, gentlepersons, induced by the enclosure of a toilet stall. Consider the preoccupation with the lower energy center, the false impression that through mechanics will come meaning . . ."

I saw it coming, but there was nothing I could do to prevent it. The entire contents of Willy's glass hit Harry square in the face, and I swear the entire bar went silent as a tomb. A slice of lime slid off his bald pate and bounced soddenly off the table onto the floor. A droplet of tonic formed on the end of his nose. If Weisberg had had an ounce of violence in him there would have been bloodshed, but he did not. Instead he slowly rose from his chair, mopped at himself with a napkin, and said with a kind of Talmudic gentleness, "Perhaps I was a bit over-bearing." Willy glared at him, then turned on his heel and stalked out.

For a few moments we all remained in place, manne-quins, immobilized. Then Harry, offering me a look of suffering and forgiveness, took the check to the bar and paid it. Helen McGinnis scuffled after him without say-ing good-bye. I muttered something about getting the tip. Frankie looked faintly amused. After a while she said (in a remarkably normal voice) "We were going to ask you to go on to dinner with us, but I guess that's kaput."

"I'll take a rain check," I said foolishly. "I still have quite a lot of preparation to do for my class tomorrow. As a matter of fact your renter, Michael Arington, gave me a fifty page manuscript that I promised to read. (Why did I keep dribbling on?) I probably ought to get to it."

"Mike is such a scene," Frankie said.

"Isn't he though? God knows why he keeps coming back. We don't see eye to eye on anything. He keeps telling me I don't read him right." (I told myself if I didn't shut my face in a minute I'd be boxing my ankles and saying "mercy, land t' goshen.")

"He tells Willy that at least you read him . . . I think the exact quote was 'with diligence if not insight,'" Frankie said. She eyed me coolly. "This whole thing tonight has upset you, hasn't it. I mean, you're really kind of freaked."

"I think it got a little out of hand," I said. "Don't you? I was amazed you could just sit there."

She shrugged. "Willy's crazy," she said.

"He did get pretty hot."

"No, I mean really crazy. When he gets all wound up about something he really thinks he believes in, and somebody puts it down, he just flips. Something snaps. He'll be okay in a couple of hours."

I found her indifference hard to believe. "Doesn't this bother you?" I said. "Don't you worry that he'll throw a drink at the wrong guy or something?"

"Sure, but what are you going to do. I used to try to talk to him about it, but when he's under a lot of strain he just clams up. In England he went to a shrink and the guy gave him some tranquilizers, but he says they make him dopey and he can't do anything when he takes them."

"He should try again. To see somebody, I mean."

"He won't. He says it costs too much."

"But does he really think he *needs* to see somebody? Admitting you've got a problem is half the battle."

"To tell you the truth, when he gets uptight he goes to see you."

I gave her a thin smile. "Great. Unfortunately that's like the blind leading the blind. And I can't dispense pills."

The wind had come up off the harbor and was blowing through the open door. Frankie shivered in her light cotton dress, and I pushed my chair back, suggesting we move inside.

"I better get home," she said. "Explain to your friend, will you, that Willy didn't mean what he did. By midnight he'll be all contrite and full of apologies."

"Harry more or less asked for it," I said, as we headed out. "Amazing. I never saw Willy like that. I'm still in somewhat of a daze."

Frankie shrugged her eyebrows as I held the door open for her. "You will still come to dinner soon, won't you? Willy would be devastated if you held this against him.

So would I 'cause I wouldn't get to know you better."

"Of course," I said. "I await an invitation."

"I'll have him call you." She smiled and held my eyes with hers for a moment longer than my role as friend of her hubsand required. There seemed a promise there, of things to talk about, the two of us, perhaps . . . but in the short run a dinner, soon, next week, Willy would confirm. As I watched her get in her car and drive away I wondered whether the attraction I felt for her was directed at a real person, Frankie Ward, flesh and blood, or merely at a place in time, resilience with a future, the freshness of her age.

Three

THE FOLLOWING WEEK, WITH THE TERM STILL IN ITS FIRST stages, I had to spend a good deal more time at the university than was my habit. There were advisees to advise, students trying to register for courses late, independent studies to get under way, and so I put my own work aside for a while, took most of my meals at the college, and more or less camped in my office. Celebrating community consciousness. Often I didn't go home to Weisberg's until ten o'clock.

One evening after an institutional supper (stewed tomatoes in bread, shredded carrots in Jell-O, foreskins in white sauce) I was sitting at my desk with the overhead lights turned off and only the small table lamp burning. On the bookcase to the left of my chair, in the empty shelf that separated two continents and two literatures (Z-Zola from A-Agee), sat a trisectioned photograph case of silver holding the black and white images of my mother and father, and the Kodacolor smile of my wife and son. The dead flanked the living, and it seemed strangely inappropriate at this particular time in my life that the ghostly expressions of those who had fashioned me should be so overpowered by the bright lips and sun-tanned cleavage of the woman into whose flesh I had invested my own, and that toothless child who combined us all. Inappropriate and sad. I suppose I was feeling my lonelines for the first time.

The contrast between the stiff formality of my parents' pose, the plain photo backdrop, the Sunday clothes, and the lounging disarray of bikinied Erica, poolside with her naked child, could be fashioned by the allegorist into a history of generational variance. What I, as allegorist, found sad was my inability to align myself with a point of view.

I had always had a certain awe, admiration, envy, and respect for my father even though I found him often intolerant. While he knew in what he believed, he did not entertain the notion of multiple possibilities or situational ethics or conduct that deviated from the scriptures (in which he otherwise did *not* believe). One did not lie, steal, cheat. One did not mistreat women and animals, or covet any but one's own. One did not drink to excess, or, for that matter, indulge in any pleasure to excess. One did not use four letter words or tell smutty stories in the presence of ladies. One always paid one's own way. And so on. Little things when taken individually, but they added up to a life that was based on convictions lived, and the liver always knew where he stood in relation to his surroundings. It was a hard act to follow.

My wife, in contrast, had come to find all forms of behavior acceptable, and to abstain absolutely from making moral judgments. She saw herself, quite possibly as a result of her undergraduate training in filmmaking, as a scientific observer whose role was simply to record the animal's habits and not to applaud or condemn. Man was driven by mysterious forces and not to be held accountable, ultimately, for his actions. So do your own thing. To be sure, she contradicted her position rather frequently (she didn't think much of Richard Nixon's thing, or the male chauvinist thing), but that oversight was easily understandable when one considered that she took most of her ideas from house organs of the radical left that were usually as vociferous in their denial of other people's thing as they were in the proclamation of their own — the kind of "it is my God-given right to deny you your God-given rights" position that left my father weak with rage. I myself float somewhere in the middle, finding Erica's liberation and my father's puritanism equally simplistic, and unable to accept either one.

Perhaps I was too harsh in my judgment of Erica. Twelve years of marriage had certainly changed me; why shouldn't it change her? She always denied that it had, claiming that she took positions contrary to mine simply to crack my introspective shell. She argued that if she couldn't get a *rise* out of me, then she couldn't talk to me about anything, because I obviously preferred the company of books and my typewriter. I denied this, though not with much conviction.

Whatever Erica's public justifications, I was convinced that she had begun in the last two years to live out her fantasies of the "new culture." Nothing that I could remember about our courtship or our first few years together suggested that this defiance of reason, this regressive behavior might take place. Or had I just been oblivious to the signs from the very beginning?

And if so, what were the signs? Signs of what? What is the problem, please? What exactly is the nature of the complaint? I don't know. Life together just doesn't seem to be working out.

I snapped the light off, locked the office, and went out of the building. I hadn't seen or talked to Erica in two weeks, not since the afternoon I left, and I decided that maybe it was time we put some things together. I suppose I'd been waiting for her to call me, but that obviously wasn't going to happen. I was going to have to make the overtures if we were going to decide what to do with ourselves, and besides, we had a joint checking account. She could bleed me dry if she got mad enough.

It was no more than a fifteen-minute walk to my house, and I thought the cold night air might do me some good, might work out some of the kinks and allow me to sleep fifteen or twenty minutes beyond my early appointment with the dawn. To avoid the lights on College Drive I walked down an old cattle trail at the bottom of a ravine that divided the north from the south parts of the campus. Redwoods gave way to madrone, bay and oak as I descended, and at the bottom the ravine widened out into ragged pastureland where I had to cross a quarter mile of ungrazed field to the main road leading into town. My socks were full of foxtails and screw grass by the time I reached the pavement, but I was so enjoying the night chill against my sweating skin, and the dry, musty smell of wild oat mixed with dust and eucalyptus and the sea, that I didn't bother to stop to pick them out. A dog barked in the begonia nursery as I walked by, triggering a chorus of increasingly distant howls. A raccoon, or possum, or maybe only a cat, ran across the road in front of me and vanished into the brush.

As I approached the first lights of the Westwood sub-division I was torn between my desire to drag out my walk by taking the long way by road around to my house and my disinclination to enter the populated and street-lit area. Being absolutely alone, with nothing but night sounds and smells and the thud of my own pulse, was the most delicious thing in the world. What I would really like to do, I decided, if I could only be released from the irritating nag of conscience, would be to retrace my steps and keep going, up into the coast range mountains, and there simply live for a time on my own with my own head for company.

Deciding to avoid the lights, I climbed over a barbed wire fence and cut across more unplowed fields. Eventually I came to the broad horse pasture that separated my place from the nearest neighbor's, and I went through the gate at the far end, noticing as I did so that both houses were dark. Erica would hardly be in bed at this hour, I thought, but it seemed unlikely that she would be out. I paused a moment to listen to the crickets and to look down across the gradual slope of the land to the ocean a half mile away. There was a partial moon, enough to illuminate the surf line and the jagged upthrust of rocks offshore. The swells boiled into white water there, and then resumed their dark inland roll.

When I went over the pasture fence, across my backyard, and up onto the porch off the den, I saw that the t.v. was on and that Sally Wilcox, our usual babysitter, was asleep on the couch. I slipped in through the sliding door and turned on a light. Sally sat up, rubbing her eyes, and then bolted to her feet when she saw me. "Oh, Mr. Warren..."

"The missus out?" I asked.

"She went... I don't know. Out. Yes." The poor girl wasn't sure how the game was played. I had no idea how much Erica might have told her, but it was clear that she understood I wasn't supposed to be around. "She should be home any minute now." Lame offer. She can tell you herself where she has been.

"Terrific," I said. "I'll wait. In fact, you can run along now, Sally, and Mrs. Warren will pay you tomorrow. I seem to be a little short, but don't worry about a thing, I'll stay right here until she gets home."

"Oh. Well, she told me . . . gee, I don't mind staying, Mr. Warren."

"She didn't by any chance tell you that if I came around you were not to let me in?"

"Well, no. Gosh, it's your house . . ."

I flashed her my Vincent Price smile. "So don't be a pain in the ass, Sally, just run along and I'll explain it all to Erica when she comes."

I made myself a drink, and after checking on Lenny to see that he was covered up, I sat down to watch the last half of the "Creature Feature" that had put Sally to sleep. It didn't take long to see why. I tried a magazine, put it down, poured myself another scotch, wandered around the house, and eventually wound up in our bedroom going through the closet to see if there were any of my clothes that I wanted to take over to Weisberg's. The familiarity of Erica's things, hanging there so forlornly in the empty house, touched me in a funny way — almost as if she had died and I was sorting through the remains, trying to decide to whom they should be bequeathed. Painful and sad. It occurred to me for the first time that these dresses and blouses and pants belonged to somebody who no longer belonged to me, that where they went and what they did and how they looked was none of my concern. I had forfeited my right to touch them, to inhale the lingering fragrance of the body they had held. What I really couldn't stand was their independence. They had no right to be happy without me, God damn it. When I bent over to inspect her shoes, standing at parade rest on their wooden rack, I spilled my drink on the closet floor.

The other thing I noticed was how old and shabby a lot of Erica's stuff was. She had never been much interested in clothes, and I used to have to beg her to go out and buy new things. We'd go together, when we were first married, and I'd pick out a dress I liked, generally some cocktail number in black with a neckline down to the navel, then debate her on the issue of price and utility. "Come on, Eliot, where would I ever wear a thing like that?"

"I'll buy you dinner. I'll take you to the opera."

"My bust is too big. I'd fall right out of it."

"Terrific."

"Oh boy. I'd look like a call girl in that thing."

"Yeah, yeah, try it on."

I had my way only once, and she turned out to be right — the occasion to wear it never arose. I think we finally used it as a stage prop in some variation on the early theme — lust crazed brute attacks pert little blond in suburban kitchen, hoists her in the air, rips off panties, assaults her on counter top between leftover meat loaf and ratatouille parmesan. I got the idea from a salesman we knew in Cambridge who insisted that whenever he returned from a trip, his not very bright wife presented herself at the door in high heeled shoes, a waitress apron, and a cold martini. She indulged his fetish for a year or two and then ran off to Philadelphia in a converted pie-van with two homosexuals from Tewksbury. But she proved his point. Offbeat sexual events are sure a good way to free up a convention-ridden mind. Erica, however, managed to make me feel like I was dibbling my lips whenever I suggested them.

She came home at two o'clock. I was sitting in Lenny's room with the door open, drink in hand, just watching him sleep, when I heard the car pull into the drive and the motor die. A few minutes passed, then feet on the gravel walkway, a man's voice, Erica's, the opening of the front door. There was brief muttering in the entryway, and Erica called for Sally.

"Yes," I said, in squeaky falsetto. Footsteps down the hall to Lenny's room.

She snapped on the light to discover me sitting on the floor with my scotch and soda in one hand, a plastic G-man special in the other. "Bang." I told her. "Bang, bang, bang."

She stared at me for a moment, as if she were trying to decide how to handle the whole deal, then said, "What did you do with Sally?"

"I fed her to the cat," I said. "What do you think I did with her?"

Erica unfolded the extra blanket at the foot of Lenny's bed and tucked it in around his shoulders. Out in the entryway I heard the discreet closing of the front door, and a minute later the car started up. "No nookie tonight," I said, addressing the darkness beyond the window. "Sorry, pal."

"You're drunk," Erica said, "and probably deranged. What do you want?"

"I'm *deranged?*" I belched. Soda tingles in the nose. "Jesus Christ! I'm missing in action for two weeks, my clothes aren't even out of the closet, and already you're bringing home tricks at two in the morning."

"You've been missing in action for a lot longer than two weeks." She was picking up Lenny's dirty clothes.

"What's that supposed to mean?"

"Figure it out."

I got to my feet, rattling the ice cubes in my glass. "You want one of these? They're good for the humors." She didn't bother to answer. "Well," I said, "you won't mind if I help myself I trust . . . since I'm still paying for it." I went out into the kitchen and poured myself a couple of fingers. Erica followed me.

"Would you mind telling me what you're doing here?" she asked. Her tone was not very cordial.

"I wouldn't mind," I said, "but first I'd like to know why you come traipsing in here in the middle of the night with some guy who sneaks off the minute he hears your husband is back?"

She gave me one of her *where do you come from* looks, and finally said, "Look, you left, not me. *You* walked out of here and haven't troubled yourself with so much as a postcard since to let me know what it is you think is up, and now you presume to want to know where I've been. Well, fuck-off!"

I kind of admired her spirit. I had expected her to be angry, but I had imagined a more self-pitying anger, one that would soon dissipate into her addiction for soul-searching explanation. *How could you do this to me? ... the best years of my life* ... etcetera. Instead I was being told to shove off. It made me want to stay. "Okay, okay," I said. "Forget it. I didn't come to get in a fight."

"What did you come for?"

"To talk to you. There are some things we need to get straightened out." Standing there looking at her in her pleated skirt and thin white blouse was making me horny. Childbearing and time hadn't actually left all that much of a mark on her figure, and even at two in the morning her face looked fresh and alive, if rather cold in the harsh kitchen light. I felt as if I were seeing her for the first time in years, and I felt more than a twinge of jealousy over the man who had just slipped out the front door.

Erica must have read the look on my face because she backed out of the kitchen and said, "If we must talk at this hour, let's at least sit down." She went into the living room, and I followed her, stopping to admire the Cantú print over the fireplace that we had bought some years back at an exhibition in New York.

"You remember when we got this?" I said. "And how we debated two days over spending fifty dollars?" Erica ran her hand through her hair and studied the rug. "Boy oh boy, the things we *didn't* buy in those days, just because fifty bucks sounded like ten thousand. You remember that acre of land on Lake George that your father practically wanted to *give* us, and we decided that it was too expensive? He was even going to lend us the money himself."

"What are you doing?" she said. She sounded very tired and a little depressed.

"What?"

"The reminiscence trip. How it was in the good old days. I remember the good old days very well, Eliot, and I remember the not so good old days even better, and what's more I don't think you came here to chat about how things used to be." She crossed her legs in a swish of nylon. God! I wondered if it would be rape.

"All business, huh?" I said. "Well, maybe you're right though I don't see anything nefarious about recalling some of the nice things we used to have. I happen to be pretty sentimental about Goose Pond and the White Mountains and playing cribbage in front of the fire on a winter night and maple syrup poured into a pail of snow and skiing through the woods with a full moon."

"I do too. I don't like those memories corrupted, used."

"You remember that night it got down to twenty below and the furnace ran out of oil, and then it snowed in the morning and Skinny L'Heureux wouldn't come out and plow our road so the tanker could get in because I refused to bribe him every few weeks with a bottle, the extortionist. Jesus, at one point there I really thought we might all freeze to death."

"Stop it, Eliot."

"I see."

"Let's just stick to now."

Well, I guess that's how it's going to be, I thought. The roles have gotten reversed and I'm rejected instead of rejecting — a metamorphosis that adds a totally new dimension to my emotional response to the situation. "I take it then that you were pleased when I left."

She stared at me. "I was not pleased. I'm just like anybody else, you know. I think of those years going down the drain. I think of a lot of things that were shared that are suddenly meaningless, I think of Lenny, I look around this house and I am constantly reminded of *us,* of *ours,* and it is not in any way *pleasing.*"

The phone started ringing, and I figured it was her date of the evening calling to see if I was out of the way. The bugger. We ignored it until it stopped.

"I'm not your chattel," she went on. "I'm not an object or an ornament. I'm like any other woman and I need to feel like one. I need to be with someone who is interested in what I think and want and do, who pretends I have a functioning intelligence that's worth listening to now and then; someone who doesn't make me feel that I'm just the fool who is around to pass the snacks and clean up the mess. I've had a lot of time to think about it in the last few weeks."

Rethinking it and telling it to me seemed to make her angry. Her mouth was set and her eyes hard.

"So if what you came around for was to see how I'm bearing up in the absence of your esteemed company, the answer is fine. And if you harbor the slightest impulse to come back, save your energy; it will take a lot more than dragging up old memories to con me."

I sat miserably, scratching my arch along the inside of my tennis shoe, unable to admit or deny even to myself my real motive for being there. Finally self-pity and my training as an only child got the best of me. Paradoxically it produced an honest response, though I admit I did my best to look small and helpless. "I guess I did harbor that impulse," I said, "I don't know. I certainly don't blame you for the way you feel. I came here tonight on a whim, really, and then when you weren't home I got to wandering around until I finally wound up sitting on the floor in the closet with your clothes draped around my head."

Erica laughed. Did I detect the possibility of mild hysteria? I laid it on. I told her she had found me in Lenny's room because I was getting a bang just out of watching him sleep. I said I was snotty about where she had been until two A.M. because I was jealous, because I thought of us not as divorced or irrevocably separated, but only taking a breather from each other to try to figure things out. I didn't want to woo her with memories, I just couldn't put *fifteen* years of being together out of my head as if it was a load of old boxes and trash being hauled out to the dump.

"Jesus, Jesus, Jesus," she said, stopping me. She sat straight in the chair, gripping its arms as if she wanted to tear them off. "Don't *play* this game with me." Her voice at least was shaky.

"I'm not," I said. "I'm not playing."

She sat still for a moment, eyes closed, waiting for her control. She was beginning to look as if she had aged ten years between the kitchen and the living room. "I wish that was so," she said, calmly, shaking her head to let me know that it was no go, "but I know you better. You're so transparent, Eliot. You're just like Lenny when some kid wants a toy of his that's broken and useless and that he hasn't looked at for ten months. You're like a four year old. You come over to the house, get half stewed, walk around in an aimless fog getting more and more sentimental, and when you discover that I'm not sitting around eating my heart out, when you're afraid that somebody else might find me fit company and that I might be able to go out and enjoy myself, you can't stand it. All of a sudden your cruddy old toy becomes real interesting."

She rose, and I saw (with some ray of hope) that her

hands were trembling. I went over to her and took hold of them and she did not pull away. "*Really* interesting," I said, knowing she was right; despising my puny soul for demanding a rematch. "Real is the wrong part of speech. What you want here is an adverb. I'm a lonely adverb. Need a good home."

"You never quit, do you," she said, her eyes closed.

"Uh-uh. Not without a struggle."

"If you come back it has to be different; it has to be open and honest and we have to be able to talk about things even if they hurt, even if they make us look foolish and weak; no more of this where you put me down and retire and I find ways to get even with you behind your back because I can't confront you with how I feel, what I want."

"Fair enough," I said. "It can be that way."

Her eyes opened and she looked at me for a long time, tired, without blinking. "Can it?" she finally said. "Let's see. Let's start with that man who brought me home to-night. I think you ought to know that I've been seeing him a little. I don't love him; I don't even respect him much. What he does, mostly, is make me realize how much I want you . . . but then I haven't had you for a long time, have I, and there are other things I need too. I can't just dry up and become an old maid because I've got a husband who decided he isn't much interested any-more. I can stop that other business anytime, but I won't do it just to become your maid service again. I thought you ought to know that."

Whatever the name of the high I had been riding, it suddenly popped like a soap bubble, and I stood there with this greasy film of awareness seeping out of my head and down through my veins to my toes. It was a state of wonderment, a marvel, a curiosity as much as a pain; hurt was in it, to be sure, and a sense of betrayal, but mostly I was amazed. I wanted to say, "I didn't think you had it in you, the courage, I didn't think you could pull something like that off. Hey, look at me with egg on my tie."

Erica was watching me. A response was obviously called for, since she had decided to test the waters by taking a flying leap off the end of the pier, but I didn't have a response at hand. Or I had ten different responses and no one seemed to manifest itself as a front runner. Finally I just shook my head and offered a feeble smile. "No more maid service," I said. "I didn't bring my toothbrush."

"I think we have an extra," she replied. "If not, you can use mine."

Four

ONE OF THE "CONDITIONS" OF MY REINSTATEMENT IN ERICA'S
bed was that I would spend more time each week with
Lenny. We hadn't gone quite so far as to formalize this arrangement with a contract, but I was on trial and my general behavior as a shareholder (Erica's term) in the company
Warren was under close scrutiny by the management. If I
could raise the net asset value per share by the close of the
period ending June 15, I might be eligible for certain in-
come dividends; otherwise my common stocks would be
liquidated for more profitable short term bonds, deben-
tures, and notes. Like the milkman, say. Anyway, that's
how *I* was beginning to see it.

Saturday was the day Erica had designated for herself;
Lenny my responsibility from breakfast to bed. If I had
left the Friday night poker game at Peterson's house at a
reasonable hour things might have gone smoothly enough
and a routine been established, but I was hungover, diar-

rheic, and tired. I missed cues that should have warned me I was on thin ice from the start. Erica moved around the kitchen with a kind of detached efficiency that indicated she was not pleased with me. She pointedly avoided any inquiry into my evening beyond asking what time I had gotten home, and I said, knowing she knew perfectly well it had been four A.M., that I guessed it had been pretty late. "We got talking. I didn't pay much attention."

"Umm."

"Pete has a few drinks and there's no turning him off."

"Oh."

"He wants to pick your brains."

"Uh-huh."

"Pleasant wife, though. Young, but very nice."

"Harry called you. Something about tennis. I told him you were taking Pickle to the boardwalk . . . in case you forgot."

"I didn't forget." The coffee water started to boil and I got up to find filter papers for the Chemex. There weren't any and I had to use paper napkins (which would fall apart by the third dunking and fill the pot with grounds. Why is it so hard to keep a few essentials in supply? But of course filter papers *weren't* essential to Erica. She could use newsprint for all she cared about the taste of her coffee). "Harry want me to call him back?" Erica shrugged. (Meaning, why bother? You're tied up.) "Maybe he'd like to go with us," I said. Erica sighed heavily through her nose. (Meaning, that is a poor idea. Meaning, if Harry goes, you spend the day with Harry and the deal is you spend the day with Lenny.) "Is something bothering you? Are you mad about something in particular?"

"Should I be?" (Meaning, you bet I am.)

"If it's about the hour I got home last night, I didn't know there was a curfew on." She said nothing. Gave me another of her *I'm not going to discuss it* shrugs. "Look,

93

Erica," I said, "I may be something of a bear to live with and all that, but I haven't been having an affair with anybody so don't go pretending the hours I keep are a big issue in our problem. Running around on you has never been one of *my* sins."

"I suppose you're going to throw that at me every time you need to feel self-righteous."

"I'm not throwing anything at you. All I'm saying is if I'm out late you don't have to do a jealous wife number on me because that isn't part of my act."

"I'm sorry. I was just feeling . . . turned on last night, and I wanted you home."

"Hey, sweetheart, I can't anticipate the random hornies, you know. I'm not a stud standing at service."

"I'll say."

"Oh Christ, let's just drop it." The telephone rang, I answered and the voice said, "Weisberg here. What's happening today, young man?" Erica went into the living room to water her plants. "I have to take the kid to the beach," I told him. "My day in the barrel, but why don't you meet me at the wharf and we'll get some lunch. I'll regale you with the story of how I made peace with my good wife and how I'm already screwing up again."

"If it has a tragic ending, I'll pay," Harry said. "Give me some previews . . . just the parts where you suffer."

It struck me then that my remark wasn't very funny, that it had, in truth, a resoundingly adolescent smack, and I told Harry to forget it. "On second thought, I'd better stick with Lenny today. It's his party . . . a kind of three week late birthday outing. But if you meet me at Gilda's at two I'll buy you a consolation beer." I hung up on him, went in to kiss Erica good-bye, and gave Lenski a piggyback ride out to the car.

I am reminded by the outing with my son of a passage

in Saul Bellow's *The Victim* where Asa Leventhal tries to find ways to entertain his visiting nephew, winds up after a series of tentative suggestions of things to do in a dull horror movie starring Boris Karloff, and concludes that he, Asa, is "out of touch" with kids. The truth is he was never *in* touch, not even when he was a kid himself.

We started out at ten-thirty in the morning at a Baskin-Robbins, eating a hot fudge sundae with cherry and extra nuts, and we progressed hour by hour through a kind of *mondo foodo* nightmare that included a sack of Fritos on the way to the beach, two hotdogs and a Big Hunk at the beach, a chocolate covered banana and an orange drink on the way to the boardwalk, a sack of popcorn and a pink, bouffant frightwig of cotton candy, a Big Mac and a fried pie during our "lunch break," and a two-pound box of saltwater taffy (the flavors picked by Lenny — peanut butter and licorice) as we strolled around the amusement park afterward. The beach had not been a particular success since there isn't much to do there but make sand pies and shoot beaver from behind the blind of your Cool-Ray, Polaroid shades. Leonard was a little young yet to lie around ogling, and so, not knowing how else to amuse him, I fed his face every time it seemed preparing itself to complain.

He wanted desperately to go on the roller coaster and found the logic of my refusal unpersuasive. I looked around frantically for a hotdog stand, and we were on the verge of another falling out when I noticed a sign on the chain link fence to which he had attached himself tooth and claw that said children under ten years of age were not permitted to ride.

"See," I said, "that's why. We can't break the law, kiddo. You wouldn't want me to wind up in the clink."

"What's a clink?"

"Jail."

"You could *say* I was ten."

"They'd know. They'd ask me for your birth certificate and when I couldn't produce it they'd throw me in the clink."

"Then let's go on the bumping cars."

"Jesus, Lenski," I reasoned. "The first time somebody clobbers you from behind all that junk you've eaten will go flying all over the place. You'll bust wide open."

"I won't either."

"Anyway, you have to be ten for the bumping cars too." Gloom. Starting to pout. "Well, what *can* we do then?"

"How about the fun house?" I suggested. "They've got to have one. You know, with the screwy mirrors and the maze and all that. What do you say we see if we can find it."

It was clearly low priority, but he agreed, and I started to congratulate myself for thinking of such a tame diversion, one where maybe I could sit down for a while and rest my aching feet without having to worry about the perils of the parachute jump, or the gastronomic effects of the rotating dive-bomber — acts that seemed to hold the greatest appeal for Lenny in spite of his diet. He didn't seem much bothered by all the trash he had consumed, but why court disaster?

My caution, of course, went for naught. We found the fun house, and entered through the plaster jowls of an enormous clown's face into a gymnasium-sized room that smelled of sweet-and-sour socks and was full of prepubescent bad news. There was a thirty-foot slide with dips and bumps and turns, a rolling barrel that one tried to run through without falling down, an escalator-like affair called "The Wave" that one walked along as it dipped, tilted, arched, fell away under one's feet, and then Lenny discovered the "Whirlygig," a huge wooden wheel that spun its load of shrieking kids slowly at first, then faster and faster, until centrifugal force flung them off into a padded canvas barrier. When the last one was dislodged from his bum-clinging perch the wheel stopped and everyone scrambled aboard again.

There was no use protesting. Resigned, I waited through three cycles of the Whirlygig, hoping against certainty that my now glassy-eyed little boy would not want still another go, would acknowledge the salty warnings of imminent nausea, would climb off of his own accord and join me on the bench where I kept a watchful eye on that secret air jet in the floor — in case some witless, miniskirt should pass over it. But I knew none would (and none did), just as I knew he wouldn't (and he didn't). He hung right in there.

And it was with rather impressive cool, I think, that I rose, when the time came, to deal with the outraged mother of some small dignitary whose birthday troop had received, all over its collective taffeta and seersucker, the backwash of Lenny's suddenly unclogged pipes. He reminded me a little bit, from his central position on the spinning disk, of one of those high pressure Rain-Bird sprinklers that you see watering broad expanses of public lawns. Or a fire hose turned on suddenly with nobody to hold its thrashing nozzle. Poor kid. The walls of the bunker in which the Whirlygig was recessed began to take on the textural and compositional features of a Paul Klee, something along the lines of, say, "The Order of High C," or perhaps a Severini, like "Dynamic Hieroglyphic of the Bal Tabarin," oil on canvas with sequins — only in our gallery it was cream soda on tarp with Big Hunk and fried pie. The chocolate banana he more or less torpedoed over the guard rail intact, where it sank harmlessly beneath the undulating swells of The Wave. A dud.

"DON'T YOU HAVE ENOUGH BRAINS TO KEEP A CHILD STUFFED WITH ALL THAT GARBAGE OUT OF HERE?" Den Mother. Enraged. Trying to soothe befouled charge with a wad of Kleenex produced from her handbag.

"What would you recommend, lady? Roto-Rooter?"

"DON'T WISE OFF TO ME, BUSTER. I'LL HAVE A COP."

Something about beggars and choosers. The operator shut off his machinery, climbed down from the controls, and produced in one well practiced motion a sign saying *Closed* and a pail with a mop stuck in it. His expression as he went by was one of such vacant resignation that it occurred to me, in a moment of whimsical light-headedness, that the sign might better be hung from his lip than the turnstile entrance for which it was intended. "Aw naw," he said, sadly inspecting the mess. "*Motherfuck!*"

I held my hands up in what I hoped was helpless confusion. "Sorry about all this."

"Shit's down inna rim. Never gonna get it out. Stink all to hell."

"Sorry," I repeated.

He made a gesture indicating his familiarity with the event. "Don't feel like the Lone Ranger, Pal, you're number four on the day. One more and I'm tellin' ya they can stick this job up their ass."

At least Weisberg was amused. When I told him about the tribulations of parenthood at Gilda's, where we sat in a back booth drinking Coors on tap with a platter of fried clams, he offered condolences and what he felt was witty advice on how to deal with equal rights amendments in the home; puns on Rockettes, suffragettes, and drum majorettes; tongue-in-cheek blasts at the political militancy of Emmeline Pankhurst and her women's union; suggestions that I deliver Lenny to Erica with an announcement that while I could not hit a child, her emancipation no longer afforded her any such courtesy — and smack her in the eye. No wonder he was single. "Actually," Harry said,

"I envy you. For a steady piece of ass I'd take picklepuss here to the boardwalk every day of his life. I'd buy stock in Disney World."

"That's funny, Weisberg," I told him. "In spite of your grotesque apearance and dismal failure with women, I've always envied *you*. Free, unencumbered, rich; in a town full of promise. I don't know how you can be so consistently morose. I'm serious, if I were in your shoes I think I'd have to live on Valium or Miltown or something just to keep myself down."

Harry chuckled sourly. "Have you ever actually looked at this town? I mean really looked? Discounting those over eighty, which is about fifty percent, it is largely peopled by underaged teenyboppers and what can only be described as rejects from the casting lot of *McCabe and Mrs. Miller* . . . the miners, forty-niners, and not so darling Clementines in their Farmer Browns and prewashed denim. I see an old-fashioned skirt these days my socks roll up and down. Speaking of rejects, how's your friend Ward? Still slaying dragons in the groves of academe?"

"I don't know. I think he decided I'm tainted by my associations and he's staying away. I haven't seen him."

"I have."

"Really?"

"He came around the office awhile ago to apologize for his outburst at the Crow's Nest; which, I have to admit, he managed in a very backhanded way."

"Ah, you kissed and made up."

Harry snorted and waved a fly off his glass. "Naw, the kid's basically a schmuk. He's got that intense, ex-doctoral candidate seeking recommendation for position with CIA gleam in his eye that makes me suspicious as hell, and I don't like him. But to give him his due, in some ways he seems bright enough."

"And how have you determined this, oh venerable one?"

"He hung around. We talked about this and that. Actually what he really wanted was to know what I thought of you."

"You're kidding."

"No. I'm not. I told him you were devious, sneaky, not very intelligent, corrupt," Harry sighed dramatically, "but he didn't buy it. He thinks you're the Messiah."

"That's why he's bright."

"Wrong again. He's bright because he's assimilated a lot of information along the way, and like any good pedant he knows how to make connections and associations. He's also dumb because he's completely on the wrong track, he's imitating someone he ain't ever going to be like, thank God, and he's driving himself crazy trying to find the combination that will change him, Shazaam, from wee weeping Willy to wild man Warren."

"Ridiculous."

"Exquisite modesty. Actually you probably do find it ridiculous because you know that fundamentally you're a putz. But the issue is not *why* Mr. Ward is obsessed by your surface glitter . . . these are questions that could only be answered through extensive analysis . . . the issue resides simply in the *fact* that he has chosen you as his guru."

"Now I know why you don't like him. You're consumed by envy."

Harry looked at me with an odd smile. "You know, the delightful and also scary thing about you is that you've never taken anything seriously in your life."

"I beg your pardon," I said. "I didn't realize our discussion was on that plane."

"What I'm trying in my clumsy fashion to get through to you is that friend Ward is a spooky young man with a lot of intensity and not much imagination. That combination spells R-O-L-A-I-D-S. Right now you're a seven course meal. You could become acid indigestion. When you fuck up and he finds out you're a sorry mortal with a cirrhotic liver and fillings in your teeth just like the rest of us, look out. You're going to reveal to him that what he thinks he wants to be just like ain't all that fancy a product."

"You know what, Harold? If you weren't the world's penultimate joke I'd be offended by your somewhat quali- fied opinion of my character."

"Yeah? Well I'm just telling you what I gleaned from our talk. The guy gives me the fantods, frankly. And there's another thing while I'm laying it out. I noticed the little eye trips you and his old lady were into. Peek-a-boo, flutter flutter. Nothing escapes the Weisberg. You be careful, man."

I reached over and zipped up Lenny's jacket. "You're an incorrigible, you know that, Harold? Your mind is totally infarcted. It's possible, believe it or not, to have commerce with a woman without wishing to molest her, and anyway, I want you to drink up, fool, because I've got to get this fry back on the streets or he'll tell his mother he spent the day in a bar."

"If you want my advice," Harry said, "keep a low profile."

Lenny was still pretty green when we drove over to the harbor to watch the boats come back in after the two-day windjammer race. I had convinced him that fresh air would do him more good than another turn at the shoot- ing gallery down at the boardwalk, and for once I didn't get an argument out of him. He seemed pretty subdued, offering only the faintest glimmer of a smile when we passed a McDonald's and I suggested he might like a couple of burgers. We parked near the fuel dock and walked out on the jetty, almost to the end, then nestled down between the rocks where the sun was still warm but the spray couldn't get us. For a while he became quite talkative, telling me about pre-school and the spelling tests where you got a red candy if you didn't miss more than one and a green candy if you didn't miss more than three. He liked the green ones best so he always tried to miss the requisite number, and I suggested that he could probably work a trade when he got red ones, thereby improving his class standing and pleasing his palate at the same time. He smacked himself on the forehead with an open palm the way Erica does when suddenly something obvious occurs to her. "Why didn't I think of that?"

After a while he fell asleep, the wind riffling the thin strands of his hair (cut too short for my taste); a tiny pulse beating in the pale veins along the side of his forehead. Clear, olive skinned. Erica's skin. Quick to tan. When he was a baby he looked like his grandfather. As he got older his features changed so that he looked less like Erica's side of the family than mine, only with her coloring. Even the shape of his skull had changed, and as I sat looking at him, sleeping, the childhood frown erased from his face, his features relaxed and uncomplicated by whatever hopes, fears, disappointments, tensions go through a child's head, I both envied and was immensely sad for him. I had done him few favors in his short life; even my attempts to alter his bad habits, like sucking his thumb, turned into oppression and meanness. Impatience. I inherited the worst of my father. I wanted Lenny to be a logical, reasoning adult at the age of four, capable of understanding cause and effect, capable of acting upon that understanding. I refused to accept impulsive and compulsive behavior in a baby who could hardly talk when my own behavior was, in the same respect, far worse. And how stupid, I thought, because I loved him in my own uncommunicative way, and now, when I took him out for a day's fun what had I done to show it but stuff him so full of sweets that he blew his cookies in the fun house.

Although Lenny seemed to think that the day had been a barrel of laughs, Erica was less delighted by his account of its events. Whatever frustrations she may have felt about motherhood, the health, education, and welfare of the child was a responsibility she took with complete seriousness, and my consorting with Harry Weisberg in a waterfront gin-mill with a four year old in tow was an offensive act. In the interests of harmony she managed to restrain herself from direct criticism of my leadership potential, but told Lenny that "Daddy" hadn't had a lot of experience with little boys' tummies, didn't always recognize their activity interests, and probably hadn't been thinking very clearly anyway because he'd been schnockered the night before and gotten home in the wee small hours. Normally such circuitous needling would have engendered the churlish response it deserved, but I was preoccupied. In one sense she was right. I wasn't thinking clearly, not at any rate about the commitments involved in a "happy marriage." I was quite depressed, as a matter of fact, and feeling put upon that at the age of forty I was required by natural law to go through an identity crisis again that didn't seem to differ in many respects from the one I'd gone through at eighteen — the tiresome "who am I and what do I want" syndrome, but with a new (and equally humdrum) routine superimposed. How did I get trapped under the weight of all these obligations? Bills? Dependencies? Requirements? My life is full of *stuff*, I thought. I drown.

Nina Allencraig had a phrase for it. Our intimacies had not yet reached the point where she had cause to use it, but they would. And, as usual, she was right. Top down and let the wind blow through the hair — if you have any. Fifth gear and rolling. Song of the open road. In her words, sports car menopause. Enjoy.

Part Three

One

I HAD NEVER HAD AN AFFAIR, EVEN A FLIRTATION, WITH ONE of my students. Inexperience resulted in my being at a total loss how to proceed beyond the refries and enchiladas Nina and I ate at the Toro Salvaje one evening, two or three weeks after she first came into my office seeking artistic release for her creative anxieties. I read the newspapers and magazines like everybody else, those articles that explain to the middle-aged the meaning of the new morality and the decline of social ritual; those obituaries to dating, necking, petting, foot-printing on the dashboard upside down, and all other medieval customs that are supposed to have disappeared with the fifties. I know that nice girls do, when they feel like it, and in bed not in the backseat of a chopped and channeled '49 Merc. (You would have loved that car.) I know that bored and stroked no longer refers to automobile engines. I keep informed. But it came as a great shock to realize that while

I might very well fall into the tipsy, inarticulate seduction of a dissatisfied housewife like Frankie, I didn't know how to make sober conversation to a sweet, good-looking twenty-year-old — a twenty-year-old whose own experience was so vast (or so it seemed to me) that she had the cool presence to walk into a university administrator's office with no clothes on and tell him he was a puritan, and then — and THEN — politely inform Weisberg's Committee on College Discipline that if they thought her body offensive or threatening to the health and welfare of the community they could test their opinion in a civil court of law — until they did, she was wasting no more of *her* time. And with Nina there in front of me all healthy innocence and strong white teeth, I couldn't judge her for it either. I guess there is a new morality, and I guess I'm never going to understand it.

The application of a fourth tequila sunrise that evening at the Toro Salvaje had no effect on my mental eclipse. Fortunately Nina was as nervous as I (I found this out much later when she confessed she thought I was constantly on the verge of a clumsy proposition), but the social jitters made her loquacious rather than mute; she never noticed my monosyllabic grunts and look of retarded abjection. Her father, she told me, was a research chemist for a firm in Los Angeles. She had grown up in Pacific Palisades with her two sisters, three brothers, and a cocker spaniel. Her mother did volunteer work at a Dominican hospital in Oxnard. In high school she had received A's and B's in everything but math, and she listed under her yearbook picture "Glee Club," "Dramatic Society," and "Youth Symphony." She had gone out with the president of the senior class for two years. She was five-feet, eight-inches, weighed a hundred and thirty pounds, and had had the German measles and two cavities as a child. How does someone who went steady with the senior class president wind up ignoring her education for six months after graduation to live with an itinerant rock musician in San Francisco and spend her days playing the flute on a sun-struck balcony in North Beach? Nina's explanation was not morally enlightening.

"What else was I going to do? Hand out Big Macs for a dollar sixty-five an hour?"

"Were you in love with the guy?"

"Oh, for about three months, I guess I was."

"I mean, couldn't you have found some other way, to ah, make ends meet?"

"What for?" she asked, all bouncy innocence and smiles. "I wanted to play the flute, not join the labor force. I wanted to wake up in the morning to nothing but a day of music, twenty-four hours of Jean-Baptiste Loeillet ahead of me . . . well, twelve maybe, you know, of playing, listening to recordings, reading everything I could get my hands on about eighteenth-century music. I really got into it. I think it was the best studying I've ever done, honest."

"Ah!"

"You know what I'd do every day?"

"Huunnn!"

"I'd get up around seven-thirty, see, because I had this terrific apartment on Green Street with a balcony that looked down over the Fisherman's Wharf part of North Beach at the bay, and it was just great to get up early. I mean, zonk, Alcatraz dead ahead, and San Quentin on the other side of the bay when the weather was clear, and Berkeley to the right . . . only maybe it was Richmond, I don't know, and Marin County on the left. The *view*, oh wow, it was worth twice the price. But anyway, I'd get up at seven-thirty every morning and put Jean Pierre Rampal on the hi-fi, you know one of those flute and guitar things with Rene Bartoli or somebody, and I'd squeeze some orange juice and grind coffee beans and while the coffee was perking I'd throw open the drapes in front of the balcony and sit there in this funny old stuffed chair, with no clothes on, and the sun coming in through these big French windows warming me all over, and I'd play the flute along with the record. I mean it, it was complacencies of the peignoir every morning, every day Sunday morning, coffee and oranges in the sunny chair. I learned that in Wiggen's modern poetry class, in case you wondered."

"And you were the cockatoo."

"Uh-uh. I was the green freedom. See, that was the whole thing, the freedom. Not just lying around and doing nothing and pretending you're free just because you're not participating in somebody else's system . . . because I worked very hard, I really did. I practiced and studied just about all day every day . . . except, you know, when I had to earn the rent and all, though John wasn't around all that much (bubbles and laughter), and I went to every one of my classes at the conservatory. But I was the freedom because I had rules and order and self-discipline." She blushed and laughed. "I have great willpower, really! And see, all the structures were imposed from the inside, by me, and so I really felt good about having enough personal strength to do something serious that didn't come easy, with nobody forcing me to perform."

We never did get around to the ostensible purpose of our meeting, her paper on Otto Rank. We talked only about Nina — or she talked and I grunted. Everything I could think of to say sounded professorial and instructive, and reminded me that I was beginning college as a sullen freshman at about the same time she was beginning the trip from ovary to uterus, that her father and I were roughly contemporaries, give or take a few years, and that I would be far more confident and comfortable laying a hand on her mother's ass than I would on hers. If *I* had a daughter in college I'd want a law passed that kept male instructors under forty-five in cages — not because their behavior is in any way extraordinary, but because there are fewer of them than there are nubile coeds under twenty, and it would be more practical. I suffered the sophomore jitters driving her home at one A.M. (wondering whether I should try kissing her good night), and closed the evening with the shaky confession that I had not fed her beans and tequila strictly because I admired her mind.

"I was never under that impression," she said.

"You weren't?"

"My mind is not what professors around here usually admire."

"You mean . . . you get asked out by other faculty members?" I don't know why I was surprised.

She thought a minute. "Well, this has been a dry year. Only three. Wiggins, Oglethorp, and Jones. Sounds like a law firm, doesn't it? And then, of course, you."

"*Ogle*thorp? You mean Martha Oglethorp?"

"Umm. But you're the only one I've gone with, if it matters. The others are all stuffy and into their fairly heavy scenes. I couldn't see any room in their space for me."

Delightful child.

We met for breakfast at a crêpe joint near the harbor, and I wrote down on a paper napkin a list of continued readings for her independent study — *Borges on Writing*, Ben Shahn's *The Shape of Content*, Conrad's letters to Ford Maddox Ford, a few other things — and after we'd eaten we went down to the beach and took a long walk along the sand, not talking much, just strolling, watching the shore break, letting the tide wash over our feet and wet our cuffs. It was a marvelously clear morning, already hot, but with enough of a breeze to dry the sweat on my back and blow a skein of fine sand across the tops of the dunes behind us. We walked for several miles, climbing

III

once over a rocky point that jutted too far out into the surf to be skirted, then along the empty expanse of beach that curves south in an unbroken line to the mouth of the Pajaro River. A few surf casters materialized in the sparkling mist, a flock of sanderlings, gulls, an occasional pelican laboring along the coast, otherwise we were alone with the day. Nina picked up sand dollars and tiny shells and tied them in the front of her shirt. I found a long kelp stalk and tried to crack it like a bullwhip; nearly succeeded in removing a piece of my ear.

I do not remember at what point our hands touched, and then touched again, and stayed together with fingers loosely intertwined. I do remember thinking that beginnings were not, after all, so very much different than they had ever been. Erica and I had fallen in love holding hands in the backseat of a car as we were returning one night from a ski trip in New England. An accident. A bump in the road and our fingers brushed. Nina and I walking on the beach, thinking of nothing in particular, the texture of the sand, the heat from the sun, the comic skitter of shorebirds chasing the backwash of a wave, and then that little accident, hands making contact, and through some tactile chemistry a need, a want, a commitment communicated. I also remember wondering why she was playing this ancient game with someone who must have seemed to her nineten and three-quarter years pretty ancient himself.

"Because I like you," she said.

"If you knew me better than you do, you might not."

"I know you well enough."

"Don't be silly," I chided. "You have no idea where I come from, what I come from, what my life has been like up until six o'clock yesterday evening." Slyly, "You don't know what my motives are for being here right now, or where I think I want to be tomorrow."

"I know you're here because you like me in the same way I like you."

"Is that all that matters?"

"That's now. So I do know about that, and as for the rest, you know, I don't even *want* to know about that . . . about 'then.' 'Then' just messes up the good things about 'now.' So don't bug me about motives and history and stuff, please, okay?"

"Okay, but suppose all I'm interested in is trying to sleep with you?"

She looked at me bemused. "The word is fuck."

"I'm acquainted with the word," I said, faintly embarrassed.

"Then why don't you use it?"

"Its connotation is a little more matter of fact than what I had in mind."

"So you see, you are interested in something else. Why get into a speculation trip?" She turned away and looked out across the water. "People sure mess around with themselves a lot."

I don't know, at that point, if she was right or not. I remember that one of the principal things on my mind was the little hideaway over Harry Weisberg's garage that I had kept for myself even after I had gone back to living at home.

There were more people on the beach around the Pajaro Dunes development when Nina and I reached it, but it still looked more like a pleasant Courbet painting of the sea near Normandy than the Anzios and Iwo Jimas closer to Santa Cruz. We found a warm hollow protected by a fringe of saw grass and lay with our faces to the sun, talking in a drowsy monotone, Nina turning her head now and then to look at me. Ice-blue eyes flecked with a poof of dandelion white around the cornea. Her hair shone dark like coffee beans against the sand. She fell asleep after a while and I lay there thinking that I was already in too deep to back off even if I wanted to — which I didn't. I conjured up Erica's possible ex-lover to justify my own excursions, and told myself that to play it safe and sane, to be rational and realistic, to consider the negatives and impossibilities, was to condemn myself *a priori* as a man whose emotional life was so controlled that it was therefore over. One of the also-rans. Third place to the weak and timid. The hell with the examined life. Better side with Picasso and Miller. Then I fell asleep too.

We walked back to the car around two o'clock, thinking about food again and debating between the Burger Pit and the Wienerschnitzel. I had only two dollars in my pants and Nina was broke. "You want to come over to my studio?" I asked. "I keep a few things in the icebox." And having asked was suddenly afraid that she would mis-read (or *read*) the invitation. What a disgustingly obvious proposition. You want to come up and see my bean sprouts and cherry tomatoes? Der wienerschnitzel? "That didn't come out right, did it? Sorry." Nina's eyes were curiously void of expression. "I'd like to explain myself to you, honest to God," I started again, "but I'm not sure what to say. I mean, I know what all this *looks* like . . ."

She took my hand and walked me along the fringe of beach bordering the parking lot. "Maybe it would be easier if I told you how *I* feel," she said. I nodded dumbly, grateful, I guess, for any help I could get. "Do you know I had a crush on you way back when I was a freshman . . ."

"Freshperson."

"I don't care for that word . . . and I'd see you around the college and think you were very dashing. But then I found out you were married and all, and I didn't think I'd ever get to know you. I even looked you up in the university directory to make sure." She laughed at herself; girlish sim-plicity. "Then the independent study happened, and your creepy friend Weisberg let drop in the middle of one of his inept passes that you were separated from your wife, and I thought to myself, Nina, maybe you've got a chance after all, maybe if you look pretty and bright he'll notice you as something more than just another boring student. I guess I was pretty obvious, huh."

"On the contrary . . ."

"I always get evaluations that say 'Nina's major strength is her candor and straightforward manner. Nina is charmingly naive.' I can't help it. I know I'm not very coy, but I don't give a damn."

"You're very beautiful," I said.

She looked bemused. "I'm all right," she said. "I'm not beautiful."

"I'm usually pretty immune to the charms of teenagers," I told her, "and I assure you I'm not in the habit of chasing around after my students, but you turned my head around in a very unusual way. Don't argue. I think you're beautiful inside and out. And I'm the professor; I'm wiser and older."

"I'm almost twenty," she cooed. "In five weeks."

"No doubt that accounts for your being so opinionated."

Suddenly she was serious again, and looking at me pensively. "What are we going to do, Eliot?"

Not understanding the question precisely, I shrugged. "About what?"

"Do you think all this is wrong?"

"Do you?" I said. This was an evasion. I didn't know if she meant "wrong" because I wasn't separated anymore, assuming she was aware of that small fact, or because I was twice her age and her teacher, or just what she had in mind. I confess I wasn't prepared to divulge any more of my personal life at that point than I had to.

"I don't know," Nina said. She sat down on a driftwood log and stared reflectively at the ocean while I kept my silence. "I guess I'm too excited to think very clearly, but I know there are a lot of things I want to do with my life that mean keeping it uninvolved. I also know that I've never felt like this before, not this strongly, and I'm afraid."

"You're a wonderful woman, you know that? And tough. What are you afraid of?"

She shook her head. "Commitment, I guess. Giving up my dreams for someone else's, or hurting someone because I'm too stubborn to give them up. I am stubborn, you know."

"Dreams?"

"Of law school and maybe politics eventually. I dream of going to Washington after I graduate to work for a few years. I dream about a career in public administration, public service of some kind, because it's something I know I'd be good at and it's something I believe in. Everybody sits around saying the world is screwed, but nobody wants to do anything about it anymore . . . not since the sixties anyway."

"What makes you so sure that falling in love with somebody presumes giving all this up?"

She was silent again for a while, then turned and faced me directly. "It's been my experience, Sir." She was obviously considering carefully what she was about to say. "See, I've had a few lovers in my life, and that's a part of me that I understand very well. I can always deal with it because I know myself that way; I know I need to be loved and have people feel good about me, and that I get my greatest pleasure by giving pleasure to a man, but when making love *with* somebody becomes making love to them, or by them, and the whole possession thing begins, then I bail out. I can't stand it when somebody is always on my case, always trying to impose their thing on mine. And it always happens that way eventually."

"Forgive me for being obtuse," I said, "but why tell me all this? I'm not out to spoil your dreams."

"You asked what I was afraid of. You're the first person I've met who could maybe do it." She stood up then and put her arms on my shoulders like a dancer about to execute a plié. "Also, I want you to know how I am."

"And now that I know?"

"We can go to your studio. One thing I never do is make love in public. But you've got to promise to take me home by six. I'm still a struggling student, remember? Got to keep up the grades."

On the way I was nervously preoccupied with the quality of my coming performance. What would I look like to her without my clothes? Was I too hairy, too stocky (in this age of slenderized males), too pale? Was my linen clean? Would I be able to sustain a marathon erection? Would I be able to get an erection at all? I had known moments of impotence in the past, embarrassing failures with women whose bedside manner was either too forceful or too passive, or whose physical imperfections, when revealed, preempted my concentration and caused a short circuit in the wires from pate to pecker. By the time we entered the garage and climbed the stairs to my hovel my anxiety was so severe that I was beginning to think of excuses to put the whole business off.

The lone can of tuna in my larder turned out to be the dark kind and intended, I think, for cats, not humans, but we worked out an arrangement with some pickle relish and mayonnaise that pretty well disguised its overbearing flavor. Anyway, food was not the first of our hungers. I was greatly relieved, when Nina came over and brushed the crumbs of French bread off my chin and gave me a heavy, slow, somewhat fishy kiss, to discover that an erection was not going to be one of my problems.

I do not wish to dwell endlessly on the subject of my general ineptitude with the younger generation (Nina was soon to help me out of that bog), but I confess that I was not in control of myself on that day, and my presentation was more swinish than swainish. I was, in short, premature in the execution of my duties, and having disgraced myself on the gentle slope of her exquisite tummy, could offer no explanation but an old joke my father used to tell about Johnny the spastic, who, when promised an ice-cream cone if he could touch both index fingers to the bridge of his nose, and who, after struggling for an hour and winning his prize, brought it to his mouth and with one convulsive jerk smashed it on his forehead.

"Oh well," Nina said, "even space shots have been known to misfire. I'm flattered, actually, you find me so stimulating."

It could be argued, I suppose, that what interested me most about Nina, what I found so "stimulating" (apart from her physical perfection), was her complete inversion of what repelled me in most other undergraduates of her age — to wit, the notion that the self is all that matters. Whatever gratifies the self, contributes to its development, its sensitivity, whatever pleases one *for the moment* in one's search for expansion and uniqueness, is okay. All behavior is okay, just as long as an appeal can be made to the constructive growth of one's consciousness, and "just so long as nobody else gets hurt along the way." Nina, on a global plane, wanted to carry everybody's cross; the poor, the black, the Vietnamese. At the same time she could perform an absurd act like walking in on Provost Dixon without any clothes because, as she put it, that was where her head was at the time and the consequences fell solely on her shoulders. "In his heart of hearts," she assured me, "he dug it, even though he was very solemn and pretended to be very offended by my disrespect. I noticed that he kept thinking of things to say to drag the whole interview out . . . when he could have left or had me removed, right? Instead he put on his shades and stuck it out like a good trooper. I don't mean he stuck *it* out (very amused by herself), I mean he *stayed around*." She did a reenactment of the whole event for me the next afternoon that was so comically lewd I rolled off the bed onto a wine glass and imbedded a shard of glass in my right buttock. It cost me thirty dollars to have it removed — an assault not only on my flesh and dignity, but my pocketbook as well.

Nina didn't take herself as seriously as other more strident defenders of the "alternative life-style," and she really didn't give a damn if I liked her attitude or not; *she* wasn't on a crusade. We argued a lot about that "just so long as nobody gets hurt" evasion. I pontificated that as a philosophical justification for behavior this was invalid because the seeker, the learner, the self-expander was really in no position to judge who or what might get racked up along the way — if he were he would already have arrived — and Nina said, "Yes, right on," and cracked a seismic yawn at the sophistical quibble. You're a regular whiz, Dad. "Who are you to be postulating moral equations, you baby raper?" she said. "I'm just a child. You're not supposed to be screwing me, you know, you're supposed to be explaining what the rhetoric of irony is all about, and anyway, I want to go down to the penny arcade and blow up some German submarines. If there's anything I hate it's kraut subs. Come on, Eliot, take me out on the town. This bed is a sewer."

Two

WHEN ERICA'S FATHER CALLED FROM HANOVER WITH THE BAD news, my solicitous participation in his daughter's concern was somewhat disingenuous. My mother-in-law, "Ma" Savage, wasn't exactly a caricature; if she had been I probably would have understood her and liked her better. She never meddled or pried into Erica's affairs, never invited herself for extended visits, never concerned herself with the quality of Lenny's upbringing. She couldn't have cared less, because she was a selfish, class-conscious, old burgher whose penultimate misery in life was that she had been born in Worcester instead of Boston and whose ultimate misery was that Erica hadn't married someone who had. Actually her ultimate misery, I suppose, was the cancer for which she was about to undergo surgery.

That I didn't care for her much was not, however, the real reason my commiseration was fraudulent. Mom's understandable self-pity led her to seek, before she died, a reconciliation with the daughter she had ignored all her life, and through Dad was imploring Erica to come East with Pickle for what one feared "might be the last time." I was imagining two weeks of high jinks with Nina. At least. "Go," I said. "This is no time to bear grudges. The woman hasn't much time, if statistics are worth anything, and I'd think you'd rather see her while she's still alive than go to a funeral."

"My brother will be there," she said a little coldly. (Her brother was the favorite; the one, in fact, Erica had been rejected for because as a child he was a scabby little turd who cried, threw tantrums in public, demanded constant attention. Later he went to Groton and Princeton, and married a Smith girl. Now he's a big turd.) "Besides, it costs a lot of money."

"Hang the money. You know your conscience is going to bother you if you don't go. *Some*day, anyway."

"Do you remember what I told you my mother said to me when I was ten years old? About how she was very sorry but she only had enough time and affection for one child, and since I was such a *good* little girl and Timmy such a *difficult* little boy, he was the one who was going to receive it. 'Your father and I want you to know there's nothing personal' she said. Now I should go and provide comfort and solace?"

"If nothing else, Erica," I said, "we could use a vacation from each other. I think it would be good for both of us."

"Now *that's* true. I hadn't thought of that."

"Well think about it. If you decide to go, I'll have one of the secretaries make the travel arrangements."

On Saturday we took the coast road to the airport, stopping in Half Moon Bay for a late lunch, and I put Erica and Pickle on the plane in San Francisco about four. Then I headed for the first phone-booth I could find. The person who answered in Nina's dorm went to look for her:

somebody else saw the receiver dangling unoccupied and hung up. Ma Bell pocketed my last thirty-five cents, and I drove home *sans* mate, *sans* date. *Sans* gasoline too. I ran out a mile before the summit on Highway 17 (from whence I could have coasted), and spent an hour and a half hitchhiking back and forth with my little red can. I left a hundred dollar watch as a deposit for a gallon of gas and it was nearly eight when I got back to the house. The front door was unlocked and all the lights blazing.

For a few moments I stood in the entryway, listening, assuring myself that I *had* locked the doors when we left, wondering why burglars, if that's what it was, would turn on all the lights, wondering why I was standing there with my thumb in my bum if it *was* burglars, and then I saw the note on the hall table.

CAN YOU COME TO DINNER TOMORROW? WILLY.

I stared at his block print letters wondering why he had found it necessary to deliver this invitation by break-ing into my house and turning on all the lights. I had not seen him since the unfortunate evening we spent at the Crow's Nest when he had flipped out, and here he came again with another symptom of screwball behavior. As I stood there trying to sort it all out, I began to get a persistent, cold tingle somewhere in the region of my neck and shoulder blades because it suddenly occurred to me that Willy was still in the house. I took off my shoes and padded down the hall toward Lenny's room. Nobody. Nobody in the bathroom either, or the kitchen, or the laundry. All empty. I searched the whole house, the closets, under the beds; then went slowly through and turned off the lights. To pacify my curiosity I called his house but there was no answer. Well, I thought, no doubt he'll have some explanation tomorrow. I called Nina's dorm, but the Saturday night evacuation had already taken place and I got no answer there either, so with nothing else to do I raided the liquor cabinet and went over to my digs above Weisberg's garage, had a snort or two and fell asleep.

Frankie met me at the door the following evening. I was an hour late and I handed over my two bottles of Sauvignon Blanc with an apology and the expressed hope that I had guessed right and she wasn't into anything like beef hearts or pig livers. "Salmon," she said. "Willy's out back immolating himself with charcoal lighter." She was dressed in a white blouse, leather pants that were flared at the bottom and tight over her accommodating little butt, and deerskin moccasins with bells tied in the fringe over the instep — a considerable improvement, I thought, over the flour sack tent I had first seen her in. Her hair was pulled away from her face and held in back by a silver barrette of Indian design, and she was wearing pale lipstick. I told her she looked terrific.

Frankie made a face and handed me a cucumber and a metal peeler. "Well, I do what I can, but when you face odds like mine it's tough. Stripped of the costly ensembles I picked up at the Re-Run, I am your basic toothpick."

"I don't know," I said. "I can't see anything to complain about."

"I did put on six pounds after I lost the baby. I think I was trying to eat myself pregnant again."

"Surely there must be an easier way."

"You ever been married to a monk trying to write a book?"

Willy came in with charcoal dust blackening his hands and went to the kitchen sink to wash them. "Finally got the sonofabitch going," he announced. "At no small risk to my personage: huffing, puffing, cardiac arrest. You want a drink? I have some of your favorite poison."

"I could maybe force myself," I told him.

He measured scotch with a one ounce shot glass, added a half-pint of water and some ice, and when he was finished I took the bottle and poured a large dollop into each drink. "To flavor the water," I said. "We are men not fish."

We left Frankie to struggle with the question of the salmon and went into the room off the kitchen that served both as living room and study. Willy's books, most of them paperbacks and literature texts, were stacked on shelves halfway up one wall, and along the opposite wall an old blanket chest, with a piece of plywood where the half tray had once been, held an amplifier, turntable, and several dozen records.

A glass doored antique bookcase held what I assumed to be especially revered texts — bookclub sets of Faulkner, Hemingway, Fitzgerald, several shelves of works devoted to Eastern religions including hardcover editions of Lobsang Rampa's *The Third Eye* and *The Saffron Robe*, Indries Shah's *Tales of the Dervishes*, *The Way of Sufi*, and *The Magic Monastery*, Thomas Merton's *Zen and the Birds of Appetite* and *Mystics and Zen Masters*. Next to what appeared to be the complete works of Alan Watts I noticed three of my own books. Curious marriage. I settled myself with a grunt onto the sofa and closed my eyes. A harpsichord played softly in the speakers suspended from the ceiling, and for a few minutes we sat and listened to the music without talking — now a pattern with us, I thought, a moment of silence to gather forces. I knew the artists, Igor Kipnis playing Gabrieli, but I could not think of the specific work. Erica had given me the record for Christmas a few years before, and briefly my mind slipped back to earlier days when life had seemed very uncomplicated and promising. I was glad she was not with me. Erica was never one to lie back and let social intercourse lapse — something in her upbringing, no doubt; always the hostess with the mostess or the con-

versational guest. Frankie's voice out in the kitchen interrupted meditation. "Goddamn this slippery fucker."

I opened my eyes in surprise. Willy grinned behind
the kaleidoscope he was screwing around and around.
"She's filleting her thumbs," he said. "She becomes rather
coarse when she bleeds."

"Ah well," I said. "It's the seventies. It's California."

"I mean, I've tried to explain that it's very déclassé to
go around cursing all the time, revealing one's linguistic
limitations, but I'm afraid you're right. We've been
undermined by time and space."

"Even in the best of homes."

"There's no sanctuary. Even the classroom has become
corrupted. I had a girl the other day discussing Christian
symbolism in 'The Wasteland' and you would have
thought she was discussing the action in a skin flick. Shock-
ing. Wouldn't have stood for that in New England."

I rattled the ice cubes in my glass to announce that I
was ready for a refill, but just then Frankie appeared in
the door to appeal for help with the fish. "Can't you do
it, Willy," she whined, handing him the knife. "I'm just
making cat food out of the damn thing."

He grunted to his feet and without looking my way
went into the kitchen. "Make the man another drink,
Franklin," he said, "and find us some horse doovers."

She took my glass and shook her head. "He thinks that's
hysterical. He thinks whore's ovaries is a cliché, right,
but horse doovers is a real ball buster. He heard it on
t.v. last night, so all day he's been going around saying
'horse doovers, horse doovers.'"

I nodded in sympathy. The poor imbecile. Through
slitted eyes I admired her perky behind as she twitched out
of the room. Imagined peaches and a wisp of panty. Oh
my. Youth. Music floated around my head, rattled my
eardrums now and then with sudden gusts of fortissimo,

faded away, a sea-wash of background noise. I really was tired, I realized; no need to fake it. And also I was getting tight. My resolution to make an early evening of it, stay sober, and avoid debates of the Weisberg/Ward genre was fading into 90-proof indifference. Anyway, I was enjoying Frankie. Refreshingly vulgar.

All of a sudden I became aware of something rooting between my legs. I jerked, and heard Frankie say, "Gopher, you asshole, get out of here." She set our drinks on the coffee table and led Gopher by his choke collar into some other part of the house. When she came back she was excessive in apology, which was odd; he hadn't eaten my dinner or anything. "He's a crotch sniffer," she said. "Habits of his mistress."

"Didn't realize you had a dog," I said, ignoring her remarks.

"Consolation prize. I didn't get a baby, so I got a puppy instead."

"I was sorry to hear about all that. I meant to say something earlier, but I thought maybe you'd rather not be reminded."

Her turn to ignore me. She leaned out of her chair to see what Willy was doing in the kitchen. "*He* was really upset," she whispered, "a lot more than I was. I was pretty sure I didn't want to be a mother all along, but what can you do when you're caught and your husband won't go for an abortion? I mean, he went absolutely bananas when I lost it, like I'd killed him in effigy or something. I was scared. I love him and all, but sometimes he's . . . I don't know. Like that afternoon at the Crow's Nest."

"My offer still stands," I said. "I can find somebody to help, and I think the university will stand some of the cost."

Frankie picked a fruit fly out of her drink and flicked

126

it into the air. Her thumb started to bleed again where she had cut it, and she wrapped a cocktail napkin around the wound to stop the flow. "I think things are going to be okay. I mean he's got a job and all, and his father figure is right here. I know that sounds patronizing, but I think when he gets that damn novel done he'll be able to be his own man for once. Won't have to rely on other people recommending him as somebody with 'promise.' What a drag, that book. Who gives a shit about another exercise in dark humor?"

Willy appeared then, wiping his hands on a ragged dishtowel. "What about dark humor? The humor of darkness? You running down my life's work again, you hag? By the way, your fish is done."

"It's your fish, sweety," Frankie said. "You're the chef, remember?"

Willy was wiping at something slimy on his shirt. "If you're still willing," he said to me, "it's about ready for you to look over. The novel, that is, not the fish. How about if I bring the draft by tomorrow?"

"Go cook the meat," I said. "Don't spoil my appetite."

Willy cooked. I helped Frankie set the table. We ate. We drank wine. We talked about this and that. There is little point in plodding step by step through the entire evening. I recall how absolutely ordinary, how utterly uneventful and quiet the whole situation was, and how impossible to read into *my* behavior, at least, any motivation beyond the exigencies of social discourse and a desire to be amiable. I say *my* behavior because Frankie's after-dinner suggestion that we dance (a bottle of wine and a nightcap or two after dinner) may have been prompted by something more complicated than the irresistible rhythms of Roberta Flack playing on the hi-fi. I don't know. Maybe she was bored by her husband's ontological groping (he had started that business after his third glass of wine) and figured the only way to get off the subject of being and becoming was to ignore him like a muffled snore. He wasn't paying much attention to her anyway, addressing his metaphysics to me, and none of us could have passed a sobriety test at a Polish picnic.

The focus of Willy's alcoholic angst (or maybe it was genuine, who knows?) was the absence in his life of sufficient testing, of physical ordeals and contemplative rites of passage that would assure him not only that he was, in fact, a man, but one passed on into the ranks of the spiritually mature. "I spent five months in a *gomchen*'s hermitage near the Lachen monastery in Tibet trying to acquaint myself with Lamaist methods of contemplation," he said. "But I don't think I could tell you what I learned except a whole lot about solitude. All I got out of a tour in Vietnam was a leg full of metal and a taste for morphine derivatives. So what . . . finally I decide that since I'm really a product of the Western World I better take another shot at its peculiar form of monastic life and go back to the university, become a disciple, an anchorite, a novitiate, append myself to Warren *Roshi*, venerable teacher, find the path to enlightenment, spiritual liberty. What do you think about that?"

"I think you forget the teachings of Buddha," I said. I poured him another glass of wine. "Buddha said to his favorite disciple, Ananda, 'be your own lamp, be your own refuge,' something like that, by which he meant rely on yourself, don't look for authorities."

"Okay, so how do you go about divesting yourself of a tradition in which the perfection of self, the transformation and elevation of self, comes only through grace. What I want to know is. . . . What I think is. . . ."

But I was being otherwise distracted. Frankie was kneeling on the floor in front of me patting Gopher, who had been readmitted and was sleepily sitting on his haunches in the protecting parenthesis of my legs and breaking wind every time he yawned. I scratched his ears. Frankie scratched his chin. Now and then her fingers would brush the back of my hand, and it became obvious after a bit that this was not an accident. Hands again. Maybe I have magnetic bones. Once or twice our eyes met and held. When the record stopped she crawled to the turntable and flipped it over. She was, I think, quite smashed.

If Willy was aware of our inattention to him, he gave no indication other than to repeat himself every so often and to pause occasionally in the midst of whatever point he was trying to make. (On the off chance, perhaps, that somebody might wish to embellish or rebut.) The points kept escaping me. Elusive as Frankie's touch. He rambled back and forth over his initial subjects. At one moment he was saying that the war we offered our modern young man was unacceptable as a challenge because it reduced him morally even as it proved him physically; at another he was insisting that all contemporary life was a vicarious association with the gunslingers of our past. "The myth of the cowboy proves my point. To understand our archetypes is to understand what we wish we were, but aren't."

What I wished to be, but wasn't, was a man home in bed. With his sweetie wrapped in his arms. Somebody's sweetie. Anybody's. But I couldn't seem to find the energy to leave. I kept flirting with the notion that if I did go I would miss something very important, something that would enlighten me, us, all, something that would resolve Willy's terror over the horizontal limits of his life, and let me off the hook for my repeated failure to play interlocutor in his quest for answers. Or maybe my inertia was more akin to Poe's than to any real expectation that something might happen. Frankie was turning me on. I stayed because I should have gone. I should not have played finger funnies with Frankie. She was nothing to me but young and pretty and flushed with her own sexuality.

From out of the gloom and false camaraderie, cigar smoke and stale whiskey, "Do you ever ask yourself . . . do you even wonder . . . if you have sold out on yourself?"

"Why should I?" (Another evasion? "Of course!" I should have said? "Of course.")

"If maybe when you accepted the security the system offers, took the safe road, the easy path, most traveled, you diminished yourself, your art, your chance to be important?"

"Your question is romantic nonsense. Art isn't the exclusive province of tormented sensitivities and the inhabitants of cold-water flats."

"So is it then in the province of total dedication, total obsession? Did you ever dare, once upon a time, to take the risk?"

The question seemed to assume, of course, that I had not. It seemed to assume, moreover, that the risk was a real one, that it was worth taking, and that no other combination or accommodation was morally legitimate, but I was too weary and drunk to instruct. Let him think what he wanted. "What I have dared," I said, "or not dared, is my business. I wouldn't bore anyone with it."

For a moment I think we glared at each other. I think Willy's expression just then was both disgusted and triumphant, as if he had finally won some Kewpie doll he wanted so badly, and mine, probably, was contemptuous. Shades of my old man. There was no victory to be had. There had been but one army on the plain. I had no patience for Willy's brand of fireside psychoanalysis, and dismissed him as a curiosity seeker, an entrail inspector, a tiresome tourist knocking at the locked gates to my soul. Can't you read the sign, bub? The museum is closed.

Frankie, sensing a break in the action, or impending hostilities once again, stood up and assumed a sort of ballroom stance. "I feel like dancing," she said, and pulled me to my feet. "You guys are deadly." It was, considering the obvious attention she had been paying me all night (the dog being a poor pretext for sitting at my feet, and her bright smile that winked on like a bar sign when I talked an implicit siding against Willy), the worst possible move she could have made. My complicity was thoughtless, and for that all the more inexcusable.

From the depths of his armchair Willy watched us shuffle around the room for a few minutes, his eyes betraying confusion and hurt. In my somewhat alcoholic state I wasn't worrying much about it. If he couldn't keep his own woman in line, that wasn't my problem. Maybe they did this kind of thing all the time. Maybe they got off watching each other come on for other people. None of my business. Belch! After a while he got up and went into the kitchen. We heard him washing the dishes, and then it was quiet in there. I thought I heard the door to the backyard open and close. Frankie turned out the light and we continued to move against each other. Unsteady. Equilibrium lost in the near dark. My mind fuzzed out like a dying bulb and I felt her lips on mine, mouth open, tongue into my throat. My hand slid up to her breast and with my thumb I rubbed her nipple erect, and she moaned softly, biting my ear lobe and pressing her hips against mine. "You're making me wet," she whispered.

Small sputter of light in my empty head. "What about Willy?" I said.

"Gone to bed."

How long we kept moving that way in the dark I don't remember, but long enough for me to realize eventually that more would be less. And impossible. "I better go," I said.

"Not yet. Please."

"This isn't going to happen, you know that."

She was quiet a minute. "I know but it feels good. The angels and trumpets number wears thin as a steady diet."

I pushed her away. "I have to go, Frankie. This is insane."

She found the light and switched it on, and we stood staring at each other foolishly, squinting, trying to read-just. "Better say good-bye to Willy," I said, backpedaling into the kitchen toward the bedroom door. He wasn't there. Nor in the bathroom either. Frankie called him and Gopher came sleepily out from under the kitchen table. "Where's Willy?" she said. Gopher yawned.

Thinking I remembered the sound of a door closing earlier, I went out onto the service porch off the kitchen. The yard seemed empty, but I noticed that the grill on which the salmon had been cooked was still glowing and emitting a heavy smoke over by the ramshackle garage, and I walked over to it wondering what on earth he was burning. It was a square box of the kind a ream of typing paper comes in, and as I peered blankly at it Frankie came up, took one look, and dumped the whole grill onto the flagstones. "Oh my God," she said, stamping around in the embers and sparks. "It's his book. Help me, for Christ's sake, he's burning up his bloody manuscript."

Three

I CAME DOWN THE BACK STEPS OF THE GARAGE ABOUT NINE-fifteen the next morning and was headed for my car when I saw old goat-boy Weisberg standing out in his little patch of veggies in his pajama bottoms scratching his pot and glaring at the dirt in front of him. I thought I might fill him in on the latest act in the Ward saga, and so wandered over. "How they hanging, Harold?"

"Fucker offed my artichoke."

"What fucker was that?"

"Gopher fucker. Look at that." He prodded a loose depression of crumbly soil with his slipper. "That was a healthy artichoke plant about two feet high, and the mother ate it."

"You have to live with those things, Hair. Gophers have to eat too."

"Why?"

"I don't know. Must have something to do with the

ecological balance. Everything's good for something."

"Yeah? Well I haven't thought of anything a gopher's good for except compost."

"Why don't you get a trap?"

"I got a trap. I got cyanide tablets, poison grain, chloride bombs, clackers, two cats, and a twelve-gauge shotgun. And I got twelve thousand gophers down there laughing their asses off at me, undermining my yard and my house with their bloody holes. The city's going to condemn me one of these days for ruining the drainage basin on the whole western side."

"That bad, huh?"

"Please! Eliot! Do me a favor and go wherever you were going. I do not wish to exchange pleasantries with death so recently visited."

"Your artichoke?"

"Also I was expecting to leave tomorrow for a weekend of meditation and enlightenment at Tassajara with a lady of my recent acquaintanceship, and she just phoned to say she can't go. Her parakeet croaked. She's distraught."

"Do I know this one?"

"I hope not. No. I met her at the DeYoung. I got dragged in there by Jerry Okker and I was so bored looking at crusty old door knockers, and samurai swords, and the soup bowls of . . . primitives . . . that I went out in the lobby and there she was. As bored as I."

"So you invited her to the Zen Center at Tassajara."

"WE WERE GOING TO SWAP SPIT AND TOUCH PEE PEES. HER BIRD DIED." He began to dance on the ground and pull at his disheveled hair.

"Jesus Christ, Harry," I said. "Cut it out, will you, think of the neighbors. No wonder we have a town-gown problem."

"Listen, you want my reservations? I can't cancel them now, it's too late, and there's no phone down there, so you might as well take that charming coos you've been shacking up with, *Miss* Allencraig, and go. There's a lot of nudity down there. She'll fit right in."

"Sometimes, Harry, it astonishes me that you've come so far with so little."

"I don't see what she sees in you."

"Ah, you're jealous."

His face collapsed in a sour grin. "Okay, all right, so? But just a little. If you want to go, it's fifty clams a day, but it's worth it. It's the other world. And lately, pal, you look like you could use some time for reflection." He looked at me closely, mild concern mapped on his face. "Do you know what you're doing, Eliot?"

"You mean with her?"

"I'm not talking about auto parts."

"I don't know. Probably not, but I'll survive."

"I'm not worried about you; I'm thinking about her. I know this girl, Miss Allencraig, and she may put out, every quiff fifteen and older does, but she's an ingenue, a naïf, my friend; for all she thinks she knows about sex she is basically an emotionally honest woman who also happens to be an incredible romantic, and she is not running around with you because she is hard up for attention."

"I'm not getting your point," I said.

"You're a big excitement in her life. You're an older man, you're smarter, more experienced; compared to the campus turkeys she's got all around her, you're a big deal. What are you going to do, Mr. Big Deal, when she falls in love with you, if she hasn't already? You going to leave your wife and kid? You going to set up housekeeping with her? You going to introduce her to all your forty-year-old friends? Or are you going to abandon them and take up with teenagers?"

"I might," I said, feeling that he was pushing me a little

hard. "What got you off this morning? Captain Krunch?"

"Hey, Eliot. It's me. Harry. Quit trying to bullshit me. And yourself. You can't exchange wrinkles for zits; it won't work."

"All the same when it's upside down, huh?"

"That isn't what I mean, and you know it. I'm talking about *your* wrinkles, fool. Right now you're thinking you haven't felt this way since you were twenty, right? Banging away three, four times a night, the old heart going pitty-pat, pitty-pat every time you see her, telling yourself your love is pure as driven snow and all the time looking in the rearview mirror to see if anybody's around that knows you and might rat on you to your old lady, but sort of hoping your old lady *does* find out so she'll throw you out on your ass and make everything all right, except that she probably wouldn't and you'd wind up living in a nastier little mess than you're already in. This is Harry you're talking to, buddy, the Margaret Mead of modern American culture. Patterns. Archetypes. If you don't believe me, ask my ex-wives."

"If I understand you correctly, Margaret," I said, "you suggested just before this latest account of my emotional dementia that I take my 'ingenue coos' to Tassajara as your stand-in in the spit swapping marathon. I don't get it."

Harry regarded me sadly. The bald spot in the middle of his kinky tangle of hair was beginning to redden with the sun. "Conflict of interest," he said. "My first thought in life is how to get laid. My second is how much does it cost."

"If you have to ask what it costs, you can't afford it," I said.

"That's a put-down, right?"

"Right."

"Okay, just for that I'm going to give you your Benny

136

Goodman record back. The one with 'Body and Soul' and 'Avalon' and 'When My Baby Smiles at Me.' Me and you are having a falling out."

"Terrific," I told him. "I never could keep two women happy at the same time."

"You don't count so good either."

That afternoon, sitting in my office writing a note to Michael Arington to try to convince him that the protagonist in his manuscript, a "brilliant" literary critic and member of the New York "establishment," tended to qualify himself unwittingly by references to things like Virgil's *Ecologues,* Tom Hardy's *Far From the Maddening Crowd,* Stern's *Tristan Shamdy,* Weisberg came in. He had his shirt open down the front and was wearing some kind of abstract wooden cross on a heavy metal chain. He had on Zorries and tie-dye bell-bottoms. "If you don't look like a perfect ass," I said. He had my Benny Goodman album, borrowed over a year ago, in his hand.

"Here, you fickle sonofabitch," he said, fawning, and handing it to me. "We're through."

"I'm going to take you up on Tassajara, Harold, you can't welch on that." The jacket cover had a tire track across the middle and the cardboard was pitted. I took the disc out and inspected a number of pencil-sized holes in the nonbreakable plastic; looked at him quizzically, dangling what was left of my famous 1938 Carnegie Hall jazz concert between my fingers. "You have some explanation for this, of course."

"Of course."

"Let's hear it."

"I have an old machine."

"I see. You need a new needle?"

"No, you have to nail the records down." Convulsed.

"Well," I said, "I guess from now on I'll have to play it by ear."

A little before five, as the secretary was locking up the main office, I came out of mine headed for the john. "Just a minute there, Ms. Cornhall," I said. "Five minutes yet. Back in your cage."

"Oh, Mr. Warren. Somebody was in and left a paper or something for you." She unlocked the door and went back to her desk, picked up a manila envelope and handed it to me. On the front in penciled letters it said WILLIAM WARD. I opened it and glanced at the first page of the manuscript, reading only "I will not be present at our scheduled meeting for today," before I stuffed it back in disgust.

Later, in my studio, I sat down to read Willy's script — a letter really, though so manic and hysterical in its way that it was not always clear whom he was addressing. In general, however, I got the message.

For the record, his swan song.

I will not be present at our scheduled meeting for today. There is no book to discuss. There is nothing to *discuss,* as I have at last learned, words and conversation merely being obfuscation with you. I was tempted to allow you to consider the whys and wherefores on your own, but that assumes an ability to project your imagination into another consciousness, and I have come to doubt that capacity in you except when that consciousness is a pure extension of yourself.

At my house when you were so kind as to bless us with your company (how exciting, we said, after all this time — finally — we have him to ourselves) a word boiled up from the soul. Onanism. The word, the soul, the soul you failed to understand, as I tried throughout the evening to give you its meaning, more sober at first, later drunk (but not you, not the Ancient Mariner who can hold so much more than I), that word boiled up from a soul all too familiar with it. Onanism. You remember? Let me reconstruct.

In the room something strange is taking place, and it is not the wine. Something else, an energy that each of us forces into the atmosphere for subtle and private reasons that will not bear exposure. Raw, onanistic energy, and yet all of us grasp at some elusive conjunction that will magnetize the soul's power into movement. But there is too much in the way, too many obstacles that prevent us from touching, too many compromises, evasions, sell-outs, and we settle for titillation, unconsummated wet dreams, all the nonsense conversations that tell us we have not even bumped in the night, the dry hump connection of empty words. Onanism.

What do we say to each other? We tell stories. I play the game. Top this one. You do. Why are we talking like this? Or, I begin to ask myself, is it me he's talking to at all? The glowing hot eyes of my wife, a mixture of her sensuality and thirst to be alive, are like a burning in the room; hot eyes familiar to me, but distant, focused on illusions, dreams, the enchantment of other worlds less mundane than the one I offer.

Or is it? I ignore the distance, the fascination. I am interested in the guest, because he has always been ambiguous, elusive, but now he is in my house, sharing my meal, and I am trying to open my soul to him and explain it, and he is not responding, he does not converse except to make stories. Why is he here if he is *not* here? I say. Why am I here? What is this energy in the air? And where is my wife? Ah yes. I see that she too is interested in the guest; her hot eyes are distant from me and expectant, waiting. But this is to be expected, is it not? The guest is new, a new friend, an anticipated event, a social evening in the midst of colorless textbooks, lectures to prepare, a novel to write, an acquaintance at a time and place where she and I have few who know us, or care, an alternative to the dullness of being home becoming, living on love alone — which is both beautiful and lucky, but not all of life that can be had.

We sit at the dinner table and talk and pick at the salmon. More wine, more wine. I do not need wine to make me talk, to crumble the barriers to my soul. We drink the wine and eat the fish, and I am talking and he takes my sentences and diverts them into stories for my wife. She laughs and takes his side. This "soul" business is faintly embarrassing. What is a soul? Only a word. A shape to fill a lack. He lacks a soul, or perhaps he simply cannot or will not assert it; would rather use another's to score off, make jokes, clowns before the hot eyes of my wife.

Talk. Talk faster, fool, and maybe they will listen. I am having to explain myself too much. Onanism. I can no longer feel my wife's presence as she sits on the floor at his feet, stroking the dog's head, just as he strokes the dog's head, and their hands meet, and I think why? Why? This is my house. Why is this man doing this in my house? I am in a play.

Later, I go into the kitchen and make coffee for myself. I tell myself that what is happening in my mind might not be happening at all, that I am allowing "vibrations" to derange me, disorient my judgment, that I am beginning to sound like a note from underground. All the "energy," all the onanism is inside *me*. *They* are eating fish and drinking wine and scratching the dog behind the ears, making the kind of conversation that normal people make. But I know that is a cop-out, a compromise, a sop I have thrown my pathetic soul to quiet its anguish. What's happening *is* happening. It is more subtle than I have managed to portray in retrospect, but in real life I am good at catching the subtleties, especially when they concern my wife. A man always in the process of becoming knows his woman far better than the man who is already there. He has to. He is insecure. He is in love. His wife is his life.

In the house she moves like a flaming feather, light, floating. No. She is sleek, dark, mystery, smoldering eyes. She puts out the lights, tunes in the music, serves more wine. I am standing in the shadows by the kitchen table. It occurs to me that she has been closer to his body all this night than to mine. They start to dance. They stop. He is dancing with her again. The record stops and they sit on the couch, close, his arm around her shoulder and hers around his waist. I look away, afraid to see them kiss, and then squat on the floor and pet the dog who has come to find me, talking to him in a voice that is loud enough to be heard but that is not heard, and then they are up again and the record is playing. Ritual. The dance.

What does it mean? When this happens in front of you should you say that it means nothing? If so, why? If not, why not? What does it mean? All right. If it means what you think it means, why the shock? Because of what it has been for her and me? Because it has been private and deep and everything else that can only be described as nuance — universal nuance — how *else* to describe it? And you are shocked at him. Why does he stay? What is he doing in your house at four o'clock in the morning with his arm around your wife? Why should this man, who by his appearance, his life-style, what he wants you to believe he is, even need to be here? Why? Does he think you don't *see?*

I am a note from underground.

I hide in the shadows while she comes in the kitchen for wine and fills but one cup. In the light of the doorway she stands inches from him, stares hotly into his face, sips slowly with lowered eyes from the cup, then refixing her stare brings the cup to his mouth for him to drink. Energy is reduced to grade-B vibrations. The obligatory stare-fuck of secret storm melodrama. Hey, we could really dig each other, yeah, but later, right? This is what the evening has been all along, you can dig it, right? and the sips say yeah, I can dig it, it's out in the open with us now, no more beating around the bush with us, yeah.

How could I be wrong? I have senses. Jesus! I have to touch myself to be sure I exist, to be sure I AM — in the room — in the kitchen — I have to piss but I don't dare leave because they will . . . what? They will do what? Touch? Really *touch?* Rub together, kiss, fondle each other's parts. I want to laugh, but I can't bear the imagination of it, I will see it through from my hole in the kitchen.

Nothing will happen. We are onanists. We pull out so that no fleshy part is damaged, soiled, touched. Only the mind; the soul. I am hurt, stupefied, erased, for me she is very much; everything, in fact, all there is of me, she is. I should walk out into the room. I should say "Would you two like to be alone?" That would clear the air. But to do that would be to admit that I see what I see, and I am unwilling still to believe that it is going on right here in front of me. I should play the incensed husband, but that would admit that he is the center of the play, and he is not. I would not give him that credit because he is now so much less than he was. He has fallen. And with his fall has brought down everything in which I believed. If I can accept my destruction as lover, I am wounded in other ways that will not be laid so quietly to rest. Too many illusions smashed.

If I cannot repair those that relate to my wife, I cannot repair those that relate to you. Where I go now, what I do, I do not know, but this is no longer any concern of yours. The book is done. The words have all been spoken. I would remind you of Tennyson's lines in Ulysses. "How dull it is to pause, to make an end/ To rust unburnished, not to shine in use/ As tho' to breathe were life."

There was, I recall, one of those moments of noticeable silence when I finished. The refrigerator clicked off, the tree frogs and crickets out in the garden all quit in unison, the highway a half mile away was suddenly devoid of all traffic noise, even the trucks that grind all day and night through their gears, especially when I lie tossing and turning with four A.M. insomnia. My initial reaction to his tirade was stunned amusement, a kind of nervous dimension more than anything else, as if I had looked down at myself on the lecture platform and discovered that I'd forgotten to put on my pants. Christ, this is just what Weisberg said would happen. I chuckled and shook my head and made noises with my mouth, but I performed these gestures in the third person, looking over my shoulder. The indictment was so feverish, so unlike any response to life's little moments that I conceived anyone capable of making, that I had trouble adjusting myself to a subjective perspective. When I did — that is, when the first person singular was reestablished in my head — amazement became injury, and very shortly I was in an indignant rage. I flung his manuscript on the desk and went to the refrigerator for a beer. To hell with the hour, I thought, this calls for a drink. That whining, self-pitying son-of-a-bitch. That rambling, repetitious bore. Not only is the accuracy of his accusation compromised by his indulgent delight in suffering, his argument is criminally monotonous. You flatter yourself, I told him in absentia, you're not a note from underground, you're a *foot*note, an *Ibid.*, an *Op. Cit.* no less. I finished my beer in about three gulps and opened another, thankful that Nina was not yet in the studio and that my mood did not require explanation.

For about an hour I sat brooding in a stuffed chair, composing rejoinders. They ran the gambit from facetious comments on his spelling, punctuation, and syntax to more or less serious attempts to deflate his hysterical logic. "Dear Sir:" I began the first one. "Forgive me for pointing out that the immaterial entity commonly associated with the faculties of emotional action and metaphysical thought you allude to so frequently in your discourse is spelled s-o-u-l, not s-o-l-e. Unless, of course, I have misunderstood you and you do, in fact, mean, when you refer to the sole (sic) I failed to understand, the undersurface of your foot. Or a flat fish commonly offered the bootless and unhorsed in second-class restaurants. I see now that the latter definition *is*, undoubtedly, that to which you address yourself (in reference to my forgetfulness), but I must demur. It is you, sir, who have forgotten. We ate salmon, though I applaud your alternative. The salmon we ate wasn't very *good* salmon, and is best forgotten. I might also point out that in common practice a comma and a semicolon are not interchangeable ... etc., etc."

And then later, when I had calmed down a little, I went back through parts of his agony in an attempt to understand the psychology of debate, but all I could come up with was contradiction and irrational assumption. I composed yet another letter. "Dear Willy: All this talk about having had a false identity, having sold out, having been a sham, presumes, does it not, that your *true* identity must at last have been discovered, and that appropriate behavioral changes are therefore in order. Hence your letter. That is, how can you know that you were a fake unless you know now that you are not? Yet you repeatedly suggest the possibility that you are dealing with fantasy and illusion, and nowhere in your monologue do I find an alternative to the old life-style (fakery) defined. You seem to have reduced yourself to an abstraction. What are we to make of this?"

Finally I was reduced, by three cans of beer and acid indigestion, to postcards. "Dear Sir: What in the hell gave you the right to set me up as your model in the first place? If you're still in the market for a father I suggest you try someone who likes children." "Sir: Who gave you the impression that I was Jesus Christ?" "Sir: Kindly bugger off!" And that was the last dismal look I planned to take at the entire affair.

Four

ON FRIDAY MORNING I WOKE AT FIVE-THIRTY AND FIXED A
bleary eye on the dark curls next to me trailing off the edge
of the bed toward the pillow fallen to the floor. For some
reason I was still wearing my shoes and socks, but the rest
of me sprawled out from under my chin, naked and pink
as the day I was born, and I watched with some mild interest the frustrations of a bug entangled in the hair on my
chest, trying with various buck-and-wing routines to extricate himself. My hangover was monumental, I eventually
realized. My tongue felt like pigs in a blanket smoked over
a goat turd fire, and my breath . . . unmentionable. Somebody had nailed an eviction notice between my eyes with a
masonry spike, and there wasn't enough left of my brain to
draw flies at a raree-show. Mercifully I lost consciousness.

At noon Nina was bouncing on the bed and telling me
we had to get a move on or we wouldn't get to Tassajara in
time to do anything but go to bed again. "I don't under-

stand why you drink, you big jerk. You're supposed to have fun when you go dancing."

"Go away," I said, dimly remembering cowboys, country music, and sweaty calisthenics at a place called the Sail Inn. Specialists in dance music and Chinese cooking. Nothing fits in California. Nina was chipper because she had sipped a glass of wine all evening, and left half of it. The water was running. I heard the coffee pot rattling on the hot plate. Nina was sitting on the bed with a cup and saucer in her hand.

"You think you can do this yourself, or you want me to spoon it to you? Usually I don't provide this service."

I sat up slowly, aware that every joint in my body was stiff and sore: propped myself against the headboard. The room was mercifully dark, though it was already hot and stuffy. "What time is it?" I took the cup from her and sipped cautiously. As usual she had made it too weak.

"Past noon. We should be on the road already."

"You make lousy coffee, kiddo."

She bounced off the bed onto the dusty floor. "Come on El, try to put it together. It takes three hours to get down there." She stood in the doorway of the closet in a pair of tennis shorts, deciding between a halter top and an athletic department T-shirt with San Quentin written across the chest. Gift from a former lover. I watched the long curve of her back; was reminded of the rich shadow and flair of highly polished instruments, cellos and violas in a darkened room, or through the window front of a closed shop on a late afternoon, with rain in the air and wind gusting the dry leaves of a plane tree along the sidewalk. Old déja vu. Mind wandering. I finished the coffee and painfully swung my legs out of bed. Nina was tucking her breasts into the halter. "I have to run up to school before we go," I told her. "It shouldn't take long." She gave me an impatient look to let me know I was a pokey drag, and I hooked my fingers in the bottom of her halter as I went by and stretched the elastic so that she fell out of it.

"Bastard."

"You ought to get those fixed, Nina. One of these days you're gonna punt one into the ocean."

"Fuck you, sweetie. No one else ever complained."

"I don't want to hear about it," I said. In the bathroom I assembled the wreckage of my face, shaved its bottom half, managed to get one last dab of toothpaste out of the tube, and ran Nina's comb through my hair. The Alka-Seltzer I dropped into a glass wouldn't fizz, but it dissolved to the size of fish food and I drank it. When I came out she was standing there holding out my sunglasses, and thus protected I drove up to the campus to deliver some papers and call Erica in Massachusetts.

Our conversation was perfunctory. Erica was depressed by her surroundings, the house was gloomsville, and it had been raining every day. Her brother was his usual insufferable self, resentful of the time wasted on his mother and accustomed to being waited on hand and foot. She was coming home in a week because if she didn't leave first *he* would, and then she'd be stuck for the summer. I suggested she take her time. I was getting along fine, I told her. "I'll bet you are," she said.

"What's that supposed to mean?"

"Why aren't you ever home? I've called a dozen times."

"Oh that. Well, you remember the termites. I thought it would be a good time to have the house sprayed while you're away, so I moved over to Weisberg's for a while to let the two-four-D or chlordane or whatever settle down."

As a liar I had not improved much since childhood. I called the Pied Piper Exterminators right after I hung up and told them I wanted the whole spread, complete with circus tent. We did have termites, as a matter of fact, so I wasn't just being flamboyant. It would not be too difficult for Erica to find out from the neighbors the exact date of this event, and then I'd have to start inventing new lies to cover the old ones, but sometimes you get lucky. I didn't spend a lot of time worrying about it.

By three o'clock we were finally underway and heading south on the coast highway, through the artichoke and strawberry country along the fringe of the Salinas Valley and into the Fort Ord dunes where the car blew a tire and Nina blew a joint and I tore the seat of my pants on a rusty bumper guard as I tried to wrench an obstinate jack handle from its wedge beneath the spare. I was a little surprised at viceless Nina getting stoned, not because I had any moral objections but because it didn't seem like part of her image. "It isn't," she assured me. "Twice a year on rare and beautiful occasions."

We bought needle and thread in a grocery store in Seaside, and I drove in my shorts while she sewed and hummed and marveled at the measure of her high. "I'm the neurosurgeon," Nina said, sucking air through her molars as she pricked her finger. "Knit one, pearl two. I'm putting all these sutures in your sad old ass. Onetwothreefourfive sixty."

"Neuro, baby, refers to the nervous system. It's from the Greek *neuron,* meaning nerve or sinew; in Old English, *sinu* or *seonu.*"

"Oh Lord! Now I know why you wear your pants around your chest."

"Don't bother to embroider them, Nina. Just sew up the hole."

At the first exit to Carmel she developed a sudden craving for peach ice-cream and instructed me to turn off. I reminded her that *she* had been the one in such a hurry to get on the road, but that was another time, and now nothing would suffice but peach ice-cream on a sugar cone. Into Carmel we went. We were sitting at a little marble table made out of plastic, with bent wire legs and matching chairs that looked like a Steinberg cartoon, when Nina suddenly remembered an exhibit of watercolors done by a friend of hers from Morro Bay, currently featured at a gallery called Village Artistry on Dolores, and there was no way around it, we absolutely had to go see them. "He's a super painter," she said, offering me a bite of her jamoca almond fudge (peach having been lost in the mind shuffle as she studied the offerings posted in *ye olde* lettering above the counter). "He does these fabulous things in tempura."

"He cooks too, does he?"

She burped with complete gentility into a paper napkin and studied my face. "What?"

"Tempera," I said. "Tempura is something you eat."

"Oh shit, you're always bringing me down."

"I thought you might like to know the difference."

"Well, they both have eggs in them, don't they?"

The gallery, happily enough, was closed, and we drove out of town and up into the Carmel Valley for a half an hour, then turned south again on the unpaved road to Tassajara. Lush meadows spotted with oak gave way to canyon brush, manzanita, madrone, bay, and as the road climbed to the higher ridges of the Los Padres Forest, pine and fir. Somewhere along the top, before the trail began to wind steeply down into the canyon, we parked the car and walked out along a grassy saddle to a promontory with an unbroken view to the east and west. On our right the Santa Lucias fell sharply away in a series of descending ridges to the Pacific; on our left the Gabilans across the Salinas Valley, and in the far distance the great western wall of the San Joaquin Valley, the Diablo Range. Steinbeck country, pastures of heaven, Jody and his red pony and the mysterious mountains where Gitano went to die. Nina listened patiently enough to my speech, but she was more moved by the "cosmic expansiveness of our space" than she was by a lesson in literary topography. In fact, she was sublimely indifferent. A creature of impulse, she wanted to make love in a patch of lupine that lay below us in a depression of the slope.

A contour map of the road descending to Tassajara would look like the scribblings of a four-year-old drunk practicing Z's. We started down, Nina singing a song called "There Ain't No Flies on Me," but before we'd gone two miles she was hanging her head out the window, dope consonance transposed into the key of N. I was unable to resist a short lesson in usage when she informed me in a shaky voice that she was "nauseous," but eventually I had to let her drive — transposing my own melody to the key of T. Terror.

At about the same time my stomach was preparing to throw in the sponge and go bottoms up, the road bottomed out and in less than a mile we were at a parking area, still a fair distance away from the Zen Center. Nina shouldered our day pack and we walked in past a garden of raised beds where three or four monks were planting seedlings and a little girl was trying to feed some weeds to a duck. Near the bottom of the mountain behind the garden a number of workers were busy terracing the lower hillside, and off to our left near the creek were several rows of small pitch-roofed cabins with kerosene lanterns hanging from pegs on the door stoop. In front of us, on one side of a stone patio, lay the Zendo, on the other, the visitors' dining room with a screened porch overlooking the creek. A few students in saffron colored robes were standing on the patio. Mostly in evidence were the summer guests permitted into the mountain center from May to September.

Nina and I checked in and just had time to stow our things in our cabin and remark on its spartan simplicity —

bed, chair, bowl of flowers, bare wood floors, old lamp, how charming — and to walk on wobbly pins over to the dining room for dinner — communal, vegetarian, bring your own wine, very delicious. We were seated at a table with a lawyer and his wife from San Luis Obispo and a writer from the *National Observer* whose girl friend attempted to instruct me in the study of *koan*. To her great frustration. "You can't analyze enigmatic sayings," she kept insisting. "A *koan* assigned you by the *Roshi* is a topic for meditation, not analysis." I told her riddles without answers aggravated my ulcer.

There were no monks in evidence until after the meal when the huge gong hanging from a scaffolding of logs at the Center's entrance sounded and they filed into the Zendo to sit in zazen and chant a few digestive *sutras*. We lay on the lawn watching the stars, listening to the infrequent tinkle of prayer bells, the evening warm and soft in the bottom land along the creek, the rock walls V-ing away from us still radiating afternoon heat. Nina sighed and nestled her head into the hollow of my shoulder, her leg thrown across my hips and pinning me now and then with gentle pressure. "This is the most wonderful place," she said, "like fairyland; like you just stepped out of time for a while and discovered that everything in the real world isn't real at all, just some novel that you've been reading and gotten all caught up in until you stop and close the book and remember it's all just fiction. Don't you feel it?"

"There is a parable in the *Lotus Sutra*," I said, "about a burning house. It goes 'Come out of the triple world, which is like a house on fire, and sit in the courtyard.' "

"Farout," said Nina. "How do you know things like that?"

"That beautiful wench with the incredible body I sat next to at dinner told me."

Nina plucked a handful of grass and threw it at me.

"Oh, you . . . " She pouted for a minute. "I didn't think her body was all that great."

"Well it wouldn't stack up to yours."

"But really, El, don't you think this place is magical?"

"Uh-huh." I did, if not in those precise terms. I could happily have expired on the spot, so utterly at peace did I feel, and if she hadn't mentioned the "real" world I don't think I would have remembered it the whole weekend. My head was a euphoric vacuum.

"I love you," she said, squeezing me. "I've never been so happy in my whole life."

Later, before sleep, we crossed the stream and joined a score of secularists pretending not to notice each other's genitalia in the hot springs pool.

And while we're on that subject . . . a half mile downstream from the Center the creek takes a sudden plunge through steep narrows of limestone and granite, drops in long chutes into a succession of clear pools and disappears around the bend of a near vertical wall. Along these chutes there are natural benches in the rock, and as the stream bed lies in an east-west direction, full sun floods this area of the canyon from morning till late afternoon. One is reminded, as one emerges from the cool, dense vegetation of the upper region and stands a moment at the head of the path leading down into the narrows, of a colony of sea lions basking on the ledges of Año Nuevo island — brown bodies draped from impossible crannies and outcroppings, lolling mindless in the bright heat.

If old seals are bereft of vanity, old humans become apprehensive in the midst of such vigorous nudity, most of it youthful, firm, resilient, and tanned, a great barbecue of pubic hair, oily muscle and flesh. Who cares to display a blown gut, or sagging tits, or the marbled meat of feed-lot thighs in the midst of all this Grecian splendor? Who can remember, at a time like this, that Tassajara is a Zen monastery, and that the center of one's being, the center of Hara, is the belly? I noticed, during the two days that Nina and I spent in the rookery, that men are only slightly less sensitive than women — all undergo the agony of decision. If they take their clothes off they feel like Davy the fat boy; if they leave them on they feel like voyeurs. Only the young are unconcerned. The old stroll back up the path and flee into the woods.

Sunday we went to the narrows around mid-morning and took our lunch. We stretched out in the sun, and when it got really hot Nina lay in the chutes and let the water pour over her. I read Turnbull's biography of Fitzgerald. Later I heard her voice among a chorus of little heroes daring each other to dive ever higher from a sloping ledge above the pools. She came back breathless and brown and with an abrasion on her left buttock where she had scraped herself on the granite. "That is so much *fun*," she panted. "It's so *scary*." She buried her face in a towel and muffled something at me. "Mmmmatwegottoeat?"

I opened the bag. Cheese, sprouts, tomatoes, bread from steel cut oats, granola cookies, an apple — all the stuff I used to get so tired of when Erica was on her vegetarian kick. What are we, gerbils? Hamsters? But the narrows imparted a different interpretation. Flavor is fifty percent ambience.

Nina perched on a rock. Kissing a tomato. "What were you like when you were a kid?" she said.

"What do you want to know for?"

Shrug. "I just wondered. I bet you were neat."

"Actually," I said, "I was sullen, uncommunicative, contemptuous of my peers, and envious of the freedoms I imagined the perquisites of the seventeen- and eighteen-year-olds I emulated and admired."

"What's a perquisite?"

"Rights and privileges."

"Go on. Skip the fancy language."

"Go on where? That's how I was."

"I mean fill in the blanks. I love you. I want to know all about you."

"I thought the past and future were out of your sphere of interest."

"That was before. I didn't know I was going to get this way about you."

I put a half eaten apple back in the bag and arranged myself against the ledge. I put a towel over my waist to keep from sunburning the machinery. "Okay. Well, let's see . . . I started my rebellion at age thirteen by smoking a pack of Lucky Strikes a day — Lucky Strikes because L. C. Smith, captain of the high school football team, smoked Luckies — and I downed my first bottle of whiskey a year later, for which I got expelled and poisoned, and I was very much in the habit of delivering opinions I picked up secondhand from one venerable or another on a wide variety of topics about which I had no information or basis for judgment. I had a dirty mouth, swearing with vigor if not much authority, resisted instruction, resented advice, and kept a razor in my gym locker to shave off the dirt I surreptitiously applied to my sallow cheeks during activities hour."

"Why?"

"Why what?"

"Why did you put dirt on your cheeks?"

"So I'd look older, more manly."

"Oh."

Obviously she didn't understand that one at all. She hadn't the slightest idea why someone would try to look more "manly." It wasn't a part of her world. And it was right about then that I suddenly realized that *most* of the social values and attitudes I had grown up with were about as comprehensible to her as the habits of a bunch of Auca Indians in the jungles of the upper Amazon basin. For almost the first time in my life I wanted to talk about myself, as if a definition of my cultural inheritance would help me justify in my own mind the tremendous differences I often felt existed in our assumptions about human behavior — differences that I could never quite pin down because Nina's self-assurance about how a person should live did not open itself for argument or debate.

An example. We began talking about sexual experience and promiscuity. It came to her as a piece of historical curiosity that girls in the '50s didn't as a general rule sleep with their boy friends because they didn't have the pill in those days and pregnancy was a real risk. "At the very least it was a case of a limited science determining public mores," I said. Nina looked blank. "Until *your* generation that's the way the world always was. What do you think all this business about release from inhibitions and ignorance is all about? The sexual revolution? Haven't you ever read any novels?" My observations were so commonplace I couldn't believe they hadn't occurred to her before. They hadn't. Her only comment was "Ugh! I'm glad I wasn't born when *you* were."

I pinched her calf. "So am I. And don't pig all those cookies, either."

When the sun dropped behind the rim people began drifting back toward the Center for afternoon meditation (public invited into the Zendo). We lingered in the narrows, watching the shadows creep down the rock walls until the last sparkle of sunlight was off the lower pools, then walked back up through the woods along the creek, wading in the shallows where tiny minnows darted from gravel beds into the protecting camouflage of sunken foliage, and skaters slid around the stalks of reeds and willows. The canyon forked to the southwest, and there was a patch of sun in an eddy of the stream and an old log half submerged in the brown water. Nina slipped out of her shift and lay on her back on its mossy hide, one leg bent, arms trailing into the pool, her breasts tilting slightly to the side, nipples pink and hard. She shut her eyes and I caught a tiny green frog which I dropped on her belly just above the tiny triangle of hair in which I intended to bury my face. Oh lover's mouth. The frog was like a tiny jade ornament appliqued against the copper gloss of her skin, sea green, motionless. She tasted of salt, marsh grass, sargasso.

Night came down soft and heavy with damp. The moon was pale, diffuse, washed in a cocooning of fog. We lay in the hot springs after supper, soaking, disengaged from ourselves, and later she took me again, more conventionally, like the good missionary (how else in such a holy place), and yet again in the early hours of the morning when the prayer gong calling the monks to sit penetrated the stillness of our cabin and woke us from an uneasy sleep, our bodies damp where they touched because the room was cold and the air beneath the blankets hot and trapped. She enclosed me with her arms and legs, whimpering, not yet fully conscious, sucking in her breath through her teeth when she felt me between her, and when I went in her she gasped, came almost immediately, crying out half in joy, half in laughter at her own delirious feelings, and then we lay for a long time on top of the covers in the icy room, drowsy once more, and I could hear the creek bubbling over the stones below the springs. Thank you, she said. I nuzzled her neck. Thank you for what? For being you. I dozed. You're welcome. Did I make too much noise? No. Sometimes I'm too loud when I feel so . . . beatific. You weren't too loud, you were wonderful . . . because you felt so good.

Later in the morning, it was still damp. Fog filled the canyon until almost noon. Before leaving we walked to a waterfall above the Center and picked wildflowers that grew in abundance in the marshy ground around its base. Nina said it was against her ecological principles but she was going to do it anyway. "On picnics I was always telling my parents to leave the flowers where they belonged, and here I am picking them myself. They thought I was weird. Not much in common, me and my parents." She handed me a tiny, purple iris. "How about you? Did you get along with yours when you were young?"

"I didn't exactly meet their expectations," I said. "As I told you yesterday, I was always trying to be somebody else . . . usually somebody neither very bright nor very decent."

"Did they like you?"

"What a funny question. I suppose so. Though I elicited a kind of exasperated contempt for my slavish dedication to plagiarized personalities. I remember my old man, in particular, was constantly being enraged by my contralto put-downs of all kinds of things I really didn't know anything about. He was sort of a thoughtful, ponderous man in his way, who operated from a number of academic premises, not the least of which was that small fry should be seen but not heard . . . especially if they were punks and churls and had only a C minus average to support their arrogances."

"Your mother was the same way?"

"My mother was less concerned about my intellectual development than my social. She was afraid I would stunt my growth, or drive myself insane with lustful thoughts, or eat peas with my knife at somebody's dinner party. So between them they found most of the things I did pretty frightening, and they put a lot of restrictions on my activities." I leaned back against a rock, twirling the stem of the iris between my fingers and staring into its indigo throat. "It's funny, you know. I've never really talked to anybody about my adolescence. I just repress it. Maybe that's why I never grew up."

"I think you did."

"No, listen . . . because my response to all this overseeing I got as a kid was to withdraw more and more into myself. I became convinced at an early age that communication is synonymous with confrontation, and I understood clearly that language was invented by people to trap other people, especially *little* people like kids and students and what have you, in lies, insolence, errors of fact and judgment, insubordination, and I got to where I could pare away conversation to monosyllabic vocables, grunts, and finally nonverbal directives with chin, eyeball, and finger. Like I'd pooch out my lips at the table to indicate I wanted the salt. I'd nod or shake my head to answer all questions. Open palms held shoulder high for get-off-my-back. I think all I did eventually was sit in my room and eat Wheat Thins. I read a lot; that was my downfall. Because now whenever I don't like myself, or what's going on around me, I can jump into a book and be somebody else. Anyway, that's what my wife tells me."

Nina averted her eyes and looked off into space, and I realized I'd let my mouth outrun my brain. My crafty little brain. I'd let the big boogeyman out of his cage. (A thousand pardons; boogeyperson.) My "wife" was something Nina was doing her best not to think about, something that did not have to be or *could* not be dealt with yet, and it was witless of me to slip it in, however accidentally. "Let's climb to the top," she said, after a while. "I want to teach you something."

We struggled up a fissure in the rock, using the gnarled roots of manzanita to help us; then traversed a narrow ledge fifty feet above the ground and scrambled over the last pitch, slippery with moss and spray, to the lip of the falls. A dozen feet from the rim Nina positioned herself in a semilotus on the grass and indicated that I was to do the same. "Okay," she said. "Now the great master, Okada Torajiro, very famous teacher of the *seiza*, which in case you don't know is the practice of sitting, said that enthusiasm and ecstasy make the blood rush to the head. We have to come down now, since we're going back to the real world. When you practice *seiza* you should keep your head quiet and cool. It should be empty to receive peace. Pay attention, Nicodemus."

She showed me how. For half an hour we sat, and for a time my mind flitted from one thing to another. I began to itch here and there, and to think about the fact that I was thinking about the fact that I was thinking, and then I passed into a period of great detachment. The moment became primary, essential, whether it was the buzzing of a fly, or the feel of the cool, mossy stones under my legs, or the smell of bay leaf in the air. Butter would not have melted on *my* head, I was so cool. Peace. She was right. I was so tranquilized that I didn't bother to point out that the only reason I could reach such a state of consciousness, could *articulate* my sensations, was that I knew they were terminal.

And so were hers. Driving back up the coast she was silent and moody, barely acknowledging the poor jokes I kept trying to interject to keep her from bringing us down. "You know what the hare-lipped dog said?" "No." "Mark." "Hmm." She was locked in the bubble of her own mind, inattentive to everything beyond. I asked her what was the matter. She shook her head and turned down the corners of her mouth. "Nothing." "Not much. What is it?" Nothing was wrong, she insisted. But I knew she was wondering about Erica, wanting to ask and not wanting the answer she was afraid she might get. Weisberg had warned me. In many ways she was a very straight-up young lady whose only problem was that her common sense occasionally became unhinged by romantic fantasies. And what was Mr. Big Deal going to do about it now? I didn't know. Anything but spoil his *own* romantic fantasies.

We were as silent back in my studio as we had been in the car. Nina made spaghetti, and I stole some lettuce from Harry's garden for a salad. The gophers couldn't get that. He'd put chicken wire under the bed. We ate, glancing at each other from time to time, questions flying around in our heads like frigate birds over the booby hatch (blue-footed booby), but nothing said. Finally I asked her if she wanted to go home. She nodded, changed her mind, foundered on middle ground. "I don't know what I want."

"Then don't spoil a great time by sulking." I pleaded.

"I think I need to be by myself for a while, that's all."

"I don't understand what's bugging you."

"Yes you do."

"My wife."

"Yeah." She let her breath out slowly.

"Well let me tell you something about . . ."

"Please," she said, putting her hand on mine and her index finger to my lips. "Don't say anything. I don't want you to have to start playing games with me. I knew what I was getting into, and I mean I'm not blaming you for how I'm feeling right now, so you don't have to say anything to cheer me up. It's just that I kidded myself at first that you weren't living at home anymore, didn't have a wife and son, and so maybe I had a chance for a life with you myself . . . but I knew that she was back east before we went to Tassajara because the note about reservations and all from your secretary is lying on the desk there, and I could tell from the way you never said anything about her that it was something you didn't want to talk about because you couldn't. There wasn't anything to say. I just went on letting myself ignore all the signs because I wanted you, even for a little while. But this morning at the waterfall I came back to earth, and I need to be alone for a while."

"You think I'm on a busman's holiday, is that it?"

"I don't think you know."

"Thank you for the vote of confidence."

"Oh Eliot, don't be sulky. Be honest with yourself," (her tone almost a question) "and me? Please?"

I wanted more than anything to say something that would make it all go away, the unhappiness, the confusions, the listlessness of the moment. I wanted to tell her I loved her, that everything would work out in time; I would get a divorce, marry her, live happily ever after, become the kind of man she thought I was. I wanted to see her smiling, laughing again, not on the verge of tears. Tears unglue me completely, coward that I am. But I am, was not, not completely without perception. You could not lie to Nina even if you wanted to; couldn't feed her hopes, possibilities, might-be's. Underneath the veneer of her dreams there was a hard headed stubbornness that was unmoved by promises of tomorrow. She believed in actions, not words. My suffering silence confirmed something for her; probably that I wasn't as wild and free a spirit as I pretended to be, or that somewhere down in my soul my father's admonition "you make your bed and you lie in it" had stuck and would not come loose.

"I don't want you to see me cry," she said. "I want to go now."

I drove her up on campus to her dorm, still struggling to think of some way out of this pit we had fallen into so suddenly. I supposed it was inevitable. You can't fly so high, I told myself, without digging a hell of a crater when your wings melt. And, of course, all the moves to crawl back out were up to me. Weisberg was right. I didn't know what I was doing, or what I was *going* to do.

In the circle in front of the college she slipped out of the car without a word. I watched her descend the steps leading through the portico until the fog swallowed her and left me staring at an opalescent halo where a single lamp glowed on its metal post in the entrance. Pale reflection of her soul. My soul, reflected by the dash lights on the windshield of my car, was darkly green and obscure.

Five

ITEMS FROM THE MORNING PAPER. WEISBERG IN TERRYCLOTH robe boogieing around my room at six-fifteen, *Chronicle* in hand, cup of tea from which he has not removed the bag in the other. Hair awry, frazzled, bald patch shining in the thicket like a shaggy dog's balls. Why are we subjected to this atrocity on the morning of our discontent?

"Listen to this, listen to this," he says.

" 'MAN SHOOTS BROTHER STRANGLING FATHER.' " Harry is beside himself. " 'Redwood City — Melvin Jenner, 50, was fatally shot by his brother, George, this morning as Melvin was strangling their seventy-five-year-old father during a family birthday party' . . . police said. Yiiieee. Listen to this, listen. 'According to Police Lt. John Heavey the three men had been bowling and drinking as part of the birthday celebration. George told police he saw Melvin strike his father and then begin choking him after an argument about a loan. George went into a bedroom, found a 38-caliber revolver and returned with the weapon' . . . Heavey said."

"Drinking and bowling: it happens every time."

"Listen. 'It was a real tragedy, Heavey said. If the gun hadn't been handy, he might have hit the guy with a chair or something.' "

"I've always wondered about stricter gun laws. Take away guns, we can kill each other with chairs."

"National Chair Wielders Association. Lobby in Washington."

"Could I ask what you're doing prancing around my room at six-fifteen in your robe? At least have the taste to tie it up or something; and Harold . . . a gentleman removes his condom after service. Or is that your foreskin?"

"Actually I came up to see if you've been abusing the premises. Since your car's gone I didn't think you were here."

"My car?"

"Listen to *this* one. Christ! 'At Market and First Streets two black welfare workers in a city car had to flee when a dozen protesters snatched the keys and tried to roll the car over. Not far from there, a Municipal Railway bus had a flat tire when it ran over some nails tossed on Market Street by demonstrators. Close by, construction worker Joe Deldumpo, wearing a hard hat and tending his cement-mixing machine said he thinks war is inevitable. *It's man's nature. The first man on earth probably got up and punched himself in the mouth . . .* Deldumpo said.' "

"What do you mean my car's gone?"

"I mean gone. As in not there." Still chuckling. *"GOT UP AND PUNCHED HIMSELF IN THE MOUTH.* Deldumpo. Wonderful."

"Quit snotting yourself and go get dressed. Somebody ripped off my wheels."

I remembered parking in the street when I returned from taking Nina to her dorm because Weisberg had been hosting a poker game and the driveway was full. I had locked the car and taken the keys with me. I still had them in my pocket when Harry finally quit reading me funnies from the morning paper and let me into the house to call the police. The City had a little dispute with the County Sheriff's Office concerning jurisdiction — a legal question complicated by the fact that the automobile had been swiped at a location other than its registered place of residence. I was eventually instructed to appear at the station in person to fill out a theft report.

The whole business took about three and a half hours (it should have taken twenty minutes), and all the while I had a discomforting vision of my poor old Ford nosing its battered fenders into the arid wastes of Baja California, while Lt. Heavey or Heavy misspelled my name, garbled my description of "the vehicle in question," burned a hole in his uniform with a cigarette, and tore up two carbons in his machine. Weisberg finally gave me a ride to school in time for my one o'clock class, where, to my additional joy I found a telegram in my box saying Erica would be home in ten days. I called Nina in the hope that she would have adjusted by now to the grand design and have dinner with me, but was told by the kid who lived across the hall that she'd left around noon with some guy for a camping trip on Point Reyes. Another one of those days.

There seemed no end to bad news. When I walked to my house that evening to get Erica's car I found the whole place encased in canvas, like one of Christo's wrappings, and I couldn't even get in the kitchen to find the keys, much less into the garage where the Citroën was parked.

Harry tried to leaven my mood with an invitation to a skin flick in San Jose ("Goldstein gives it a four on the peter-meter"), but I had had it with the world and went to bed early with a book. At least there are a few things you can rely on.

To my amazement a Sheriff's Deputy showed up at Harry's door the following morning to report that my car had been found in a vacant lot in Corralitos, not twenty miles from where it had been taken. Weisberg thundered up the garage stairs to let me know, and waited impatiently while I found my clothes and got dressed. "The Constable thinks it was a couple of teenaged joyriders," he announced, driving me over to pick it up. "Good thing you're such a cheap shit you never put more than a bucks worth of gas in it. No telling how far they would have gotten."

The police had taken the car to the volunteer fire department, and when we got there I filled out a form and went out to check the damages. No new dents. The radio was still in it. The engine started on the first try. Then Harry found, lodged down behind the front seat cushion, a paperback copy of *The Upanishads*. "This yours?" he asked, holding it up.

I shook my head. "Nope. But you see Harold, all is for the best in this best of all worlds. At least I get a book out of the deal."

He flipped through the pages, then leaned against the car door, pulling at his lip. "No name in it," he said. "You think it belongs to anybody you know?"

"It's probably Nina's," I told him. "It must have slipped behind there on our way back from Tassajara."

"Did you see her at Tassajara with it?"

"No."

"Then it could belong to whoever stole your car."

I conjured amazement. "Yeah, wow Harry, you're

a real Inspector Maigret. Only since there's no name in it I'd say you're about through, so why don't we truck on out of here."

"My dear Watson, let me put it to you this way . . ."

"You want me to bend over?"

". . . how many teenage joyriders of your acquaint-anceship are likely to be reading *The Upanishads?*"

I smiled at him indulgently. "We don't know, do we, that the person or persons who filched my car were teen-aged joyriders. That is an assumption on the part of certain officials who don't wish to pursue the matter further."

"Precisely."

"What are you getting at, Harold?"

"Whom do you know that *is* interested in Hinduism?"

"About half the freaks in Santa Cruz."

"Willy Ward?"

I stared at him, considering. "That's ridiculous."

"Odd coincidence though, isn't it."

"Much too odd."

But the effect of Harry's sleuthing, though I wanted to reject it out of hand, was to force me, reluctantly, to bite the bullet. If for no other reason than to dispel the last nagging doubt, I decided finally to confront the beast in his lair.

That afternoon I called Willy's house and got a recorded message about *the number you have dialed is no longer in service*. I drove slowly across town, half hoping that I would find the place empty and a notice on the door that the tenants had moved to Swaziland, but I was in no such luck. Frankie was in the backyard shaking radish seeds along a row in a freshly dug garden plot and chanting some unintelligible incantation over her business as she patted down the dirt. She was attended by two freaks who were sprawled in a patch of pennywort and crabgrass that had once been a lawn, a six-pack of Burgie half-quarts between them, and a joint passing back and forth in an alligator clip. I regarded this pastoral scene from the driveway for a few moments, until one of these subordinates happened to look over the low grapestake fence that divided us and gloomily announced to no one in particular the presence of company.

"Oh, hi," Frankie said. "Long time no see, and like all that."

I offered something about a busy schedule and how time flies when one is working.

"This is very L.A." one freak said to the other. He looked at me and asked if I'd like to buy a crate of postholes. Something about his insolent manner, the gratuitous insult provoked by nothing more than our difference in age and attire, infuriated me, and I stepped over the fence and grabbed him by his ponytail, crab-walked him to his feet and propelled him out into the driveway with his head jerked back on the horizontal. "Get lost, Bonzo, I want to talk with the lady." His buddy scrambled up behind us.

"What's coming DOWN here, man? What IS this shit?"

I looked at him coldly; considered the pleasure of peeling his scalp from sideburn to sideburn. He backed away, realizing that even the two of them were no match. "Take a walk." I told him, and watched them down the drive until they turned onto the street.

Frankie was standing in her radish patch looking apprehensive, ready to flee. "What's happening? Wow! How come you're so hostile?"

"Is Willy here?"

"Uh-uh."

"Where then?"

"I don't know exactly. After that night you were over we went through about three days of nonstop soul searching and I finally told him that I thought what we had going wasn't all that worth preserving. So after he got through beating me up, he left."

I sat down on the porch steps and studied my shoes; considered pointing out that if she had taken my advice a long time ago and tried to convince him he needed help none of this might have happened. But then that was rather pointlessly self-righteous and didn't have much to do with the real issue anyway. "I'm sorry," I said. "Obviously I'm responsible for this whole mess."

"Are you kidding?" she said. She joined me on the porch and tucked the bottom yard of her long skirt under her knees. "Listen, Willy isn't your ordinary, run-of-the-mill moralist. He's a nut, a fanatic. He sees things only in terms of absolutes. The 'mess' began the day I married him . . . which I shouldn't have done, since I only knew him three weeks. He has a very arcane attitude toward marriage."

"To anyone under twenty-five, maybe. It seems pretty traditional to me."

Frankie didn't answer. The sun was beating down into the dried out backyard and the glare was giving me a headache. When she sugested a beer I gratefully accepted. We went into the house where a cool breeze was blowing in through the open front door. The sink was piled with unwashed dishes, and the dog had left a down payment on the linoleum by the stove, and Frankie cursed him like a top sergeant as she picked it up in a piece of newspaper and deposited it in the garbage. The whole place was in need of a thorough scrubbing, and I noticed a sleeping bag on the couch in the living room that looked as if it had been used as a chimney swab. Frankie saw me looking at it. "Michael's moved out of the garage," she said. She took a can of beer from the refrigerator, opened it, and handed it to me.

"You're not having one?"

She shook her head, reaching behind the sugar cannister on the counter and picking up a small brown box with carving on its lid. "I'm going to roll a number, unless you object."

I shook my head and leaned against the wall, sipping my beer.

"One of the delights of being single again," she said, smiling, licking the gum on a paper. "Willy's forays into mysticism didn't induce a tolerance for dopers." She lit her joint at the stove and inhaled deeply. "You know what his book was about?" she said, in a high, strained voice. "It was about Augustine Baker. You know who he was?"

I shook my head.

"Well Augustine Baker was a sixteenth-century mystic who converted to Catholicism and joined the Benedictines. He was the director of nuns in France and apparently a real oddball and a kind of recluse and I don't remember all the details, but the point is, according to Willy, who spent all his time over in England doing this research, Baker was a dude whose ideas and habits were two centuries *behind* his times. Which is why Willy found him so fascinating. I just thought I'd give you the general drift since there's no novel left to read. You sure you don't want a hit on this?"

"No," I said. "I'm afraid my dope is still gin."

Frankie folded one arm beneath her breasts and tucked her hand under her armpit. She held the joint up in front of her face like a torch, studied it, then looked around the kitchen. "You want to sit down or something? The living room is kind of a mess since Mike came in, but we could move his stuff."

"I'm fine," I told her. "Only I'm curious about something."

"Yeah?"

"Why did you marry Willy in the first place? In this day and age it seems sort of unnecessary as a first step."

She blew a faint breath of uningested smoke up at the ceiling. "It was the only way he'd have it. I was working for this repossession outfit in New York and I'd just broken up with this guy and I'd had an abortion which I owed four hundred bucks on still, and I met Willy. We started going around, and he fell in love with me. I liked him pretty well. God. I wanted out of New York so bad I couldn't stand it, and he seemed to me the answer to all my problems." She reflected a moment on the nail of her little finger. "I mean that sounds pretty cold and calculating now, but that's how I see it. I guess I saw it a little more romantically then."

"Couldn't you have just gone with him, lived with him?"

"I told you. Willy's a regular Augustine Baker. A man behind his times. And anyway, you know what he used to tell me? She had a funny little half smile on her face. "He used to tell me about you and your wife, whatshername."

"Erica."

"Erica. The model marriage." She grinned. "I don't think he had the right angle, did he?"

"I don't know," I said. "I don't suppose any relationship is as uncomplicated or idyllic as it sometimes appears."

"I mean if you were all that happy, right? we wouldn't have had that little thing with each other the other night."

I was tempted to suggest that there were a number of ways that little 'thing' might have been avoided the other night, but I let it go. "Listen Frankie," I said, "you're sure you haven't heard or seen Willy for the last three weeks?"

"Nope."

"Do you think you will?"

"I don't think so. We pretty much severed the cord. Why?"

"I need to talk to him. He sent me a long diatribe more or less saying that by coming over here to dinner that night and finding you more than ordinarily attractive I destroyed your relationship and wrecked his life. I'd kind of like to discuss that with him."

She whipped her head back and forth as if the whole idea were so preposterous she couldn't believe it. "I told him fifty times we didn't do anything. Not that I wouldn't have liked to."

"To Willy," I pointed out, "acts of omission are often more serious than acts of commission."

She studied my face for a long time, her expression changing from fuzzy to sleepy indifference, and I had a little flash on the harmonics that had gotten us into this in the first place. "We could be hung for sheep as well as goats," she giggled.

I almost smiled as I tossed my empty can in the trash. "If Willy does show up, do me a favor and get in touch."

"Well," she said vaguely, "you can't blame a girl for trying."

I was rather touched to learn later that evening, as I sat in Harry's study drinking a scotch and water and listening to Poulenc's opera *Dialogue of the Carmelites,* that he had spent his day researching solutions to the problem of Willy Ward, and that he had done so because he was genuinely concerned about my health and well-being. He had talked to his lawyer, the Sheriff's Department, the mental health people at the County Health Department, and his buddy, the District Attorney. I got the distinct impression that he had something to propose but was hanging back because he knew I wasn't going to like it. Also he was tired. To relax he was listening over and over to the last act of Poulenc's grisly little drama where the nuns get beheaded and what starts out as a chorus ends up as a solo. He was lying in his Barcalounger with his eyes closed saying *THRWOK* every time the guillotine announced the passion of another sister of the sacred heart.

I, for my part, was confusing myself, whenever I was sure he wasn't looking, with periodic slugs of Johnny Walker straight from the bottle on the sideboard behind me. I nursed the weak drink in my hand when he *was* looking to assure him that I was attentive to my options and soberly contemplating all the possibilities for redemption and salvation which he tossed out between decapitations. In truth, given Erica's pending return, Nina's departure to Point Reyes, and Willy's denunciations of my manners and morals, I didn't know what I should start thinking about first, and anyway, I was losing interest in circuitous problems for which there seemed to be no solutions. After a while I was losing interest in consciousness altogether. Harry went *THRRRWOK*, and I took a hit of Red Label. It was like ten little Indians. I dozed off when it got down to a quartet and missed a couple of *thrrwoks* because then there were only two, and it wasn't George and Tammy singing *God's Gonna Getcha For That, THRWOK,* one more lost in the pile of Z's stacking up around my chair, not Loretta, either, nor Dolly, nor Wanda, just one little bitty nun on her way up the scaffold to meet the Lord, morning Lord, Clitora Cummings here, physical therapist for menopausal men, friend of the Weisberg, and very happy in my work too, my work gives me time for creative ventures such as writing the poetry, article, and book, which I hope are published. Once I jumped out of a coffin, but I never jumped out of a cake. *THRRWOK.*

I awoke to the sound of the needle washing in the groove. Harry was staring at me through the gunsight he had made with the toes of his shoes, and we regarded each other for a few moments waiting to see who was going to turn the machine off. "You're closer," I said.

"As the crow flies, yes. But I have farther to go to get up, and I'd have to go around the desk on the left because the wastebasket is on the right, so actually you're closer."

"I think you're lying about the wastebasket," I said. "I don't see it. Anyway, you could step over it."

"I couldn't really."

"Why is that?"

"I don't have my shoes on."

"That's absurd."

"I'll tell you what. The plug is right there by your hand. If you pull it out, in a minute I'll get up and make us a ham sandwich."

"I'll think about it."

"I have dill pickles. And Monterey Jack."

"I'm weakening."

"Go for it, man. I got Heinekens."

"Sonofabitch," I said, yanking on the cord. "That was unfair."

Ham and cheese at three A.M. Feed a drunk, starve a hangover. Or something. We were into our second sandwich and the last two bottles of beer in Harry's refrigerator when he finally got around to telling me what was really on his mind concerning Willy. "The truth of it is," he said, "you don't have much in the way of choice. You can file a complaint with the police and the Department of Mental Health, but in the absence of any specific evidence that Ward is a threat to the public in general, or himself in particular, they won't do anything. As a matter of fact, they won't even keep an eye on him."

"How could they keep an eye on him?" I said. "Nobody can even find him."

He chewed thoughtfully for a while and then licked a smear of mustard off his fingers. "You ever hear of a Peace Bond?"

"No."

"A Peace Bond is what they used to use in rural communities in New England when one farmer would get in a bruha with another, and one of them wasn't big enough or tough enough to get into a punchout. The little guy would tell it to the judge and the judge would call them both in and issue a Peace Bond. What it said, in effect, was the next time the big guy pushed the little guy in the mud it was going to cost the big guy a grand."

"Only in this case I'm the big guy, Harry. And this isn't rural New England in the nineteenth century. And Willy hasn't done anything that is threatening . . . as you point out yourself."

Harry looked at me shrewdly through the hole he'd poked in his napkin. "True," he said. "But he might, and if he does there is a way I can help you. We are not entirely without precedent here."

"Go on."

"I am still a member of the American Psychiatric Association. I teach rather than practice, but my profession gives me credibility in certain areas. I am boarded, after all."

"I'm not following this, Hair."

"Let me try it another way. Any peace officer in this country, if he arrests somebody he thinks is dingey, has the authority to put that person away for seventy-two hours in the mental ward of a hospital. They calm the nut down with Thorazine or lithium, and try to persuade him to commit himself voluntarily for treatment. If he won't buy it, and there's evidence that he really is a loony, a judge can send him to Atascadero for ninety-day stretches until the court is finally convinced he's stable enough to return to society. Now my point is, the judges in this county tend to take the word of the district attorney on these matters, and the district attorney happens to be a good friend of mine who respects my professional opinion. He also owes me a few."

"Jesus Christ, Harry," I said, appalled. "I'm not about

to railroad Willy into the nuthouse just because he's a pest. You may have no ethics, but I do."

"A pest? Listen, my friend, today's pest is tomorrow's parolee. And what's in question here is not my ethics, but your ability to judge character. I knew Willy was headed for big trouble the first time I saw him, just by the way he looks at people, like he's not seeing *them* but some weird translation in his head of what he thinks they *are*, and those are the kind of guys that start trying to rearrange the world to fit their fucked-up image of what it should be, not what it is. They are sometimes dangerous, and compassion for the predicament should not translate into ignoring their potential."

"Okay, okay," I said.

"In any case," Harry said, "the boy needs help, and that's a fact. The rest is hypothetical. *If* he should put himself in the way of having assistance forced on him, I am prepared to use what influence I have to see that he gets it."

I yawned. From where I was sitting in Harry's kitchen I could see out the breakfast nook window and across the garden plot to the garage and the single forty-watt bulb that was burning at the foot of the steps to my studio. The wind was blowing and the branches of a eucalyptus tree were shadowed movement on the pale clapboard wall beyond. For a moment I thought I saw a figure pass in front of the light and disappear into the darkness. It was late, and I realized I was letting Harry's paranoia get to me. All I needed was to start seeing ghosts every time something moved in the periphery of my vision, every time a tree limb scraped along the side of the building when the wind came up off the sea. I could imagine the state of my nerves if I succumbed to that. "I believe," I said, rising, "that it's time to let this matter rest. I'm going to crap out."

"Alone?" Harry wiggled his eyebrows.

"Alone."

"I'm not going to ask," Harry said. "I'm merely going to applaud your good sense and judgment. She was such a honey I know it was a tough decision."

"Well, as Dorothy Parker said, Hair, candy's dandy, but sex rots your teeth."

"Frankly, that's not a problem I've considered. My own problem, which I admit is only faintly related, is why little girls who are made of sugar and spice and everything nice taste like anchovies?"

"Good night, Harold."

"Sweet dreams."

There may be flies on some of you guys, but there ain't no flies on me. Nina's tune. *Oh the night was dark and dreary/ Wind and rain and sleet/ When Daddy joined the Ku Klux/ And Mamma lost her sheet.* I was humming it as I went up the steps to my room, mainly to keep the darkness back a little and assure myself with some noise that the world was still with us. Either because I was still wrecked from the Johnny Walker or because it was pitch black on the landing in front of my door I had trouble fitting the key in the lock. Keep singing, kid. *Mamma's in the kitchen, switchin' and pitchin'/ Daddy's in the cellar, grousin' and bitchin'/ And I'm upstairs kicking the dog for eeeyou — phoria.* I finally got the door opened, stepped inside, whistled shave and a haircut, and stopped dead in my tracks. I suddenly realized that the reason it was so dark on the steps was that somebody had turned the light off. Five minutes earlier, from Weisberg's kitchen, I had seen it on.

Did my flesh crawl? My spine chill? The hairs on my neck snap to attention? None of that. I did get a tremendous rush of adrenaline knowing he was somewhere in the room, and my heart rate shot into overdrive, but I was relieved at the same time that our confrontation had come and I could finally take him by the throat and throttle him — or persuade him through gentle argument and rational discourse to go piss up somebody else's rope. "Willy," I said, "I don't know what this game is all about, but if you've got some move to make you'd better make it quick, because I'm going to climb on you like ugly on an ape."

There was no answer. I thought I heard movement over by the bed. I moved quietly to the bookcase behind the open door where the lamp was. The switch was broken, and I was reaching carefully down through the spokes of the shade to twist the bulb, when my visitor spoke. "I love you," she said. "Don't turn on the light. Just come and hold me."

Six

WE ENTER NOW THE TANGLEWOOD. IN THE TREATMENT FOR the screenplay it says the lovers meet by guttering candle-light, their whispered sighs echoed in the wind outside. They come together to come apart, but love proves stronger than duty, and in the end, haggard but happy, they ride off into the sunset, popping their bubblegum and singing "We've only just begun to live." Oh yeah.

What we had, in fact, was a momentary relapse. Nina's attempt to start forgetting me by going off camping with someone else had only reminded her that college boys are neither very interesting nor very proficient, when it comes right down to it, and that being impatiently groped when you have been patiently loved is not an altogether satisfying experience. There were more important reasons why she came back, but a couple of noisy orgasms and a cold dawn brightening the paisley of my drug rehab furniture served to remind her all over again of Hank Williams's immortal classic, "Back Street Affair," and by the time your cheatin' heart was breaking for a bit of breakfast she was back on the skids. "We've got to stop this. This is tearing me to pieces."

It was a litany that was to become a bit tiresome, particularly since it elicited only the most obvious and transparently stupid response. "What's wrong, for God's sake, with two people in love showing it?" I said. "The damage has been done. If there was a mistake it was getting involved in the first place. And anyway, I don't regard this as a mistake."

"What's wrong is you're married."

"I'm aware of that. In case I forget I know you'll remind me."

"And you love your wife."

"Now wait a minute. That's an assumption you make with no basis for judgment. You don't know a thing about my relationship with my wife."

"I don't have to know anything. I'm not stupid. I know what you *don't* say; I know what you avoid talking about." She fished under the bed for a box of Kleenex and blew her nose. "Okay, so things are maybe a little dull right now; you've fallen into some pretty boring routines after fifteen years, but that doesn't erase what you started with, that doesn't cancel out the past, and when she gets back you're going to figure you owe those years a chance. And then it's going to occur to you that you've accumulated quite a lot of mutual stuff that isn't so easily abandoned. And I don't mean the furniture."

"What makes you such an expert on the psychology of marital relationships?" I asked.

"It's pretty conventional, Eliot."

"Conventional! Christ almighty, the convention is to leave your tired-out, used-up wife and run off with your honey."

"Yeah . . . but the thing is you're such an egotistical bastard that to do what everybody else does would really stick in your craw. You couldn't live with it because that would make you just one of the boys."

"Nina, do us both a favor and quit it," I said. "If what you came down here for was to lay a number on me, then I accept responsibilty for the way you feel, but I would sure as hell like to forego the love-hate transmogrification."

"Can't you ever just use a simple word?"

"No."

If I could find a simple word for the variations on a theme we went through I would certainly use it and spare us all from show and tell. We suffered daily bouts of cardiac arrest, followed by short-term pacemaker implants. We would see each other at ten A.M. and cruise along comfortably for an hour or two before some remark or gesture infused five cc's of reality into the vein and the patient lost control. Neurological dysfunction. Upper respiratory collapse. I would thunder home swearing never again to trust anyone under thirty, and twenty minutes later I'd be on the phone. Nina would insist at breakfast, brunch, lunch, and dinner that after long and careful thought (and a vigorous, health restoring run on the beach) she had finally come to accept the inevitability of the impossible; that difficult as a platonic friendship was going to be it was the only way to preserve our sanity — and keep her from flunking out of school. An hour later she'd be glued to me in a mad embrace that left us transported, but more frustrated than ever.

After three days of this *démarche* we had exhausted every possible avenue of resolution and found ourselves in precisely the same place we had started. Communication was pointless. We wound up sitting in various local diners consuming gallons of coffee and staring at each other without an inkling of what more to say. Nina finally "opined" that since platonism wasn't working, and a love affair with her in the role of mistress was impossible, we should not see each other anymore. "No calls, no nothing. Cold turkey."

"Fine with me," I said, knowing the impossibility of that. "I've about had it with your peculiar brand of ethics anyway."

"Fine. Then it's fifty-fifty and neither one of us will be hurt."

"Fine. I certainly won't."

"Fine."

Gloom. Silence. Another quart of coffee. Both green with nausea. I've got the drizzlies. Overdosed on caffeine. *THWOK.* Nina has one red eye that peers at me like a startled rooster. And I'm the earwig trying to find a crack in the log. She hasn't washed her hair since she cleaned the frying pan with it out on Point Reyes.

"I wish you could go to the waltz with me tonight."

"The WALTZ?"

"The end of the year waltz up at school. Oh, it's just beautiful, Eliot, the way they decorate the room with streamers and balloons and the great big glass ball they shine colored lights on. There's a live band, and everybody dresses up in fabulous costumes, and they dance the night away. It's just absolutely the most romantic thing you ever saw in your whole life. All the seniors get drunk and everybody cries a lot because they're all going away pretty soon and never going to see each other again probably, and when the sun starts to come up and the band plays the last waltz it's like a greenhouse in there it's so humid."

"You wish I could go, but I can't?"

"Right."

"Why can't I?"

"Because we just decided we weren't going to see each

other anymore . . . for a while. Besides, I have a date. I go to the waltz with this same boy every year, because it's kind of a special thing with us. If I stood him up and went with you he'd punch you out . . . except he's quite a lot littler." Finally, something struck her as amusing.

"You want some more coffee?" I asked.

She hiccuped into her hand, consulted the menu, and threw it down. "Oh God, why not? I'm so wired now it can't make any difference. But Eliot . . . could I also have, you think, an order of fries?"

"FRIES?"

"Yum."

Perhaps it was the influence of the period craze for the 1950's, but what was happening to me during all that floundering around was a sense of having regressed to my teens when "puppy love" was in flower and Dear Abby counseled nice girls not to pet on the first date. Leave the puppy at home, girls. What I remember most vividly about growing up at mid-century is a weekend affliction known to the endocrinologist as elephantiasis of the scrotum and to the layman, standing knee-deep in the mud of Maidenhead Lane trying to clean and jerk the front end of his old man's car, as lover's nuts. An ailment contracted, generally, in the backseat of an automobile between eleven-thirty and one A.M. Severely aggravated by tight Levi's and Frisco jeans: cured only by immediate pulverization of the dreaded nematode (*Wuchereria bancrofti*). That recreant worm. Fifth columnist! Responsible for obstruction of the lymphatic passion. *THWOK!* Recent sufferers are to be found in the halls of local high schools, around lockers, where they assiduously sniff index fingers and proffer sexual misinformation to fellow trucklers and oafs. Complete cure, restoration to a normal, fulfilling life, is unheard of.

Or at least that is how it used to be. I was under the

impression that post-modernism had all but eradicated such adolescent ailments, and that I, most certainly, would never again find myself inching down a midnight street like a ruptured hurdler, looking for a handy bumper. There is a certain irony therefore, in the following spectacle — the rake and rambling boy, aged forty, and the promiscuous young lady, aged twenty, spending their last five uninterrupted days together on a Goodwill special, wearing all their clothes, and titillating themselves backward in time and space.

Because what happened, as I knew it would, was that our resolution to stay away from each other lasted from about three o'clock Saturday afternoon to three o'clock Sunday morning (green freedoms, cockatoos and all) when, after skulking around the peripheries of the last waltz in Santa Cruz, nipping off a pint of Boone's Farm Ollalaberry wine and peeing into the fuschia bushes to avoid entering the dance hall and risking early detection, I made my appearance like William Wilson's doppelgänger and spirited her off into the night. We made for my apartment. Between kisses we agreed that we were insane, that we couldn't stay together, that we couldn't stay apart, that all was hopeless, in the best Brontë sisters tradition, and that we would destroy each other completely if we didn't find strength and will to resist. We compromised by going to bed with our clothes on.

Actually it wasn't my idea. My argument, delivered between thrashings and gnashings, was that having taken the plunge in the first place, having gotten involved with one another and gone to bed and made love, etcetera, etcetera, one could not return to GO and pretend that an after the fact celibacy would restore everything to an uncomplicated state of grace. There were various kinds of infidelity, I pointed out, of which brand X (as in sex) was the *least* serious. Omitting sex from our relationship was pointless because it didn't speak to the real issue, psychological and emotional infidelity; merely eschewed its most visible manifestation. Rather like throwing the Peace Corps out of Panama because you don't like American involvement in the Canal Zone, I said. Where is the logic in maintaining an emotional commitment and denying yourself its expression? That's like a cancer victim going to a surgeon to have his ears pierced. Going to a five star restaurant and ordering a corn-dog. Small Pepsi, I said.

Nina's answer was far more complicated. "I love you. All this hurts a lot."

So we clutched each other's clothes for the rest of the night. There were tears, clinches, recriminations, anguished tossings and turnings. She wanted me as badly as I wanted her, but she wasn't going to disappoint herself by a weakness. At one point it looked as if I were going to mate with the flap-crotch of my Toga II, Slim-guy, cotton bagger briefs, but as that didn't happen I wound up in the wee small hours with a genital condition that recalled the road apple rodeo of my younger days. Then, when Nina was finally sleeping, I crawled into the bathroom to unprime the pump, but wound up sitting on the biffy with my head in my hands and the absurd conviction that to abuse myself at my age was not only degenerate and demeaning, but a terrible violation of our love and the very real pain I had caused us both.

I don't know why I choose to be cute about it. I suppose I am so suspicious of my underdeveloped emotions that to say out loud that I loved her, and that my gibbous heart was heavy indeed with the suffering my dishonesty had brought on, is to raise all the hags, harridans, and crones that plague my most ingenuous remarks and cause those wretched ladies to point their fingers at me in denial. The hell with them. I did love her. I was miserable.

Because it was not so easy, I discovered, to make the kinds of decisions that seemed to come so obviously to one's friends. Boring marriage: terminate it. In love with another woman: change partners. There was much to what Harry had once said when he asked me whose crowd we were going to join, hers or mine? Among other things, watching her with her own at the waltz had informed me how little I was attracted to reliving that station. And what would we subsist on after I got through paying Erica's bills? I wasn't quite mean enough to desert her economically, make her sell the house and lower her standard of living. And what about Lenny? He was at just the wrong age to find himself without a father — even one like me. Right now stability was his due.

I suppose the real reason I dragged my feet at the thought of starting over was Erica. Something about the devils you know are better than the devils you don't. We had our problems, true enough, but I was willing to admit that most of them were of my making. All I had done for our marriage after she had taken me back was immediately run out and get involved with someone else. Our talks about truth and honesty and openness had gone whistling right through the hole between my ears, and there was no way I could pretend she was responsible for what I was into now. How could I do this to her? The best years of her life . . . and so forth. I believed all that.

Ah, but my God Nina was lovely. Nina was young and fresh and full of beans. Nina was a collector's item in bed. Wwhhuunnggg and aarrgghhh. Nina adored me in a way it seemed Erica never had, and knowing what a perfectly contemptible swine I was beneath my plastic wrap surface I was flattered by her love to the bottom of my flat-footed soul. She was an unending source of amazement because she was in no way my creation, and it was clear that she was too proud, too self-aware, too intelligent ever to allow herself to become an extension of me. Over the years Erica had become an appendage of Eliot Warren. Nina would always be Nina.

When I told her all this she just looked at me with a funny expression on her face and said, "It seems to me pretty odd for the quintessential sexist to worship such independence in his woman."

"Not so," I told her. "For the quintessential sexist to have such an independent soul devoted to him is the ultimate confirmation of his most selfish assumptions." (At least I was becoming more honest.)

"Well, I'm *not* devoted to you anymore, so get your hand off my leg."

We continued to toss and turn, fret and grope, sleep in snatches and eat nothing. Nina was no tower of rationality, in spite of her resolve, and weariness didn't help her consistency. At one point she decided she *did* want me to leave Erica. "What *are* you going to do?" she said. "If you love me the way you say you do, if things are so rotten at home as you pretend they are, why do you stay? Any normal man would leave." Then she would pout. "I'd sell out my dreams, I'd share my life with you, but you, you bastard, you want us both. You want it all."

"You think I'm just after the captain's paradise, huh? Fire and slippers and mom's home cooking Tuesday, Thursday, and Saturday? Hot time in the old town on the off nights?"

"Yes."

"Well, you're full of shit."

"No I'm not. That's *exactly* what you want." She sat up in bed, angry with herself for being such a dope. "I can't believe I'm even doing this . . . letting myself be used like this. Look, jerk, you're going to have to figure this mess out, not me. I'm not married. I'm not trucking around with two husbands."

"What about the guy you went to Point Reyes with? What did you do out there with him? Take snapshots of the surf? Watch birds? I mean, you aren't exactly sitting around pining for me . . . not that I've noticed."

She rolled over on the bed and pushed herself to her knees. She was incredulous. "Just fuck you! What does that have to do with anything? I'm not *married* to anybody, remember? I can go wherever I want and I don't have to pretend anything to anybody. What am I supposed to do? Cut myself off from every guy I ever knew and liked just on the off chance you'll have some time to devote to me between office hours and going home to supper? That isn't a thing you ask somebody you love to do."

"Office hours and supper! I've been with you every damn day for the last month . . . ever since I met you."

"Yeah, and what about Friday? When your wife comes home? The big bird descends from the sky, what then? Do I get to see you every day then, and sleep with you, and wake up to you in the morning? Do I get my share?"

"I don't know. I won't know until it happens."

"Oh well fine, because I know. On Friday it's bye-bye Nina, it's been nice knowing you. You were a swell piece of ass but now I got to get my act straightened out."

I lay in the dark for a few moments, staring up at the ceiling and trying to count the number of holes in the plaster where the lathing showed darkly through. "So that's it," I finally said. "That's why we're not making love anymore. We're punishing the chauvinist for the limitations of his interest."

She turned on the lamp beside the bed and propped her head on her arm, looking down at me as if I were some curiously befuddled bug crawling through the tangle of a thickly seeded lawn. "You don't understand this at all, do you? You don't understand that I'm upset and confused and mad because I love you, even though I think you're the worst thing that ever happened to me. I can't help myself. I'm scared, Eliot, because I'm afraid I might not be able to get over you, and because I know I'm going to lose, and because I know my ego isn't going to take rejection very well. I'm really unhappy, you fucker, because you made me fall in love with you like I could never imagine feeling about somebody, and sleeping with you just makes it worse. You don't understand any of that, do you? Or you don't care."

"I care. Quit accusing me of that, at least."

"See, in the end, I'm going to get creamed. So what I'm trying to do is save a little bit of myself so I'll have some strength left when it happens."

"Why do you insist you're going to lose, damn it?"

"If I'm wrong, buddy, there's one easy way to prove it. And then we can spend the rest of our lives making love."

But at another point — I don't remember which day or night, time got so warped — she insisted she wouldn't stand for my leaving Erica. "Home wrecking isn't one of my pastimes. If I did something like that I think I'd hate myself for the rest of my life. If somebody did that to me it would destroy me, and so I can't do it to somebody else, no way. I mean one of the few absolutes I have is that you don't do unto others what you wouldn't have done unto yourself."

"That's very poetic."

"I don't care what it is, it's something you'll never talk me out of."

"The only trouble with your code," I said, "is that you aren't doing unto anyone. I am. It's my problem, as you're fond of pointing out, not yours."

"Oh no. Because that's the trouble with the whole world. Everything that's honest and right is an anachronism because people try to assign responsibility for actions that aren't prima facie their own to somebody else."

"Now who's trotting out the Clydesdales to haul a little thought?"

"I'm not as stupid as I look. And anyway, it's not a little thought. You could afford to reflect on it." She snuggled down on the bed and pulled the quilt up under her chin. Her breathing was soft and even, and after a few minutes what began as simulation of a dreamless sleep turned into the real thing.

I was not entirely witless and without occasional moments of insight. As I lay there night after night, thinking about my sins and contemplating the darkness of darkness, I began to wonder what it actually *would* be like to be married to Nina, to spend the last of my sports car years before true menopause watching her slowly grow into the slack frustrations of her own middle age. Erica was once just as bouncy and resilient. Would I love Nina in the same way when the stretch marks began to appear, the atrophied muscles, infarcted tissues, calcified joints, veins popping to the surface? Three big ones for the purple throb of decay. Or, growing fat and bald, a rheumatoid arthritic with aching piles and a heart condition, would I gleefully foul my diaper in the knowledge that even Nina, lovely Nina, could grow old and stupid and die? The thought was of some comfort to me when I would wake in the middle of the night with my arms mysteriously dead, the circulation cut off, numb flesh tingling ever so faintly, and my bladder full again, even though I had emptied it three hours earlier. You too, kiddo, I would think.

But seriously, what if I could bring myself to divorce Erica, give her the house and whatever unreal estate we had accumulated during our fifteen years together, settle a monthly allotment for living expenses and child support, and start all over with another woman? Would the result, in the long run, be any different? How long before Nina's unqualified candor would begin to surface again, and she would see me not as that fascinating older gentleman with the body of a light heavyweight, the mind of a philosopher, the soul of a poet, the rapier wit of a . . . oh well. She would begin to see me as the potbellied scramble of neurotic contradictions and sleazy paranoia that I really am.

Friday came in fifteen minutes. Or was it two hundred years? It happened to be graduation day and Nina, who still had a term to go to complete the requirements for the degree, was nevertheless involved in such pomp and circumstance as a "modern, experimental, innovative, progressive" institution in the California system of higher education could still muster. Which wasn't much. Still, there were parties to attend, lovers (ex- and ex-officio) to bid adieu, classmates and friends to wish a lot of luck out there in the jobless, indifferent world where they were now certified exiles. I dropped Nina off in front of her college with a promise to call her in a day or so with some kind of resolution — a promise which she ignored as she stared intently (and with a curious brightness in her burned out eyes) at the gaggle of parents who swarmed over the campus, parking their cars illegally in the faculty lots. The pricks. I couldn't even kiss her good-bye in such a mob. We left the formalities hanging along with everything else, and I went home, changed, and started driving for the airport.

The plane was two hours late. I had time, happily, to pour a couple of overpriced drinks into myself in the Pagoda Room and to buy some flowers and a Tonka dump truck for my arrivees. Airports depress me, generally, unless I happen to be the one with a ticket, but this afternoon was worse than most. Between drinks I made a trip from the bar to the men's room and came back three minutes later to find that somebody had stolen the Tonka truck and left me one red rose stuck by its foreshortened stem into my scotch and water. I plodded into the gift shop and remade my purchases.

When Erica's plane did arrive, she was delayed another

twenty minutes by a jammed forward hatch, but finally she appeared on the ramp, Lenny in hand, and we were once again a united front. I thought her kiss a little perfunctory and cool, considering the flowers I bestowed on her, but I didn't find out the reason until we were almost over the mountain and descending to the coast road near Half Moon Bay. Up to that point we made small talk about New England and her mother's condition and a penicillin allergy Lenny turned out to have, and I offered a résumé of my academic activities through the last month of the year. I confessed that I had been too much occupied by students to get a lick of work done on my book. Then I made a mistake and tried to get personal. "Did you miss me back there in our old stomping grounds?" I asked.

"More than you missed me."

Did I detect innuendo in that controlled voice? Pulse RPM up to five thousand. "What's that supposed to mean?"

"I'd rather talk about it later," she said, gesturing with her head toward the backseat.

"I think what'shisname is asleep. You can tell me now."

She turned around and looked at Lenny, stretched out on the seat with his arm curled affectionately around his bright yellow truck. "It's too funny," she said, satisfied that he was out. "One of the big reasons I didn't want to go to mother's in the first place was I thought maybe we had reached rock bottom and were about to find a way to climb back up. I didn't want to take a chance on losing what little ground we had gained." She had turned with her arm crooked over the back of the seat and was looking directly into what I assumed was my flaming right ear. (Maybe it was a cabbage. RPM's red-lined.) "So yes, at first I missed you like crazy . . . not because you're such a prince to be around, but because I wanted to get on with *us*, and I was trying to figure out a way to get out of there as fast as possible. Actually, I had a reservation a week ago. I was going to fly home and surprise you. Only you know what happened, Eliot?" (Go on, I thought. The block's cracked anyway; the head gasket's blown. Might as well burn up the valves so we can junk it.) "I had a visit from Willy Ward."

I turned and looked at her, stunned. "That's impossible," I said.

"No. As a matter of fact he was in New York for his mother's wedding and he came up to Boston to see his uncle. I don't know how he knew I was in Worcester, but where there's a will there's a way, huh? He's moving back to New Hampshire, or maybe Vermont. I rather thought you'd know all this . . . since you're so well acquainted with his wife."

"Now just hold on a minute here," I said, my temperature taking a sudden rise. "I don't know what that crackpot told you but there is absolutely nothing, *nothing,* between me and Willy's wife, nor was there *ever* anything between us, nor *will* there ever be anything . . ."

"Oh I know that, sweetie," Erica said, cool as ice. "I didn't mean to imply there was something going on. Women have a feeling about these things you know. I could tell that his need to crucify you was more complicated than that."

"Well good," I said hotly. "Because there isn't anything between us and never was. I wouldn't touch Frankie Ward with a Fudgsicle."

"I'm sure you wouldn't, dear. I imagine your little playmate Nina would hand you your head on a plate if you did."

Thwok!

Part Four

One

SUSPENDED ANIMATION. SPRING INTO SUMMER. EQUINOX TO solstice. The sun moved higher until it spent most of its morning risings on the vertical behind the liquid amber, and my study window no longer received full exposure. The azaleas and the rhododendrons bloomed, the hedge of mock orange between my neighbor's house and mine gave up a perfume that made me dopey with nostalgia for my Santa Barbara origins — those few fragrant years before my family moved north out of the citrus country to the damp fogs and urban sprawl of the Bay Area.

With the school term ended and my life in somewhat of a mess, I shut myself up in my study once more and went back to work on my book. Erica and I maintained a guarded truce. I had condemned Willy's visit as the product of a psychopathic liar and substantiated my disclaimer with a full account of his behavior since coming to the West Coast. For reasons that no doubt had more to do with self-protection than indifference or lack of curiosity, she chose not to debate me. Nina was no longer a distraction because she had taken off the same day I went to the airport to pick up Erica and was spending the summer in the fortress of her family home in Pacific Palisades. Or so she said in the note she left under the door of my office. Rather than pursue her I decided to immerse myself in my solitary fictions to see if a stint at the typewriter might not ease the contortions of my unrestful soul. I wound up writing her into the story, and so continued to tongue the jagged edge of my broken molars.

But at least things were moving. By the end of July I had finished a hundred pages I'd had sitting around in draft, and written at least fifty more. I knew where things were going next; even had enough confidence in their propriety to take a break and crank out an article on San Simeon I had agreed six months earlier to do for *Travel and Leisure*. Traveled leisurely down the coast for a few days to refresh the memory. Full of narrative energy I composed a rather comic blast at my university and its obsession with what it euphemistically considers "experimental inroads in higher education" and sent it off to an old friend of mine at *Change*. When she accepted it, I had a change of my own — of heart — and decided it was really unnecessary to fire yet one more missile at that crumbling structure just to satisfy one's desire to say "I told you so." It would fall down of its own weight anyway. When I told Weisberg what a good boy I had been he collapsed in hysterics. "You raving bullshitter. You just read in the papers how this place is in trouble with the legislature anyway and they talk of closing it. You were protecting your undeserved salary."

"Not so," I said, offended. "I realized that I was on an ego trip. It was unbecoming in one as restrained and tasteful as I."

"Ego! You don't *have* an ego, man. You are a solid lump of throbbing, pre-frontal Id. You are the original Mister *I-want-it-because-I-need-it-because-I-have-to-have-it.*"

"You're suggesting I'm childlike?"

"In all respects but innocence. You were born corrupt."

"I think that's a bit harsh, Harold."

In August I persuaded him to go on a backpacking trip with me and Lenny in Yosemite Valley — an all male outing that was actually my idea, not Erica's. His own son, with whom he shared an uneasy month every summer, was to be brought down from Portland by the ex-wife, and we planned to spend a day or so with the boys getting the gear together and then take off for a week in the back country. The dads would carry the grub and cooking equipment and the kids could carry their own sleeping bags and clothes. We'd do an easy loop out of the valley: something like Nevada Falls to Merced Lake and back by way of Cloud's Rest. Nothing too strenuous. I did that stuff with my old man when I was a kid. Yes, Harry, an easy trip. Remember every step of the way.

Harry was enthusiastic but skeptical. "It would give me something to do with Jerome besides sit around and suffer his reproachful silences (his mother devotes July to slandering my memory), but Jesus, Eliot, I don't think I've walked more than a hundred yards consecutively in the last twenty years."

"It'll do you good. Besides, Jerome's getting to the age where you can't buy him off with movies and a ride on the boardwalk. It's time you taught him a few things about survival."

"Believe me, pal, his mother teaches him all he needs to know about that. Could I take a lady on this trek?"

"This is fathers and sons, wiseguy. This is men against the mountains, not some hoochy-kootchy show. Hell no, you can't take a lady."

"Will we have a tent?"

"Do you want to carry it?"

"I don't know. How much does it weigh?"

"Seven or eight pounds?"

"That's not much."

Perversity nearly got the better of me, but I decided why be cruel. "We don't need it. It's August. It hasn't rained in the Sierra in August since before Christ."

"You know what I don't like about this whole deal?" Harry said.

"No, what?"

"I have to trust you."

The expedition nearly folded when we went to Berkeley one afternoon toward the end of July to buy pack frames and sleeping bags. I explained to Weisberg, as I tried patiently to coax him off his knees, that goose down had gone up a little in price since the army surplus days of the late '40s, but that a good North Face or Sierra Design bag would last him the rest of his life. If he really was seriously upset about it he could present the one he was going to buy Jerome as an early Christmas present. I bought him a drink in some joint on San Pablo and after a while he calmed down; in fact he got stewed and when we found ourselves in REI looking for reasonably priced pack frames he wanted to buy every gadget and thingamabob in the place: egg carriers, collapsible water bottles, wind resistant matches, biosuds, a sven saw, a safari compass filled with green liquid and sporting luminescent points, space blanket, wilderness storm kit, snakebite kit. He was a kid turned loose in F.A.O. Schwarz. At one point I found him over in the climbing equipment section discussing the virtues of the Stubai Nanga Parbat Extreme over the Interlap Sentinelle Rouge. "We don't need an ice ax, Hair," I told him, "nor the avalanche cord, nor the Austrian nut and ice hammer, nor the crampons. We're not going to Katmandu."

"How do you know what's up there?"

"Because I've been up there."

With great reluctance he put it all back, consoling himself with fifty-six-dollar climbing boots (replete with scree collar and Montagna soles) that weighed about a hundred pounds apiece and looked as if they'd give him blisters just trying them on. There was no talking him into a nice pair of tennis shoes, though I did manage to suppress his longing for zippered gaiters.

On the eleventh his son arrived and it was immediately clear to me why Harry dreaded having to play dad for a month. Jerome was not a prepossessing adolescent. Even in Santa Cruz, where every variety of unnatural act walks unmolested on the public streets, Jerome was an eyesore. It was not just his complexion (picture aerial photographs of fire bombing over Dresden), nor his slouch, nor his stoop, nor his psychic lordosis, nor his sullen, petulant contempt for any remark addressed to the RFD in his mind, nor even his indescribable fright wig bound by a do-rag to the top of his head — none of these alone elicited one's support for increased experimentation in eugenics (or a legalized program of euthanasia), rather it was the whole anthology of offenses, the blitzkrieg assault on aesthetics his composite shortcomings expressed, that made one want to kick him. When Harry said we were going to the mountains for a week he curled his lip and slowly closed his eyes. His father shrugged and looked embarrassed. "It's a stage," he said.

We left late on Friday afternoon in the hope that the boys, who we assumed would be completely off the wall with excitement, might get tired after a few hours of driving and fall asleep. In contrast to Jerome, Lenny was a model prisoner. Jerome had a sinus condition that he refused to accommodate with a handkerchief, preferring instead to make noises like a honey-bucket siphon in the bottom of a septic tank, until eventually his father came down on him and threatened to put him out of the car. Thenceforth he snuffled every fifteen seconds and looked put upon. When we reached the valley at midnight and laid out our sleeping bags in the dark, I made a point of locating my quarters as far from *Chez* Weisberg as I could. Wasted energy. After an hour on the ground Jerome moved into the backseat of the car.

In the morning I opened my eyes on the towering slab of Half Dome, rimmed by the palest suggestion of dawn, a cuticle moon still glimmering off to the left in the direction of Tenaya Canyon. I took a hit on the cold mountain air, redolent of pine and wood smoke, and snuggled back into my nest, indulging myself in various impossible fantasies that were all the more pleasurable because they were impossible. I would give up writing, stop teaching, quit grumbling about indifferent youth, sell my possessions, and buy a string of mules. Become a packer. Get into a Bailey straw and a plug of Day's Work and truck city folk to the end of the rainbow. Trout. Western man. How high *is* that moon? Up there like a Christmas ornament in the top of a Ponderosa pine? Nina as cowgirl in tight faded Levi's and denim shirt with snap pearl buttons. Freedom.

I sat up again an hour later. The sun was down in Bridgeport on the eastern side of the Sierra, and the valley floor still dark, but a few campers were now up and about, wisps of ghost smoke drifting into the trees, mountain greenery visibly replaced by Winnebagos, Bizi-Bodis, Kozi-Kars, international day-glo orange tents, and various constructions of hanging blankets, towels, and dirty laundry to protect the privacy of cheek and jowl. Out of my bag and over to kick Harry, who grunts and burrows deeper into rip-stop nylon and duck feathers. Please excuse the interruptus, Coitus, but I'm on my way to Curry Village to buy some wood for our breakfast fire because the last twig in this valley disappeared in 1914 along with John Muir, and while I'm all for retarding pollution and preserving the ecology we forgot the petrol for our jim-dandy backpacker's stove. Not to concern yourself, Harold. Leave everything to me. Flap jacks and weenies and a pot of java so black it'll take the enamel off your tooth. In the mountains anything tastes good.

I bought eggs and sausages and a bundle of wood at the Camp Curry store, and then started back through the trees to my sleeping companions. The light was still bad and at one point I stumbled over a root and fell to my knees knocking my glasses off in an attempt to juggle my firewood and keep from dropping the bag with the eggs. I found them immediately but discovered I had knocked the right lens out of the frame. Rather than fool with it there I put it in my pocket and trekked the last quarter mile in waltz time. Then a strange thing happened which I could not attribute entirely to 20/40 vision.

About fifty feet from our campsite there was a block building that housed toilets and a wash station. As I approached I noticed a man in a navy blue parka standing at one corner, his back to me, his gaze apparently fixed intently on the compound in which our car and equipment were located. There was something familiar about him, but with only one good eye I could not decide what it was, and in any case I didn't pay much attention until I got closer and for an instant he turned his head to look at me. What he saw startled him and he moved quickly around the edge of the building, keeping it between us as he hurried away through the woods. I cannot claim a shock of recognition, only an instinct. I had the strange sensation that it was Willy Ward.

There was no point, I decided, in activating Harry's natural paranoia by telling him what I thought I had seen. Obviously I was wrong, Willy was probably halfway to

Tibet, and one hysteric with sensory-motor disorders was enough in any expeditionary force. Not only was there no reason for Willy to shadow me, there was no way in the world for him to know where I was, and I finally calmed myself by realizing how preposterous my suspicions were.

Rather than think about it further I built a fire and began preparing breakfast. The smell of sizzling sausage brought the others out — Harry beating his chest and saying things like "Oh boy, smell like a washday" (whatever Dickens thought that was supposed to mean) — and even Jerome condescended to walk over to the comfort station and fill the coffeepot with water. By the time we squatted in the pine needles to eat, Willy had been forgotten.

"Hey Jerome," Harry said, a gleam in his eye and a smile on his kiss. "How about these sausages, huh? You ever eat anything so good?"

Jerome looked miserably at his plate and snuffled. "They look like moose turds," he said. Thereby establishing the tone of his day.

The easy loop trip I had defined from memory turned out defective. The trip *and* the memory. Perhaps there had been glacial action in the twenty-five year interval since my last visit; faulting, tilting of the earth's crust in a more precipitously vertical manner. It's thirteen miles from the valley floor to Merced Lake, with an elevation gain of thirty-five hundred feet. I knew that, but I had forgotten the implications. I had also forgotten that all the elevation gain takes place in the first three and a half miles. So there we were — one flat footed Jewish intellectual accustomed to the topography of Manhattan Island, his heteromorphic son, a five year old who insisted on leaning out over every precipice we came to, and wading in every puddle, pond and stream crossing, and rolling rocks back down the canyon at the juncture of every switchback — and me, Edmund Hillary *Noir*. Upward we toiled. The fifty pounds on my back began to feel like five hundred. Harry struggled under a similar load, plus fifty on each foot, plus another twenty when Jerome collapsed at Vernal Falls and declared he would go no farther. To emphasize his point he fed his lunch to the chipmunks. Harry's assumption of the prodigal's burden was not entirely altruistic. "If you're going to stay here that's fine with me, but I'm going to see you freeze your ass off if you do."

By two o'clock, blistered and very sore in the muscle, we reached the summit at Nevada Falls. Harry's spirits were erected by the sight of a modestly endowed girl sunning herself, topless, on a slab of granite near the trail, but I refused to stop. The trail marker promised a short mile to the campsite in Little Yosemite Valley, and I knew if we didn't keep going we would turn to stone. It took a good hour, even on level ground, but by mid-afternoon we were there. I revised my fantasies (perhaps I would not become a packer after all), and Harry, once he had recovered sufficiently to look around him, asked what the steel cables strung here and there between the trees were for.

"To hang up your food," I told him. "So the bears won't get it."

He regarded me with a gimlet-eye. Sigh of resignation. "The bears," he said. "Ah, yes, of course. The bears."

Lenny was not so pacific. He wanted to see one "RIGHT NOW," and was pretty crestfallen when I told him the cable business was all forest service nonsense. "If there's any bear who can stand the company of all these people," I told him, waving my arms at the fifty or sixty campers jammed into that one small space, "I will personally kink his tail, Lenski, and hand you his ass."

I had the opportunity to eat humble pie. It seemed more a question whether the people could stand the company of the bears — all four hundred and eight of them — swarming around like flies on a dung heap. Jerome was nearly catatonic with glee when his father's pack was dragged off shortly after dark, before we'd had a chance to hang it, and we lost half our rations. It meant, he guessed, a shorter trip. He was rendered comatose by the din that went up all night from the various campsites along the river as people banged pots and pans, blew whistles, yelled, and injured themselves with the rocks they threw at dark shadows in the trees. Things were looking up as far as Jerome was concerned. The possibility that somebody might get eaten, mauled, or clobbered in the head brightened up his evening considerably.

It's peculiar how the combination of nervous energy and physical exhaustion will play tricks with your mind. I'm not absolutely sure about this, but I think somewhere around four in the morning Harry shook me awake to tell me there was something moving on the far side of what had been our campfire. I groped in my half sleep for glasses and flashlight. The glasses were wet with dew, the flashlight weak, and in any case our food was securely hanging between two trees. If I did see anything it didn't matter very much to me at that point. I knew I smelled too bad to appeal to any *Ursidae* appetite, and therefore went back almost immediately to sleep. But in the morning I had the sensation, just the merest snatch of dream vision, that somebody in a blue parka had passed during the night through the camp.

"So what happens when it all starts up again in the fall?" Harry asked the next morning. We were stretched out under a cedar tree along the bank of the Merced River, sharing a chocolate bar for energy we had no intention of expending, watching the boys try to rig a kind of bosun's chair with one of the cables and haul themselves up into the air. It was comfortably warm, several peaks of the Clark range loomed in the backdrop, the river dappled along over a gemlike matrix of stones and bottom sand, and Harry had convinced me that a layover day would be much more pleasant than getting out there and slogging along with all the others on what he was pleased to call the John Manure Trail. It did seem to have become a major highway for pack animals.

"You tell *me*, Harry," I said. "You've had more experience with tragic romance than I have."

He shook his head and popped another piece of chocolate in his mouth. "Uh-uh. My marriage was kaput the day it started. When Lil and I got around to realizing it six years later there wasn't any choice to make. It wasn't should I or shouldn't I. It was thanks for nothing, goodbye."

"How do you know mine's any different?"

"Look," Harry said. "There's two things that happen when you think you've fallen in love with somebody other than your wife. You get divorced, or you don't."

"That simple, huh."

"Yeah. After all the bullshit and stale rhetoric about honor, obligation, the children, etcetera, it's that simple. Oh, you'll try to find a way to have it both ways; you'll start talking about conventional relationships as a product of outmoded puritanism, religious dogma, pre-birth-control inhibitions, you name it. You'll start telling yourself it's possible to love two people at the same time and in the same way, and develop fantastic arguments to support yourself and give yourself encouragement . . . like, 'If I love my children equally why can't I love my wife and mistress equally.' All of which, incidentally, might even be true, except for one thing; neither your wife nor your mistress will stand for that shit. You'll start wishing you were an Arab or a Mormon, and you'll stew around in your own juice until *finally* you will perceive that you either fish or cut bait. You either leave your wife and take up with your mistress, or you leave your mistress and go back to your wife."

"So, what do you recommend?"

Harry looked at me as if I were as ridiculous as I sounded. Which I was. "You know, if you could detach yourself from self-pity and *angst* long enough to be dispassionate about this, you'd realize that what you're into is the oldest, most repeated, most clichéd situation man has ever found himself in. I mean, the thing is so bloody predictable it's a wonder anybody who goes through it imagines he has a problem. It doesn't make a bit of difference what you do. If you replace Erica with Nina, Nina becomes Erica. You change the china and hang different pictures on the wall, but ultimately you haven't solved a damn thing because what you're after is freedom, the last chance, a little whoopee before you croak."

"There is such a thing as love," I observed.

"That's what you think." He chucked a flat stone out into the river but the current was too swift for it to skip. "Okay, if it's love, then you still have no problem. You take the one you love and leave the one you don't. But that isn't your story, bub, or you wouldn't still be at home."

"Well, let me ask you this, know-it-all," I said. "Just for the sake of argument let us suppose you're right. What's wrong with freedom and the last chance for whoopee?"

"Nothing. You have to accept the fact, though, that you look ridiculous to anyone watching you sport through the meadow green. There's no fool like an old fool, as they always say. As a matter of fact I think it was you who made a few scathing comments about post-adolescence when Bill Miller bought himself some beads and leather pants and kissed off his old lady for a graduate student; something about drawing-room comedy, *opéra bouffe*, the farce of the flaccid fossil, wasn't it?"

"He's fifty-two years old."

"That certainly does make a difference." Harry tried his luck with another stone and succeeded in missing the river entirely, firing his missile straight through the mosquito netting of somebody's tent on the other side. Nobody home, fortunately. "And there is another thing. One of the curiosities of the love triangle is that there are people involved, and what you generally do is hurt a couple of them while you're busy indulging your tyrannical gonads. There's that."

"Yes," I agreed, offering a stagy sigh. "There is that. But thanks anyway, Harry."

"For nothing."

"No, actually the whole subject is pretty boring, but even having somebody explain the obvious to you helps."

"Helps what?"

"I don't know."

The following day we moved our camp another seven or eight miles along the trail. Merced Lake was only slightly less crowded, the bear problem no better, but the boys had a chance to fish for nonexistent trout and therefore less time to loll around camp eating our diminished provisions. Lenny and I spent a pleasant afternoon throwing spinners into likely looking pools, and even though we caught nothing we were together in an enterprise that seemed to elicit a lot of manly mythology. I know he thought he was having the time of his life, and I rather thought so too.

Even Jerome began to manage complete sentences now and then. Since Lenny had no sartorial prejudice to nurse, the two boys got on well in spite of their age difference (I suspect this was because Jerome's social development stopped about the time he reached the second grade), and I only heard one complaint in five days about there being nothing to do. Harry made friends with some neighboring campers, who gave him a piece of moleskin for his blisters. He too was relieved of almost everything he could find to grumble about. On the sixth day he looked around him for the first time and became a convert. "My God," he said. "I had no idea all this existed . . . these mountains. When are we going to do this again?"

"Let's just get through this one trip, Hair," I told him, "before we leave on the next."

Because on the seventh day it rained. Not one of those quick summer thunder storms that springs up suddenly and with a lot of dramatic bashing of cloud masses and bolts of lightning and dumps an hour or two on your head before vanishing over the nearest range of peaks. The sky turned solidly gray, and about nine o'clock it began to pour. We huddled under ponchos and told ourselves it would blow over. By eleven it was clear it wouldn't. The boys grew sullen, and then began to whine; Harry made snide comments about its not having done this in the Sierra in August since before Christ; eventually I suggested we admit defeat and slog back down into the valley. "The bad news is thirteen miles. The good news is downhill." (I saw no reason to be offensive and point out that going downhill is harder on the legs than going uphill.) "When we get there we can maybe get a room in the lodge. Hot shower. I'll buy us all a steak."

It took five and a half soggy hours, and when we were out nobody felt like steak anyway. Harry, who had been grimly silent for the last couple of miles, sat down on the bridge into Happy Isles and removed his boots, and it was clear why he didn't feel like stepping out for a spree. He left most of his feet in his socks. Jerome looked as if somebody had hit him eight or ten times upside the head with a mallet, and Lenny promptly lay down under a tree and went to sleep.

"How far to the car?" Harry groaned.

I looked at the map and took a guess. "About a half mile,

maybe." Rain was pouring down my neck off my hat, which had melted around my ears, and I was bone tired and cold. "Look, I'll leave my pack here and go for it. No point in all of us suffering."

Harry handed me the keys with a grin that turned to a grimace. "Thanks, pal. I'll make it up to you."

"I don't think you'd make it on those feet or I'd suggest you go," I said.

"I think I'll hang 'em in a tree so they don't attract bears."

There were long shadows over the parking lot when I finally reached it and started looking for the car. I thought I remembered leaving it on the far side, nearest to Camp Curry, but after a few befuddled moments I saw it back near the trail head where I had emerged from the trees. "Well, you were wrong," I told myself out loud, feeling pretty sure that I wasn't, and I confess I approached somewhat warily. There was nobody around. I got in and started it up, drove to Happy Isles where Harry and the boys were waiting, and we loaded our gear into the trunk. It wasn't until almost an hour later, as we were pulling into a motel in Mariposa (the valley being full), that Lenny leaned forward with something in his hand. "What's this, Dad?"

"I don't know," I said. "Let me see it."

He handed me an oddly shaped object made of quilted nylon, and I sat with it in my hand, looking at it, wondering what is was, until Harry turned on the dome light and suddenly it became clear. It was the hood to a parka, the kind that fastens to the collar with snaps, and it was dark blue.

I still said nothing to Harry about the phantoms that flitted around in my head, but I was beginning to wonder if some form of repressed guilt wasn't turning me into a psychotic. How could Willy be in Boston and California, Yosemite Valley and Vermont, at the same time? Absurd. Nevertheless, I tried once more to track down my fantasies by again interviewing Frankie, but Frankie had adopted, along with other attitudes from the California dream dump, certain "laid-back" qualities that prevented her from locating in the realm of spatial and temporal phenomena. Which is to say that she was now so perpetually stoned on Mexican gage and Percodan she couldn't remember clearly where she was presently living, or how long it had been since she had moved from the cottage she and Willy once rented. I visited her three or four times on Front Street where she was working as a barmaid, but each time she found the walls of her mind impossible to scale. I learned only that she was cohabiting with Michael Arington in the back of a purple Metro van he had entitled Uriah's Heap, and that together with the young poet Kirchner and *his* old lady (a switch-hitter entitled Doohickey) they were trying to sew up the dope franchise at the University of California. They bought and sold in a variety of cosmic powders and grasses. They hoped to make enough in the next six months to get into hot tubs and go straight. Michael wanted to run for city council. Politics, he had decided, not literature was his bag. Yes, she had heard from Willy. One card. It was postmarked Boston and said he was on his way to Vermont, but she didn't know how long ago it had been mailed because the stamp was blurred. She suggested he was back into his hermit trip. I had a strange moment of affinity with Mr. Ward at that moment. If you can't get a boy, get a clean old man. If they both turn you down, get a hippy.

How to account for that parka hood? I was stymied. I spent days in my study going over and over it in my mind, trying to reconstruct the events of the trip, step by step. Did I really see somebody by the washrooms. Was there actually someone in camp that night, or was it a bear, a dream, a consensual twitch? Where did I park that car? Why couldn't I get my mind off the whole damn thing? Then, at last, *pour fin,* good old Harold T. Wisenberger came through. He called me and with a lot of ahems and ahas asked if I recalled that blue hood we'd found in the back of my car. I told him I thought I remembered something like that. "At Merced Lake," he said, "Jerome went into some guy's tent and stole his parka. Also a Swiss army knife, a pack of cigarettes and eight bucks in bills. He had it all stuffed down in the bottom of his pack. I was cleaning it out this morning to do the laundry and I found it."

Well, a hearty *thwok* to you, my man.

I used what was left of August to work on the book, and in early September, attentive to the twinges of my ulcer, began to consider the course I would teach during the term that would shortly begin. I was not looking forward to it, as usual, and for all the normal reasons — like a lack of commitment to the discipline, indifference to the perils of puerility, resentment at the encroachments on my time to pursue the sullen art. Also the hour was aproaching when I would obviously need to resume or resolve my situation with Nina. Very soon she would be in proximity to something more than daydreams.

The truth is I was strangely comfortable in limbo — not the "out of sight, out of mind" sort of thing, just out of town, out of tension. No swiving, no sweating. I could visit Mnemosyne without the stricture of conscience. I didn't care for her any the less, I knew that, but with the pressure of decisions and justifications off I realized how much pressure had been *on* — including the need to appear in my own eyes as some kind of responsible, decent human being concerned primarily for the happiness of the woman (women?) I loved. That was some row to hoe. I hadn't been good at it, and I didn't miss the daily annunciation of my limitations.

Whether relief had anything to do with my transforming relationship with Erica or not I don't really know, but things were working better during the summer than they had almost ever worked before. Allowing myself an obvious insight, it has always appeared to me that women, be they wives, lovers, or potential one-night-stands, are pretty intuitive about a man's post-adolescent growth and that particular moment in his life when he has a sudden propensity to wander. I, quite obviously, was giving off vibrations and odors peculiar to my phylum because I began to notice that I was getting quite a lot of eye contact and suggestive winks from a variety of barflies, foxes, and ladies at the parties Erica and I occasionally attended. Erica, perhaps because of an awareness that I was outwardly appealing to others in *her* phylum, began to take renewed interest. She had had her fling (or flings). For reasons opaque to reader and writer she had decided I was still the chosen. Feminism lost ground to femininity. I noticed a bit of lace here, a décolletage there, that I had not seen before, a "spa" membership fee appeared in the check ledger. She gave considerable attention to the larder, and banished the dust puppies and spiderwebs from the corners of the house.

I suspect my response was more typical than *Ms.* magazine would like to believe. I started to cook meals and tow the vacuum cleaner around the house myself. I suggested a part-time job for Erica, and began making inquiries of people I knew to help her find one. I took Lenny off her hands three or four afternoons a week and we had a fine time building a tree house in the cypress below the pasture. And I began to talk in a way that at first completely flabbergasted her. "I really think," I said one afternoon on the lawn (we were drinking gin and tonics and lying in the grass), "that a lot of your frustration with me, and to a certain extent Lenny, comes from frustration with yourself. Your life is blowing by and it isn't going anywhere and you resent what you see as the two big obstacles holding you back."

"Forgive me, Eliot," she said, "if I tell you that observation is not very profound. The same general complaint has been around for some years now."

"Yeah, well, a lot of things that have been around that are pretty obvious to other people are just getting through to me now, so you have to forgive *me* for being a little slow, a little obtuse, but have patience. I'll get there."

"Is this *you* speaking?"

"I think you should go back to work, or back to school. Whatever you want to do."

"Really?"

"Yes, really."

"But you always resisted unto death. . . ."

"I can change just like anyone else, right? I think you should start thinking about what would satisfy *you*, not me."

"But to find any editorial work," she said, still somewhat dazed, "I'd have to go over the hill, and I don't know if it would be worth it for only a half day."

"Do it full time then," I argued.

"What about Lenny?"

"He'll be in regular school pretty soon. I can get him off in the morning, and work my schedule so I'm here when he gets home."

She was doubtful, but obviously pleased. Her protests became academic. "I can't give up all my responsibilities around here just to indulge myself."

"Its time you were responsible to yourself," I said. "It's *time* you indulged yourself, if that's what it is. We can make out, Lenny and I, and if you feel guilty you can use some of your salary to hire a house cleaner once a week."

I admit, of course, there's a possibility that I was saying all this simply to assuage my own rather deeply seated sense of guilt. But I don't think so. Not entirely. Whatever the ulterior motives, if any, the result was a peaceful coexistence that had not really been in evidence since the days we lived in Cambridge as "promising graduate student" and "working wife." Erica did, rather quickly, find a job doing editorial work for a textbook firm in Palo Alto, but she could work at home, as it happened, and only had to appear in the office once or twice a week. No major adjustments in the pattern of our lives had to be made. It seemed reasonable, therefore, to leave questions of *ultima thule* in abeyance.

Two

EARLY IN SEPTEMBER I WENT TO SCHOOL ONE MORNING ABOUT six-thirty to pick up my mail and to hunt through my files for some old course notes that I thought I might be able to use. The fog hung in thick around the courtyard, and for purely nostalgic reasons I put the mail aside, including Nina's letter, which I laid carefully on top, and made mysef a cup of coffee. Then I stood at the window and tried to conjure up a vision — two nubile sweethearts walking jauntily across toward the Provost's office without a stitch to protect them from the damp and cold — the first time I had laid eyes on the recalcitrant Miss Allencraig. It didn't work. There was nothing out there but swirling mist. I sat and opened my copy of *Publishers Weekly,* started thumbing through it, still titillating myself with delicious delay. Then, suddenly, I came across an announcement in the "Trade News" section that galvanized me to my chair.

McLean editor, Harold Nathan, scouting talent at the Bread-loaf Writer's Conference in Vermont, signed to contract a new novel by a member of the conference kitchen staff who met Nathan while waiting on his table. William Ward's fiction original, *Confessions of an Onanist: A Note from Underground,* will be published by McLean's in December.

Stunned, I read it again. I recalled advice from an old pool shark who said when the cue was cold to put it down and walk around the table three times. I made a tour of the steno pool, with a stop at the drinking fountain; picked up *Publishers Weekly* and read the page again. What are the odds on this? Nine off the eleven a sure scratch shot and the bloody hustler banged it right in. They broke Paul Newman's fingers for less. Confessions of an *onanist?* I sat down again in the secretary's chair, staring at the print like a catatonic Mongoloid. Then I began to grin, began to chuckle, began to laugh, oh the irony, the paradox, oh sweet mother of Christ. I began to howl. I smacked my pant leg, snotted my lip, beat the desk, kicked the trash basket. I might actually have broken something had a janitor not come in to see what all the fuss was about. He regarded me impassively for a moment before deciding I was just a harmless, crazy professor. " 'Scuse me," he said. "All that ruckus, thought we had us some radicals in here . . ."

"No," I said. "Just a little joke."

What else should I have done but laugh? What *could* I have done? Absolutely nothing.

When I finally recovered my wits I took Nina's letter down to my office, turned on the desk lamp, and sat down to read it. Thank God, my dear girl, for you, I thought. A moment of purity, of light, on this most dismal, dark, dank, depressing day. Diddly-dee, diddly-dum.

Love of my life,

It seems incredibly unfair that we should always have to play games with each other and pretend that we feel one way when we feel another. I've been hiding out all summer trying to make myself understand that something I once had is over and that the start of a new school year will mark the start of new perceptions about what happened, and that I'll be able to get back on the course of my dreams. But my dreams are of you. God, I miss you. Everywhere I go I carry around in my head an image of you, wishing you were here to share the days and nights with me — the beach, Baja, San Diego and the zoo, everything. I swear, every man I go out with I call Eliot and get all confused when I don't concentrate about who I'm sitting with in the movie, or dancing with, or eating dinner with. A friend of mine took me to a Mexican restaurant the other night and when he ordered Dos Equis beer I burst into tears right at the table. The poor guy thought I was getting my period. In a funny way all my thoughts of you seem very safe with you so far away, but they hurt nevertheless because I know we can never share a life.

Forgive me for being sentimental. There are times when reality intrudes and I am aware that memories *are* the past, that emotional distance grows, that sharing each other isn't what we can do anymore, but in spite of it all I miss your love. I keep waiting for a magic moment in which the walls we've been forced to build will come crashing down, but I know that they won't. I know, too, that I can't just shrug it all off, as I thought I might if I got away from you. If I come back to school I'm going to live with constant hurt that won't be assuaged by distance.

So . . . I want to graduate, but I've decided I can do my last three courses as independent study, and that won't require my living in Santa Cruz. So I'm going to register and then come back here as quickly as possible. I want to see you; I know this letter is not the way to wrap it all up, but I wanted you to know before I came so that I wouldn't have to explain it all and risk breaking down in the process of spinning out words. I know how you like weepy women.

Love,
NINA

My chickens all come home to roost.

There is really no way to describe my feelings when I finished reading that letter — not self-pity, as Harry would have insisted, but self-loathing. I sat in my office for nearly two hours, watching the sun burn off the fog, swiveling around and around in my chair and alternately constructing arguments to pursuade Nina to come back ("I won't see you, call you, write you, talk to you." "I'll take a leave of absence and quit the area myself." "I'll devote myself to becoming such a whining, mewing, spineless lump of Jell-O that you can start hating me and be cured.") and letting my mind drift in blank eddies of gray, unfocused gloom. Finally I went over to Harry's house to unburden myself and see if an hour or two of his sardonic humor might not lift my spirits.

When I walked in, Jerome was sitting in the front room eating toast and trying to make a bread knife stick in the wall to wall carpet. He didn't trouble himself to look up. "Hello kid," I said. "Pulled the wings off any flies lately?" No response. "Where's your old man?" Jerome cocked a thumb in the general direction of the kitchen. "Thanks. Nice talking to you." I walked through the house and found Weisberg sitting at the kitchen table reading *Penthouse* and jingling the change in his pocket.

"You think these letters people write in to the editor are a put-on?" he said. "I mean this lady who calls herself a free-lance fellatrice claims she digs blowing her husband's poker buddies under the table while the game is going on. Everybody knows she's there, see, and the trick is for the guy who's getting it off to not let on, just go ahead betting and raising and calling. If she can make him let on he's the one she gets the next pot he wins. You think that's true?"

"No."

"It could be, though. Jesus, can you imagine that?"

He pinched his lips together with his thumb and index finger and looked reflectively at the ceiling. "I wonder if anybody in my group has an old lady who'd be up for that?"

"You could ask. Listen Harry, I didn't come over to discuss your sexual fantasies. I have real problems on my hands. For one thing Nina isn't coming back to school."

"I'd say your problems are over."

"She isn't coming back because of *me*."

"So I would assume. Which means she's got a lot more sense than you do. She's willing to act on her convictions."

"Harry, I can't let her assume the burden of decision. I can't make her alter her life just because I'm the one more permanently installed in this town."

Harry closed the magazine and sat there snapping the pages and looking at me. "You know something? I like you a lot, old buddy. You're an asshole, but generally speaking you're pretty bright, attractively sardonic, and your bilious personality appeals to my sense of the grotesque. However, on the subject of this lady I find you obtuse, insensitive, and boring. You dug yourself a hole, and then you looked down and said 'My goodness, look at that hole I dug myself there,' and then you rolled up your eyes to heaven and fell in that hole, accidentally on purpose, and now I don't know what it is you want. Sympathy? Condolences? Applause? You're not quite like what's-their-names in *The Great Gatsby*. You're not sufficiently amoral to walk away and leave others to clean up your messes. But you're not like Caraway either. You're inert. You're not tough enough to extricate yourself from a relationship that you know is unfair to everybody concerned. So there really isn't anything I can tell you, no advice to be given."

I sat in gloomy silence, fiddling with a coffee spoon until

I dropped it and it clattered on the floor. Harry ran his hands through his wiry hair and rubbed his bald spot with his palm. "Look," he said. "I appreciate the fact that you really love this girl. I mean, I believe you do. And your wife too, probably, even though you've let your relationship go to seed over the years and it's not quite clear if or when you can get it back together. There's your kid, your job, Nina's desire to avoid becoming just another *Hausfrau,* her ambition — and even if she thinks right now that she'd settle for three hots and a cot if she could have you, she'd regret it by the time she's thirty. Or twenty-two. There's all that *stuff,* man, and there's not a damn thing to be done about it. So I dig the problem, you understand, but there's nothing I can tell you you don't know already."

"I suppose."

"Now, what else can I do for you?"

I studied my palm, thinking, what was it? — *When you fall into another man's power, bestir yourself, save yourself like a bird from the grasp of the fowler?* "Nothing else," I said.

Harry was right about all but one thing — inertia. As soon as I left his house I went up to school and bullied my way into a spur-of-the-moment interview with the Dean of Humanities. I don't know if it was the allusion to Nick Caraway, or simply that I had finally been painted into the last corner of the house, and there was nothing left to do but bust through the walls, but I extracted from the confused dean a promise of emergency leave, should my "personal and family situation" demand it (and with the understanding that I would double my course load during winter term), and by noon I was at the airport in Monterey buying a ticket for Los Angeles. I said nothing to Erica because I could think of nothing to say before the fact. I simply left. The time had come to clean up.

From the airport I drove a rented car up Lincoln Boulevard for a few miles and cut over to the coast at Venice. I had no plan to speak of. Mostly this was an impulsive act, deliberate only in the sense of moving, and in my conscious refusal to rehearse a speech. For too many years I had ignored the possibilities of the ad lib. In a coffeehouse, while I consumed a bagel and a cappucino, I looked up Allencraig in the phone book and prepared myself for the eventuality that someone other than Nina would pick up the phone and ask who was calling. My story, I decided, was that her senior thesis advisor was arranging his fall quarter and needed to know whether she would be wanting a directed study under his supervision. Ho ho. I was so wiggy at that point the irony escaped me. My subterfuge was unnecessary; Nina answered.

I recall expressions of astonishment, great excitement, hesitation, apprehension — in that order. I told her it was imperative I see her before she made her plans, that I refused to take no for an answer, and reluctantly she agreed to meet me at a beach between Santa Monica and Castellammare. "But please, Eliot," she said, just before we hung up, "don't play any games with me. I've got my mind made up about what's best, and I don't need any more confusion in my life right now."

"No games," I promised. "I didn't come for that."

But our meeting was a Parker Brothers anthology. According to Hoyle. And Dr. Bern. Actually we looked like a couple of mating storks in an Everglade swamp, stalking this way and that, performing little dances, bobbing, weaving. We approached and retreated, stood on one leg and preened, turned our backs and pretended indifference, clacked our bills in a mock duel. Eventually she looked into my eyes and shook her head in slow mystification. What did you expect, after all? Thunder la boom? "Oh shit," she said, and her arms went around me, her face into the hollow of my neck. We held each other for what seemed like moments and eternities, then sank down on the sand in an attitude of prayer, our knees and foreheads touching, our fingers entwined, saying nothing and feeling nothing but electric confusion and a kind of exquisite sadness.

After a while she pulled away and lay down on her back in the sand. I sat hugging my legs, alternately watching her expressionless face and the breakers that boomed in on a rising tide. There was a slight haze over the beach, approaching fog banks, and a heavy smell of kelp in the air that reminded me for some reason of a summer I spent as a child in Gloucester. The beach in front of our cottage was a shingle of pebbles and broken shells upon which all kinds of marvelous things would wash ashore — an unidentifiable bottle, pieces of float cork, a broken lobster trap with thirty or forty feet of line attached that was useful for tying up the retarded sister of one of my cronies down the road. I found there, once, amidst a tangle of seaweed and bits of driftwood, a small wooden cask that was full of what I assumed to be rum from some shipwrecked schooner lying silent in the deep waters off the Grand Banks. (My father had been reading me "The Reef of Norman's Woe" and my head was full of romance.) The liquid in the cask turned out to be sea water, a good deal of which the dim-witted captive and I hopefully drank and regurgitated in a wood shed behind the garage, and I have never been able to divest myself of the memory of that occasion when I smell salt air.

"I dunno," Nina said after a while. She addressed herself to space, and whipped her head back and forth. "I dunno. I thought I had it together."

I kept quiet for a minute, hoping she would go on, but she didn't. "What together?" I said.

"Me. Us."

"I didn't come down to start it all over again," I said.

"So you told me. But you see when we *see* each other . . . in a way it starts all over again whether we want it to or not." A reflective pause. "Among other things that's why I'm not going back up to school."

"You've got to go back to school. I won't be the cause of your leaving."

"Well that's tough. You are." She rolled over and lay with her head on her extended arm. "Anyway, it's no big deal. I can do what I need to do from here."

"Yes, maybe. Though it's hardly the same is it? Missing out on the last of your senior year, friends, people you've been through it all with, graduation, not to mention what-ever benefits are derived from having your thesis director nearby, and a library, and somebody to talk with when you get stuck."

She watched me with wide, unblinking eyes, and then shook her head. "No. I told you I made up my mind. Be-cause if I go back all that won't amount to anything. Eliot, I haven't done fuck-all with my studies since the day I met you, and you're not really any different now; you just proved it. I'm not exactly over you either. I've been trying all summer to fall in love with every twerp my sisters drag home for me, but . . . well . . . usually I'm goo-goo-eyed over somebody, and that makes me full of energy and life, even when I know it's temporary. In fact, *especially* when I know it's temporary. But I'm beginning to be afraid you're not temporary, that in some ways I'm not ever going to get over you, and that makes me really very sad. I want you to be a happy memory, not a constant pain."

"So you keep four hundred miles between us and that makes it all okay?"

"It makes it better, sure. At least I don't have to spend my life going through that business of wondering if I'm going to see you today, or if you're going to call, or why you didn't call, or if you're mad because I'm out trying to preserve my sanity with somebody else. I can function just fine when I don't have a big set of expectations to deal with all the time." The thought of being kept on a string infused her with a kind of wry vexation, and she sat up suddenly and threw a handful of sand at my chest. "I don't even know why I CARE! You LOUSE! You're the most conniving sonofabitch I ever met, and you PROMISED you wouldn't do this to me, you promised not to play games and try to sweet-talk me back into your . . . web, you . . . CREEP!"

I laughed at her peevish outburst, and happily my amusement proved infectious. She started to smile and then hid her face in her hands to keep from cracking up, rocked a few moments, then regained control. She looked at me with her face screwed up into a question. "Why do I love you so much? Why? You're terrible."

I kissed her in my most paternal manner, befitting the occasion, and then not so paternally as the mood changed in mid-embrace. Nobody ever told Nina it was possible to kiss with closed lips, and I tasted the faint, ever-present flavor of candy cane in her mouth. "I want you to come back," I murmured.

She ran her tongue along the ridge of my jaw and then to my neck.

"D'jew 'ear me?"

"Hmmm. No."

"I said . . ."

"I heard you. I meant no, I won't come back."

"There's no reason not to."

She pulled away and parodied a smile. "Of course not."

"I'm serious. I'm not going to be there so you won't have to worry. I've gotten a leave to finish my book, and I'm going to spend it at the MacDowell Colony in New Hampshire (this was a lie, but only a little one; I would go somewhere). So there'll be nothing to complicate your life as far as I'm concerned." I waited through a long silence for my altruism to sink in.

"You did this for me?" she finally asked.

"No. It just came up and I . . ."

"You did, didn't you."

It seemed pointless to pretend. "Yes."

"Why?"

"Because I couldn't live with myself if you ran away from something that means so much to you . . . because you had to avoid me."

"Oh." She sat back in the sand, a gloomy study. "It isn't just that . . . exactly." The fog had crept in almost to the surf line, wisps beginning to tear loose from the main bank and drift in over the beach. Goose bumps on the russet skin of bare arms. Soft strands of hair blew lightly around her face, her nipples hardened beneath the thin cotton of her T-shirt, and with a shiver she returned from whatever reverie had absorbed her. "We're crazy, you know. All this 'This town ain't big enough for the two of us' crap . . . I mean, the next thing is we strap on our forty-fives and shoot it out to see who gets to make the big sacrifice. Only we're going to kill each other over who gets to go instead of who gets to stay."

"Uh-uh. We can both go, or you can stay, but my part of it is decided."

"What does your wife say about this big scheme of yours?"

I shrugged that one off since I had not had time to consult my wife. It occurred to me that I had not really had time to consult myself, for that matter, to consider carefully whether I really intended flight or not, but the important thing was to get Nina straightened around. The rest could wait. To change the subject I looked at my watch and then out to sea where the sun was a diffused wafer behind the wall of fog. "We ought to think about moving," I said.

"What time is it?"

"Nearly six."

"Oh Lord, I've got to run."

"Mom holding din-din?"

"No, Mom's with Pop at a convention. But I've got an . . . engagement."

"Shot down again."

"You didn't give me much warning."

Neither did she offer to break her date. We walked back up to the parking lot, Nina holding back her blowing hair with her fists, and I holding back the sulks. Without success. That I should begin to pout because I faced the evening alone was completely inconsistent with the spirit of my mission, but I couldn't help it. It seemed to me she could at least *offer*. Then I could refuse and feel virtuous.

At her car she turned and held me loosely around the waist. "I'm sorry I can't be with you tonight, but this is a friend who's driving up from San Diego, and there's no way to get hold of him. Anyway . . . it's probably better. We'd just wind up doing something stupid."

I nodded a gloomy agreement.

"And thanks for what you did."

"I'll be around for a day or two," I said, playing it by ear. "Want to see a couple of people since I'm down here, so I'll give you a buzz sometime tomorrow. If by any chance you want to drive back with me, there's plenty of room."

"I'll see," she said. Meaning no. "And give yourself a hug tonight. I'll think about you."

It was getting dark when I finally found a motel that looked run down enough to be affordable, yet opulent enough to still offer t.v. and free phones. The Malibu

Palace was somebody's Disneyland fantasy fouled in both conception and execution, so that what had been intended to resemble the gumdrop and frosting abode of fairy godmothers and golden damsels turned into a deformed lump of pinkish stucco with a very obviously phony cap of plaster thatch. A home movie Castle Rackrent. I was assigned 26B, which had cute little gothic windows with leaded panes, a shower stall designed to look like a small cave, and a standard sized double bed which, judging from its tensile properties, had once served as the nuptial couch for a couple of four hundred pound fattys before the innkeeper at the Malibu Palace picked it up in a garage sale. All for sixteen dollars a night. And free phones. I availed myself of this service and called Erica to try to explain my absence.

Somewhat later, reconstructing the conversation I had with her (I was huddled in my cave with a glass of scotch, alternately freezing and scalding under the quixotic plash of water that emerged cleverly through a fissure in the rock), I decided that I had probably not selected the best time to try to explain myself and my impulsive behavior — at the very least I should have reconsidered and done it *before* I left for Los Angeles, and most certainly not with half a bottle of booze in me and no very definite plans for return.

"I thought all that never existed. Willy *invented* it," she said bravely, through her obvious tears. We had already passed through *concern* ("My God, where are you? I thought you'd been in an accident), *anger* ("You're WHERE? How could you POSSIBLY go to LOS ANGELES without letting me know. Didn't it OCCUR to you I'd worry myself sick?"), *suspicion* ("So there is somebody else . . ."), and silence. We moved then to *misery* and *humiliation* ("How could I have been such a fool, such a dupe?").

"It's over," I pleaded, once I was able to break in. "I'm just cleaning up the mess I made. It's something I have to do."

"What about the mess you've made of us?"

"I'll try to clean that one up too."

"When? After you've had your fun in Los Angeles?"

"This begins to sound like soap opera."

"It is soap opera, for God's sake."

"I'll be home tomorrow night, or Thursday at the latest."

"Never mind. Don't bother."

"Will you please cut it out. For once in my life I'm trying to straighten things out and be honest."

"You don't know how."

"I didn't have to call and tell you this, you know. I could have made up some story."

"Sure, you could have just vanished into thin air, too."

"I could have lied."

"I wish you *had,* you bastard."

And so forth and so on. The dialogue was anything but brilliant, and I didn't feel smug or virtuous or cleansed afterward, just tired of the whole goddamn business and looking forward to my seventy-fifth birthday when all I'd have to concern me was the color of my urine, the texture of my stool, and how to eat Pablum without having my teeth fall out on the plate. I went to bed at eight-thirty.

Wednesday was one of those southern California days when the smog warnings go up and the kiddies stay home attached to their respirators lest tender lungs ingest too many carcinogens and an entire generation fall to big C before puberty. I drove up the coast to Santa Barbara to get away from it (and to kill time), and paid a visit to the old estate in Montecito where my parents had rented the gardener's cottage (four bedrooms, three baths) in 1945-46, and I had built forts and waged mudball wars from the towering ice plant banks that marked the eastern boundary of the property. Hi there, Brambilla, you Tahitian warlord. I still have a lump on my forehead where you coldcocked me with that hidden chunk of granite. And how's the eye I almost put out with a matchstick from my BB-gun?

The estate had long ago fallen to developers and was now an impression of paisley-patterned drives and cul-de-sacs, neat hundred and fifty thousand dollar ranch houses with shake roofs and shaved lawns. The half mile of beach where I used to swim and watch the cormorants through a Christmas spyglass had ominous signs promising instant arrest and prosecution for any nonresident bum who set foot on it, but I was able to traverse the back side of the land along the railroad track and emerge at my ultimate destination — the terrace bar of the Miramar. My "winter dreams" occurred there as a busboy and general factotum to the elegant ladies whose elasticized swimsuits used to galvanize my eyeballs (and other keepsakes) as I carried dirty glasses and club sandwich scraps from poolside to kitchen, and whose tips kept me in touch with the latest adventures of Captain Marvel and Wonderwoman through the long summer before *V-J* Day. This time, however, I lounged and some other truckler trucked the trash.

From my table, where I sat nursing a post lunch cognac and looking south along the curve of the coast to Carpinteria, I had difficulty recognizing what had been for several years — the most impressionable years of my life — a daily vista. The beach that had then been a long, clean sweep of sand inhabited mainly by shorebirds and small boys was dotted with umbrellas and canvas chairs. Along the cliffs the picture windows of new bungalows reflected blankly in the sun. Even the horizon had changed. Where we used to have an unobstructed view of San Miguel, Santa Rosa, Santa Cruz islands I now looked at oil rigs floating in the channel and out beyond to a gray backwash of air pollution fanning away from Los Angeles. I remarked on the vagaries and vicissitudes of time to my counterpart as he cleared my table, but received only a hopeful, uncomprehending grin for my wisdom. The bigger the grin, the bigger the tip. Step's credo. Some things remain the same.

I left when the mid-afternoon sun began to cook my brains and started back toward Malibu. In a drugstore in Ventura I bought a pair of shades against the glare, and toasted nostalgia with a cherry Coke. There was a policeman at the magazine rack reading comic books and placidly ignoring the sign that said *This is not a library*. Two small boys hardly tall enough to reach the counter were shoplifting Snickers bars when the waitress turned her back, and a pharmacist was dozing on a stool behind his cache of condoms and appliances for Fem-Hygiene. I had a second Coke and phoned Nina. Exchanged a few pleasantries before getting to the point. No, she hadn't changed her mind. Yes, she supposed it would be fun to have dinner together if I was really planning to be around anyway. Could I pick her up about seven at her parents' house? I could, but how would we explain . . . ? Relax, she was no longer required to introduce her men friends. Besides, she was alone. Peachy. I hung up and drove on down to Parody Palace.

With several hours yet to waste I showered and shaved and then turned on the t.v. set, flipping idly through reruns of "Get Smart," "Gilligan's Island," "The Three Stooges," and "The Mickey Mouse Club," until finally Cronkite came on with the national obituary. After twenty minutes of disaster footage CBS must have decided we all needed a little chuckle because Charles Kurralt steamed onto the screen in his "on the road" van and gave us a human interest feature, "The Love Story of Maxine and Tools Twitty."

"Maxine and Tools Twitty," growled Kurralt, "have been in love since they were eleven. He was on the Brentwood Elementary traffic patrol; she was a milk monitor. Today they got married."

Cut to a shot of Maxine and Tools emerging from the office of a Justice of the Peace. Tools wears a blue serge that barely stretches over his ample belly; Maxine sports a knit pant suit that rides up in the crotch. They climb into an old LTD and wave frantically at Kurralt as they drive away.

Cut to the Twitty living room; angle on Kurralt. "This is no ordinary marriage," he informs us, "this is no run-of-the-mill love affair. Their wedding today marks the third time Tools and Maxine have been to the altar since their first nuptials at the age of fourteen. In the interim their bliss has only been marred by two divorces, two shootings, one stabbing, and three jail terms. All of this mayhem," beams Kurralt, "inflicted by one upon the other."

Close-up on Tools. He tugs shyly at one sideburn and looks first at Maxine, who is seated on his left, then at a thirteen- or fourteen-year-old lout who is openly picking his nose in the catbird's seat to the right.

"It's kind of sickening," Tools says. But he is not, apparently, referring to the lout; rather to some vague impropriety he senses in having married the same woman three times. "Ever'time I'd go off an leave her after we'd have a fallin' out, they's just sumpin keep drawin' me back."

Maxine gives him an "aw shucks" pat on the thigh, and giggles. "Our boy there got to be his daddy's best man twicet."

Our boy removes his index finger from his nostril. "I think it's funny," he says. Everyone holds a moment to see if he has anything more to contribute, but the light departs from his eyes, they glaze over, he peers sightlessly at the camera like a dead flounder on the bottom of a fishing boat.

"When I was young," Maxine says brightly, "there weren't no way to fight with a man like they is now. So I'd just take his car, which was the thing nearest and dearest to his heart, and wreck it."

Tools guffaws. "She totaled out two bran' new Lincolns on me, 'for I divorced her."

Angle again on Kurralt. Filling in the blanks. The Twitty's have no capacity for sustained narration. "You got married again in 1970 and less than a year later big trouble began, am I right?"

"Right. Maxine and me had a knockdown, drag out, and she shot me three times in the leg. I was pretty pee-ode and pressed charges, but layin' there in the hospital I thought about how I was to blame too . . . hell, I'd knocked her bridge work into the trash compactor . . . and I tried to drop charges. Only the state wouldn't have it."

"They convicted me of intentional shooting to wound," says Maxine, "but I only got two years probation. I had to go to the rehabilitation program."

"She went nights and finished high school," Tools says proudly.

Kurralt looks at them both, then fixes on Maxine. "Did you get rehabilitated?"

Maxine sighs, looks wistful. "I don't guess it took."

"What happened?"

"Well, me and Tools were at my brother's for a party about a year later and they got in a big argument and Tools stuck some sewing scissors in my brother, and then I shot Tools in the leg again."

"That time we both wound up in the can," Tools laughs.

"We got divorced again," says Maxine.

Long pause. Kurralt pondering the mysteries of humanity. "You just got married for a third time. What makes you think things will work now?"

Maxine sits up straight, chest out, shoulders back. She looks smugly at Tools, eyes brimming. "Cause I *found* it," she says.

Mr. Twitty tugs at his sideburn. "I found it too," he twangs.

"Found it?" inquires Kurralt.

"Jesus."

Cut to van speeding down the highway. Voice-over. *"And ruin'd love, when it is built anew / Grows fairer than at first, more strong, far greater.* This is Charles Kurralt, on the road, somewhere in California."

Was there a message for me hidden in that special feature? Or was it just another of life's little conundrums? Love: a problem admitting of no satisfactory solution. Actually, my credulity was so foxed that as I sat there staring at the ads between Cronkite and the local news I had a hard time finding my thumb to pop it in my mouth.

I met Nina at seven and we drove into Santa Monica, then up Wilshire Boulevard to some place she knew about near the Los Angeles Museum and the La Brea tar pits that was heavy with atmosphere and liberal with the gin in the martini. I was a little surprised to discover her familiarity with the hard stuff. "Since when did you take up this habit?" I asked.

She stared at me for a minute without answering, trying to think of some witty riposte, no doubt. Then she said, "A guy who's teaching me to play golf introduced me to the nineteenth hole."

"Golf!"

She giggled. "He says I look more like I'm killing snakes. But you wait, I'll get it together. I'm very athletically inclined."

"So I've noticed," I said sourly. "And now that you're

part of the country club set you've gotten into swilling straight gin."

"Not straight," she said, completely serious. "It's sad, you know. It's like very few bartenders are concerned anymore with the proper marriage of gin and vermouth. For instance I know a place where eighty-proof gin is actually mixed at a rate of eleven to one with something that approximates cooking sherry, and this item is served to you with a pickled onion, *God,* to disguise the inferiority of the product. Can you imagine? They should have their license pulled."

"It's absolutely beyond belief."

"Now in this place," she said. "I've instructed them. Three point seven to one, and hold the fruit salad. But even here if you don't ask for a twist they'll put this fucking giant olive with a pimiento in it or something. This big . . . marinated testicle. I don't know, you really can't be too careful. What are you laughing about?"

We had dinner at a Japanese restaurant (another of Nina's recent discoveries and passions), and I was prevented from ordering either of the two items I was able to recognize on the menu (beef teriyaki and shrimp tempura) by another short lecture on the contemptible, uneducated eater. I suavely suggested she do the ordering and was instructed in suimono, tsukemono, and nigiri sushi. Nina had tekka mahi. My education did not include an explanation of what any of this stuff was, though I'm afraid I recognized the raw squid for the fishy little cephalopod it is, and buried a good deal of it under a bank of sticky rice. The waiter smiled familiarly at Nina as he cleared away our plates. "Don't think your father likes squid," he said.

The only mistake Nina and I made that evening was having too good a time together. We were finally able to get off the "what are we going to do" theme — or at least

I was. Nina didn't seem to have much new to say on that subject — and talk like normal human beings about common everyday matters. We had a close, convivial evening. We were appeased into a false complacency, an unexamined feeling that everything was back on the right track, the riddles had been solved, we were whole again, and it led to a cozy ride back up the coast to Malibu with Nina sitting close to me in the car, her head resting on my shoulder and the index finger of her right hand idly twisting the hair on my chest through the gap between the buttons of my shirt. Scenes from a fifties romance. The windows were open and a warm, scented night blew through the car. I think even the Beach Boys were making doo-doo-waa noises on the radio. I suggested a nightcap at the motel. She nodded drowsily, her hair tickling my cheek.

And so I poured the last of my scotch into two glasses, apologized for the lack of ice provided by the management, and sat down in the only chair in the room. Nina stretched crossways on the bed, kicking her feet in slow count to a muted song that drifted in the open door. I tried to find the rhythm in a klatch of crickets piping in the darkness beyond the parking lot. Ten o'clock and still warm. A moth wobbled in, searching drunkenly for a pathway to the light burning in the bathroom. From my neighbor on the left the gurgle and gulp of a flushing toilet. "You can hear the surf," Nina said.

Thinking this a joke, I nevertheless listened for a few minutes and found she was right. Hummed agreement. "Do you want to walk down to the beach?"

"I should probably get going."

"Why?"

"Because you and me and bedrooms lead to strange happenings."

"Okay, so let's walk on the beach."

237

She sipped her drink and offered a noncommittal "hmmm." The crickets piped on, and a car went slowly past, down the line of rooms and stopped. I heard the engine die, and after a while the door slam shut. Late revels or late travels. A burst of gunfire from the television set next door, and somewhere down the highway a real cop turned on his real siren. We listened to him coming up the coast, another burst of automatic weapon fire, and then he wailed past, blowing north through the sand dunes and arid windies of my mind. I was tired and at the same time afflicted with a terrible restlessness to get on with it. "You want me to take you home?" I said — just to get past that fiction.

A moment of silence. "Yes," she said.

I sucked my teeth and wondered if I had imagined her voice. It seemed she had actually spoken. "Really?"

"Really." She rolled over on her stomach and I could see her eyes shining out of what seemed to be immeasurable layers of dust particles stirred up by her movement. Filthy motel.

"I don't get it," I said, confused.

"I know. I've just begun to realize that. It was dumb of me to go to dinner with you. I'm sorry."

"Why? For what?"

She sat up and placed her hands carefully in her lap. "I haven't handled this very well," she said, slowly. "I didn't want to hurt you, and so I said okay, but that was wrong of me, dishonest . . . and God knows it isn't that you don't have an effect on me . . . I wouldn't be here now if you didn't . . . but it's over, Eliot. Truly."

"I know that," I said defensively. "That's one of the reasons I came down here, remember? To point that out and convince you you didn't have to run away."

She looked at me with a little crooked smile. "That's why you *think* you came down here. You want it to end

. . . but you also don't want it to end. You want me to accept the inevitable but remain available. Anyway, it doesn't matter who's right or wrong or kidding themselves about what." She bent her head over her hands. "See, the thing is I haven't been very honest with myself lately . . . and because of that I haven't been exactly honest with you. I'm not running away. I sort of tried to tell you, to show you, tonight that I haven't got me to a nunnery. But I blew it. I should have just said it straight out."

A glimmer of understanding finally pierced the cortex of my impossible mind. "I guess maybe you're referring to the Ben Hogan of the nineteenth hole. I guess you're trying to tell me you have become otherwise involved."

She still looked at me with that sad, twisted smile. "You remember once I told you about making love *with* somebody, not *to* them? And about my fear of emotional commitments?"

"Vaguely."

"Well you see Mr. Hogan of the nineteenth tee is someone who can't destroy my dreams." She stood up and kissed me softly on the cheek. "But then neither, anymore, can you."

Three

FIVE-THIRTY, AND MY PSYCHIC ALARM CLOCK WENT OFF, MY
eyes popped open, and I found myself looking through the
windshield of my rented car, over the edge of the pulloff
where I'd stopped, exhausted, unable to drive another
mile, and down two thousand feet of rocky cliffs to the
sea. The gnarled old Monterey pines canting back from
the precipice were still in the early morning calm, dripping
slow tears of fog from the tips of their feathered branches,
and a red-tailed hawk hung motionless on the coastal up-
draft not fifty feet in front of me and off to my left. I
watched it through gritty lids until, activated by some
mysterious impulse, it slid with an imperceptible movement of its wings down along the headland and vanished
into gray seasmoke. Closed my eyes and let the unbroken
rumble of the surf away below lull me back into fitful
sleep. Dreamed that Willy and Nina were emerging from
the arched portico of an ancient gothic church and that I

was sitting in a broad patch of ivy across the street in a shopping center and pulling weeds for a dollar-fifty an hour. Nina wore a white wedding gown, and as they passed near me I heard her say "he's simply going to have to figure it out for himself. God knows, I can't."

A banging, like somebody hitting metal with a hammer, drowned out the reply, and when I rearranged my references I was awake and there was a hippy peering in the passenger side window and knocking with a heavy ring on the roof of the car. "Hey man, you going north?" I drove him as far as Carmel where I bought him breakfast and lent him a dollar and dropped him on the road by Fort Ord to Salinas.

Back in Santa Cruz, and in a mood of nonequivocation, I called Erica to tell her I was home and that I would be along just as soon as I could turn in the rented car and walk up to Mission Street where I could catch a ride the rest of the way with somebody going to the campus. "For heaven's sake," she said, "I'll come down and pick you up."

An auspicious beginning. "You just did," I told her. "You're not still mad at me then?"

"Yes . . . no." She sighed audibly into the mouthpiece. "I don't know what I am with you anymore, Eliot."

"What I mean is, is there still room to talk about things?"

"I said I'd come get you. I wasn't suggesting anything beyond that." Her voice had a slight quiver to it.

"I have a lot of things to explain to you."

"I think that's probably true."

"I would hope there's some redemption possible."

There was a momentary silence at her end, and I confess to fleeting irritation with this process of judgment. Revising one's defenses, I told myself, would take time. "I guess what I want you to know," she said, "is that I was pretty desperate after you called the other night. My only thought was that to give you a dose of your own medicine would do me good." Again silence. She seemed somewhat lost.

"That seems to be everybody's remedy when it comes to me," I said. My spirit sank. I seemed to have been through this before with Erica, and had the same feelings of betrayal. All my good intentions, reformations, seemed very much beside the point.

Her voice was small. "You bring it on yourself."

I tried to sound neither belligerent nor hurt, but an awareness that one is not entitled to certain emotional impulses does not prevent their visitation. "How do you feel about it now?"

"Kind of empty. Blank."

"It didn't do you any good, this dose of medicine?"

"I don't know. I guess not."

It was my turn to sigh. A diversion. I didn't know what to think. In terms of consciousness I didn't know if I was senseless or senile, and I told her as much.

"I know the feeling," she said.

"Hey kiddo," I said. "The truth is I don't quite know even what it is we're talking about, but I know it feels pretty dumb to be doing it on the telephone. Can we ..." I started to stammer, "... are we so far gone that we can't try to pick up the pieces?"

She didn't answer for almost a minute, while I stood there in that stupid metal booth with its stupid metal seat and its cartoon ad for the yellow pages, dreading what she might say, half nauseated by heat and hunger, not sure whether to plead or curse the world or run out into the traffic and smash the bejesus out of the first thing on wheels I could encounter with my head. And then it was all right. Erica had not been thinking it over, she had been crying, and it had taken her time to find her voice. "I hope not," she said. "God, I hope not. I've waited a long time."

"I'll be home as quick as I can," I said. I almost yelled

whoopee. "Don't come get me, though. I need to walk, I need to stretch my wings. I'm going to fly, Erica. I'm going to astound the multitudes."

I zipped out of the telephone booth and started up the hill, repeating over and over in my head a foolish jingle for Alka-Seltzer, "plop plop, fizz fizz, oh what a relief it is," and then I stopped, appalled at myself. Precisely what everyone would expect. Just what Willy Ward accused me of. Bad jokes. Frivolity. But neither did I just then choose to consider what he would have wanted me to consider — responsibility, culpability, self-judgment, the progress of my soul. Screw it. I just jogged home in a kind of two-step with a boogie beat. I felt free, elated, stoned on possibilities. I felt like Pilgrim when he finally busted through; like Red Cross making his comeback. Hummed ditties to myself going up the hill. *Tempted and tried we're oft made to wander.* Tempted and tried, only a few survive. Me. (With a little help from my friends.)

In the front yard, in a sandbox I had built a year and a half ago, Lenny was playing with his Tonka dump truck, the one I had given him at the airport, and I watched him for a few minutes from the driveway as he filled the bed with dirt and then motored along with a lot of growls, grunts, and glottal stops, across vast and imaginary vistas to the final dumping grounds. Back and forth. So completely absorbed that he never once looked up to see me standing there. A wet wave of sentiment broke over me, but I was too close to the edge, too tired and worn out and feeling the proscriptions of my age. I restrained my impulse to pick him up and hold on to him, and after a moment I went into the house to try to make a closing peace.